CAPTIVES

BY

ROSEMARY THOMAS

Other Titles by Rosemary Thomas

From The Kiwi Kingdom Series:

- Under the Blowholes Spray
- Islands
- The Driftwood Shore
- Beneath the Long White Cloud

Rosemary Thomas trained as a Community Nurse in her native New Zealand. The Kiwi Kingdom Series is based in Westland where she was born and brought up. After marriage and two children in Australia, completed a Nursing Degree. In retirement, making craft for charity keeps her busy, a long with her mother's love of writing. The Kiwi Kingdom series began with a dream that was still present the next morning. "Captives" also began with dreams that insisted they be told.

CAPTIVES

For all the women who have their drinks spiked then suffer sexual assault. Also those who are trafficked and kept in captivity as sexual slaves. Some are killed. This story set in Australia and Europe is dedicated to them.

DAVE'S

BUSINESS

CANDY'S CAPTURE

Candy looked around as she entered the bar. The Sunday session was on. She was here to meet her friend Lola, who she hadn't seen for several months. Candy had made friends with Lola at university, but their lives had gone in different directions since then.

Lola had a position in a lawyer's office, while Candy freelanced making adverts and commercials for an advertising firm. Her glance round the room told Candy she had arrived first. She perched on a stool at the bar and waited for the barman to be available to order her drink. Candy didn't realise it, but her long curly auburn tresses cascading over her shoulders drew many admiring glances in the room.

"A Cider please." Candy asked when he came.

"Allow me to pay for this. Do you come here often?"

The smooth tone came from a male who stood next to her in the crowd. Candy looked up at the solid figure, now looking down at her with a smile. Blonde/grey short hair, regular features and clean shaven; was relaxed in smart casual attire.

"Thank you." Candy looked around at the door as she spoke.

The Barman delivered the cider and glass as she looked around to see whether Lola was here yet.

"I'm waiting for a friend of mine to join me."

When Candy looked back, the cider had been poured into her glass. Just then, a message came to

Candy's phone. It was Lola. She was very sorry, but she couldn't come after all. She would be in touch to catch up next time.

"She can't come after all." Candy explained to the stranger after a quick look at her phone. "I'm Candy, by the way."

"I'm Dave."

Their conversation flowed easily, but after her glass of Cider, Candy decided it was time to go home.

"Can I give you a lift home?" Dave offered.

"Thank you." Candy smiled her appreciation.

As Candy sank into the leather seat of the Forde Falcon, she lapsed into unconsciousness.

Barry looked around the rooms of the house one last time before he left for his nearby flat to change into his sergeants uniform and headed for work. Checking his phone, Barry smiled at the unconscious figure now installed and locked in her room.

"collecting" her had been much easier than he had expected. Barry had taken advantage of Candy's "compliant" state to broadcast to his clients his first sex session with her. Filming sex sessions with captives were lucrative, but the real financial gain was with the children they made available to the paedophile community, who were always looking for new bodies — the younger the better.

The sex session had started with cutting Candy's clothes off her body to reveal her nudity. The controls of the room camera were used to take close-ups of her breasts, which were fondled, squeezed and pummelled before journeying down to her pubic area. Candy's legs were tied, by ropes to hooks on the ceiling while he raped her.

Barry knew that once Candy woke up and became aware of her situation, she wouldn't be half as co-operative. A pair of metal cuffs had already been applied to her wrists and ankles. A GPS chip had been implanted under her skin in her back where Candy couldn't reach it. If Candy managed to escape, he would be notified immediately.

It had taken a year and lots of hard work to make the house how he needed it to be, for his business. Set behind a high wall, bushes and trees hid the front rooms from view. The driveway now secured by an electronic gate. Triple glazing on the windows, and shutters to prevent a view of the interior, along with heavy iron bars to secure the front door were the only indication that this wasn't a normal residence.

The back yard which once sloped steeply from the back door, so all the surrounding neighbours could see everything on the grassy slope, had been transformed into one that was completely private.

A large concrete patio area surrounded by gardens hid a burial ground, which was connected to a dungeon under the house. This was accessed by a hidden door in the hallway cupboard.

After seeing others attempt similar businesses on the dark web, that had failed by moving their charges around and also their disposal places exposed, he had organised to keep all activities on site.

Cameras were set up in every room for Barry to

monitor activity in the house. Most important of all, Barry took precautions so he wouldn't be able to be identified. Barry had bought a head mask with completely different facial features, hair colour and style to his own. He also kept media devices for the business separate to those for his own personal use.

CANDY'S FIRST DAY

Candy woke to soft daylight. With some anxiety she looked around to find she was in a strange room. Her memory of the evening before came flooding back. She remembered meeting Dave at the bar and getting into his car for a lift home – She didn't remember telling him her address. Had she really got so drunk that he had to take her to his home? Candy was feeling mortified as she brought her hands out of the bedclothes. What she saw made her blood run cold and her anxiety turn to panic!

On her wrists were metal bracelets – the sort that would be used for a prisoner! Is that what she now was? – Dave's prisoner!

Candy looked around the room. On her bedside table sat crockery and cutlery. A refrigerator was next to it. There was no sign of her bag or phone! Was he emptying her bank account? Or had they been disposed of? Across the room was a tiled ensuite which was open to the room. The other walls were bare except for a screen on the wall by the door. The single window had fixed wooden slats, with a very limited view of a side fence. Candy noticed that around her, both inside and outside the house was silent. Looking up at the ceiling, her anxiety increased. In the centre of the room was a dark disc that she recognised as a 360 degree camera.

Above her bed were four large hooks with ropes attached to them! As Candy pulled the covers back to stand up, she noticed two things. Her clothes had been replaced by a see-through negligée and metal bracelets had also been placed on her ankles!

Candy's hand brushed her breast as she supported herself to sit up. She noticed it was tender. Checking her other breast, it felt the same. Feeling dampness on her inner thighs, Candy put her hand down to wipe and smell it. She recognised the smell of semen!

Candy had some boyfriends in the past. Most of them had been out for a good time, with no intention of a serious relationship. Candy was now concentrating on her career. She wasn't relying on a man to complete her life.

Realising that she had been sexually assaulted and raped, Candy padded across the bare wood floor to the ensuite for a much needed soothing shower.

While she was in the shower, the screen flickered to life. Several men were now watching her! Candy turned her back on them. It seemed that she now was to live her life in a gold fish bowl! There was no sign of any clean clothing to wear. Reluctantly Candy put the negligee back on and returned to sit on the bed, facing the window as she took stock of her situation.

Candy wondered whether anyone was missing her yet. Her only contact with the outside world was the voyeurs on the dark web. They certainly wouldn't be telling anyone who could help her, where she was. She could only hope that her phone was in the house and that a trace could be put on it before the battery ran out. Candy turned round to face the men on the screen.

She studied their faces. Some had looks of expectation, others were curious.

"Show us your tits!" came the demand from one. Inwardly she shuddered and was glad she wasn't his prisoner. Glaring at the screen, Candy retorted

"You can already see them!"

"I'm not paying for you to be coy!"

Candy gave a little smile. "If you are stupid enough to pay for something that isn't given freely, that's your problem, not mine! Please get a refund and ogle someone else!"

There were titters of laughter from the other viewers. Candy was pleased to see the viewer remove himself from view. She hoped he wouldn't return!

"So where are we all from?" Candy smiled at the camera, before facing the screen. "I'm from Australia."

Some of the viewers immediately became nervous and withdrew. Others gave a smile, but shook their heads.

"You should know that its taboo to mention places on here." one gently chided her.

"No, I don't know." Candy was immediately serious. "I went out to meet a friend at a bar. They didn't show. Somehow my drink was spiked. I woke this morning to find myself here, as a prisoner!" Candy showed the bracelets on her arms and legs. She was starting to feel overwhelmed.

"You will have to excuse me; I need time to adjust."

With that Candy turned her back on them and began to cry. Once she had cried herself out, Candy realised that she was hungry. Her watch was gone, so she had no idea what time it was. The light from the window didn't give any indication what time it was either.

In the fridge, there was cereal, milk, a sandwich

and some bottles of water. Candy would have loved a cup of coffee, but realised that she wouldn't be seeing one of those any time soon. Dave had been very careful to make sure there wasn't anything here that could be used to harm. Having consumed the cereal, she started on the sandwich. A voice behind her, reminded Candy that she wasn't alone.

"What's your name?"

Candy looked around. Only one face remained.

"I'm Candy."

"Have you any idea where you are?"

"No. It is completely quiet here. There is nothing to indicate where I am at all."

The face nodded and withdrew. Candy tried not to feel any hope that here was someone who was on her side.

Candy realised that this room was to be her world for quite some time. If she was to remain sane and in reasonable physical health, she needed to start looking after herself – in between looking at ways to escape!

While the screen was quiet, Candy did a check of every surface of the room, including the door and window. The door didn't budge an inch. – it obviously had more than one lock! On checking the window, she now understood why the outside was so quiet. – It was triple glazed. The shutters were locked into position as well. She looked at the floor boards. It sounded hollow underneath. Was there a way out under the house? Candy was about to check the ceiling when a familiar voice came from the screen.

"I see you're checking out your new home. You know there is no escape until I'm ready to let you go."

"What do you want from me?"

Candy ignored his statement that there was no escape. She was also disconcerted to see, that Dave was able to talk to her without revealing himself.

"This house is a business. You are expected to pay your way by co-operating."

"And if I don't?"

"Privileges such as food, and toiletries will be withdrawn. If you try to escape, I will be able to track you and bring you back to the dungeon. The only escape from there will be to your grave."

"What about children? Are they part of your business? If not you will need to use birth control."

"Of course I expect you to produce children. They will be the biggest money earner."

The lack of emotion in Dave's voice made her blood run cold. Candy realised she was dealing with both a paedophile and a sadistic killer! She kept all emotion out of her voice.

"I see. Is that all?"

There was no reply, so Candy settled herself on the floor and started some meditation.

"What are you doing?"

Candy looked at the camera with a stony face.

"This room is now my world. How do you expect me to spend my time when I am alone?"

There was no reply, so Candy carried on with her meditation until she felt calm. She then started some exercises. The screen immediately came to life. With an inward sigh and grim determination, Candy carried on to the accompaniment of wolf whistles and requests to bend this way and that.

"Sorry boys!" Candy smiled at the camera. "This is for my benefit, not yours!"

Afterwards, she tried walking on single boards, then on the cracks between, to wisecracks about the amount of drinks she had had. There was banter back and forth about cocktails Candy was drinking – one viewer made and lined up all the cocktails she suggested and drank them for her.

The sound of the front door slamming alerted Candy that her pleasant session was now over and it was time for her to "perform". The screen fell silent as the viewers saw Candy's demeanour change. She turned towards the door and waited.

Barry turned on the business computer to see the interactions Candy had been having with his clients. He smiled at the income she was generating. It seemed she had a following already. There were two incidents he wasn't happy about. The first was when she told a client to go ogle someone else! – she would have to be punished for that! The second was her interaction with a client who asked her name and whether she knew her whereabouts. He recognised that here was a police hacker and immediately blocked his access.

Dave unlocked the door to Candy's room to throw a box of Pizza in on the floor before locking it again. Candy swooped on the pizza and ate it as swiftly as she could. She had a feeling she was in trouble for something, but wasn't sure what.

Candy was puzzling over what she had done when the door opened again. Dave had a whip in his hand.

Candy put a hand up to protect herself. The other she kept ready to grab the whip! It was going to be the first and last time he did it to her!

"When a client tells you to do something, you do it! – not tell them to take their money and ogle someone else!"

The whip cracked as it stung and snaked around her arm. To the viewers surprise and Dave's fury, Candy grabbed the whip with both hands and yanked it off him.

"I get it." Candy replied coolly as she swiftly coiled up the whip. "You strike me with one of these ever again, it will be you that dies!"

With that she ran over to the toilet and pushed it around the S bend. Candy heard Dave behind her, so she quickly reached up and pressed the flush button so he couldn't retrieve it.

A punch to the side of her jaw knocked Candy out cold. When she regained consciousness, both her arms and legs were strung up with the ropes and she was being raped again, completely naked. Candy tried to keep as relaxed as she could so she wouldn't be injured. Then Dave's phone rang. Candy heard enough to make out that Dave was actually Barry. He was being called in to work to help search for an escaped prisoner.

"I'm coming."

While Barry was away, the viewers called to Candy, asking if she was okay.

Feeling fuzzy from the punch, and knowing Barry would be viewing any interactions she had with them, she didn't answer. When Barry returned some hours later to release Candy from the ropes, she collapsed onto the bed exhausted. The blood flow to both her hands and legs had been compromised and felt completely numb as they flopped onto the bed. It was some time before her circulation returned enough, for Candy to get up to stagger to the ensuite.

Mentally Candy was still feeling spaced out from the punch she had received earlier. A glance at the screen showed some viewers still watching with concern.

"Isn't it your bedtime yet?" Candy asked as she adjusted the water for her shower. In the water, it hurt more than it soothed. Looking down, Candy could see she was covered in bruises. She also had a deep cut to her arm from the whip. After her shower, Candy looked for her gown.

"He's taken it away."

"He's taken everything out of the fridge except some water."

"Was it worth all this?" came one smart remark.

Candy glared at the offender. "Wash your mouth out!"

With as much dignity as she could muster, Candy strode over to the bed and gingerly laid down with her back to the camera. Eventually the light was turned out and Candy was able to shed the tears she had been holding back.

THE SEARCH FOR CANDY BEGINS

By Monday lunch time, Max the Manager at the advertising firm was concerned.

"Has anyone heard from Candy yet? I sent her an email, but she hasn't replied."

"She was meeting a school friend yesterday. Perhaps she's still hung over?" the reply came from Jerry, one of the office workers who was keen on Candy. The manager returned to his office and called Candy's phone.

"This phone cannot be reached. Please check the number." Came the recorded reply.   This message alarmed the manager. There was no ability to contact her. This was completely unlike Candy. He knew that something was wrong. He turned to his assistant.

"Marianne, Have you got Candy's address?" She nodded as she pulled out her book with employee and freelance contractor details. "Put all calls to answering machine and come with me!" Marianne swiftly obeyed and followed him out the door.

At the apartment building they rode the lift to Candy's floor. At her apartment the curtains to the living area were open. They could see right through to the doors of the balcony on the opposite side of the building.

"Perhaps she is in her bedroom?" Marianne asked. She began knocking loudly on the door. The only response came from the next door neighbour who came out to see what the noise was about.

"If you're looking for Candy, she hasn't come home yet."

"When did you last see her go out?"

"Yesterday afternoon." He saw the concerned looks on their faces. "You think something has happened?"

"We do! We will call the police."

"I will let the building manager know. The police will be wanting access."

A few hours later the advertising agency was visited by Geoff and Ken from CIB, to obtain details of what they knew of Candy's disappearance.

"Do you know where she was meeting her friend?"

"We understand she went to the "Hare and Hound.""

"Thanks. We will be in touch if we have any news or need to ask anything further."

Out of the office, Geoff called the "Hare and Hound." "Do you have the tapes from yesterday afternoon? Excellent! I'll be there shortly."

Ken called Telecom. "Can you give me the GPS movements of a mobile belonging to Candy Payne yesterday?"

By the end of the afternoon, they had the footage of Candy and "Dave" at the bar and her leaving with him. An interview with the barman was revealing.

"Yes, I remember those two. I saw him eyeing her up before offering to buy her a drink. He was really slick about pouring it too, while she wasn't looking. I think she called him Dave. There was something about him that wasn't quite right, but I can't put my finger on it."

"If you see him again, can you get his glass or whatever he's drinking from and give us a call?"

The detectives also had the GPS of Candy's phone, which travelled a short distance from the bar before being disconnected from the network. At the spot where her phone was disconnected, there was evidence of a phone being destroyed.

"This "Dave" definitely doesn't want her to be found. The question is; Is she still alive?"

"It's time to start a profile of him. I have a feeling there will be others that he will be targeting."

They visited Candys apartment block, first speaking to the Manager, who was unhappy to hear Candy was missing. Candy was one of their best tenants, always keeping her apartment immaculate and paid her rent and utilities on time. She checked her records, advising the detectives that Candy was paid up till the end of the month. Could the detectives please contact Candy's family and advise them that if there was no sign of her by then, they would have to clear her unit so it could be relet. If there was no contact with family, she would have to implement their "abandoned unit" protocol.

The detectives visit to Candy's unit revealed little out of the ordinary, except a letter and some photos from her sister who had an eighteen month old daughter. They noted her address to pay her a visit.

On Tuesday morning before Geoff visited Candy's sister, he received a call.

"Have you seen the latest offering on "Dark Sex" site? Her name is Candy. I was bumped off."

"Is this her?" Geoff sent him a screen shot from the Bar camera.

"That's her! – and him as well! He's got her as a

sex slave. Charming bloke. Threw her pizza on the floor at her. Not long after that my access was denied. He must have seen footage of me talking to her when no-one else was around."

"Is there anything else can you tell us?" "She remembers getting in his car for a lift home, but woke up in the room she is being kept captive. She has no idea where she is. The house is sound proofed, so she can't get any external clues.

"Thanks. I will get Bill onto it."

Jillian was playing with Eliza on the lounge room rug when she saw a strange car come into their driveway and two men in suits walk up to the door. She put Eliza on her hip as she went to answer their knock on her door.

The impassive looks on their faces gave Jillian no clue why they were here. They pulled out their police badges to show her.

"We are Geoff and Ken from CIB. You are Jillian? Candy Payne's sister? And are you her next of kin?"

"Our parents are in a remote area of Papua New Guinea. We have to wait for them to contact us on their monthly trips to Port Moresby. What has happened? Please come in."

"Candy is missing. When did you last have contact with her?"

Jillian couldn't keep a look of horror off her face, which made Eliza cry. She knew that something was wrong with mum. Jillian cuddled and soothed Eliza before answering.

"She came to visit us on Saturday. She also texted me on Sunday morning about attending a fair next weekend."

The detectives then explained how Candy had been picked up at the bar and that it had been her employer who had contacted them when they couldn't contact her on the Monday.

They also advised of their visit to Candy's unit where Jillian's address was found, and passed on the Apartment Manager's request for the unit to be emptied if Candy hadn't returned when her rent was next due at the end of the month. This brought tears to Jillian's eyes, which she wiped away before Eliza saw them. By now Ken was distracting her with a toy.

"We have only one good bit of news for you. We know Candy is alive, but we haven't any clues where she is yet. The bad news is that she is being kept captive."

"How do you know?"

"A colleague saw her on a dark web sex site."

As Jillian's face began to crumble, Geoff hastened to add "You need someone to support you and look after your little one. Is there any neighbours we can get or someone we can call to be with you?"

"Muriel and Mac across the road at number 10."

Ken picked Eliza up and took her with him out the door. Eliza started crying as she saw mum was upset again and she was being taken away from her.

Muriel their retired neighbour had seen the arrival of the two men and wondered what was up. After seeing one of them bring Eliza out and head for her house, she came out to meet them and took Eliza into her arms. Eliza's tears quickly dried up at the sight of a familiar face.

"I'm from CIB." Ken introduced himself as he handed Eliza over. "We've had to give Jillian some bad news. Can you come and give her some support?"

"Of course! I will just get Mac."

When the detectives departed, they had left their contact details and a promise to get in touch.

CANDY'S SECOND DAY

When Candy woke, there was one thought on her mind – Escape! But how? Candy looked at the ceiling, being careful not to study it too carefully. She pretended to doze between checking for joins in the plaster board and giving an occasional sigh.

Eventually she had to make a trip to the ensuite. As Candy sat up her head spun, she also felt sick. Feeling herself start to black out, she lay down again. Once it passed, she tried again, only much slower. Candy managed the walk across the room to the ensuite. She splashed water on her face, which made her feel better. Her jaw still felt sore from the punch she had received the previous evening. There were no mirrors in the room, so a comb was used to brush her hair back before styling it into a plait that she had used before.

Her new style elicited some wolf whistles from the now watching audience. She glanced towards and gave a small smile to the screen. Candy was feeling hungry, but knew she had to ignore the hunger pangs. A check of the fridge showed her that the viewers had been right. Only water remained. Grabbing two bottles, Candy returned to bed and after hydrating, laid under the bedclothes, much to their disappointment.

"You aren't going to talk to us?" One called out.
Candy gave a big smile to the camera.

"I will later. I'm on water rations today, so I have to conserve my energy. Besides, I'm still recovering after he used me for a punching bag last night." With that Candy settled down for a sleep.

Candy woke to find her bedclothes had been pulled back and she was being shaken violently. She gave a scream as the pain of electricity surged through her. Barry was using a cattle prod on her. She tried to sit up quickly, but blacked out and fell on the floor on the opposite side of the bed.

As Candy came round, Barry was standing over her. In the background, there was a loud chorus of angry voices telling him to stop. Very slowly Candy made her shaking body move. Ignoring the outstretched hand, she used the bed to pull herself up to her feet.

With a dignity she didn't know she possessed; Candy faced him. There was no mistaking the anger in her tone.

"I know you are trying to break me, both physically and mentally. You may break me physically, but I will die before you break me mentally! If you do break me, it will defeat the reason you brought me here!" Candy saw Barry's raised eyebrows and continued.

"You brought me here to make you money. I won't be able to entertain your clients if you break me! There isn't anything sexy in all the bruises and injuries you have done to me! Give me back my gown! I need regular food too, if I am to nurture the children you expect me to carry for your...."

"Enough!" Barry interrupted her. "If you don't perform by getting pregnant, you will be going straight to the dungeon to be eliminated! Now, get on the bed!"

Candy kept an impassive face as she obeyed. For once, Barry didn't tie her up, which she was grateful for. But his vigorous thrusting sent her head crashing into the headboard. She immediately blacked out again.

It was only when he had finished that Barry realised that Candy was unconscious. He gave her a good shake with no response. He was about to reach for the cattle prod again when a shout from the screen stopped him.

"STOP!!! You are killing her!!!

Barry turned to the screen, feeling irritated.

"How would you know? What makes you such an expert? Stop interfering!"

"I'm a Medic!" The viewer replied in an authoritive tone. "You gave her a bad case of concussion with that punch to her jaw yesterday. You have just given her an extra injury. Her head needs to be kept still for the next week at least. – that means no more sex until she has recovered!"

Barry gave him a glare, but left the room to bring back another gown and a bag of food which he placed in the fridge. When he returned, Candy had her head over the side of the bed, vomiting.

"Don't expect me to clean that lot up!" Barry growled as he threw the gown on the bed and left the house. Tomorrow he needed to find another girl to keep the viewers coming back to his site,

"I wasn't." Candy managed to say as he passed her.

While Candy was negotiating with Barry, conversations were being held among some of the viewers.

"Location anyone?"

"G (GMT) plus 7"

"Count me in." came three replies.

"Skills?"

"All locks, alarms etc."

"Wheels."

"Weapons."

"Message "Hoodie" now."

While "Hoodie" was arranging to break Candy out, another two were conferring.

"You were right, she is special! I will take her for our program. Her eyes and hair tell me her heritage is special too. Contact "Hoodie". Offer them $50k for her."

Amongst all the viewers was Bill, who quietly was filming proceedings and had directional mics to pick up any conversation among the viewers.

When Bill reported back to Geoff and Ken the next morning, they weren't happy that Candy now had serious injuries. They needed to involve immigration, customs and Interpol. Overnight Bill had contacted European colleagues. The viewer offering the $50k was identified as a trafficker of girls to the high end of the market. A call was put out to all Australian ports and Airports to investigate the arrival or departure of any superyachts or private planes.

After Barry had stormed out of the house. Candy looked up at the camera with steely determination.

"I'm sorry about this."

She looked at the screen to find that most of the viewers had removed themselves from view. With a little sigh, Candy gingerly sat up. Spotting the gown, she smiled and threw it over her shoulder. Carefully making her way over to the ensuite for the toilet roll, to wipe up the mess she had made.

"Do you know what day it is?" a voice asked from

the screen.

"That's a risky thing to ask on here!" Candy replied without looking around. "He will probably block you."

"I'm a medic. I'm just checking you haven't any memory problems after he knocked you out again. What day is it?" the medic persisted.

Candy looked at the screen. They were all looking at her intently, so couldn't tell which viewer he was. She looked at the camera.

"I think it is Tuesday."

"Time of day?"

"Its dark outside, so its evening."

"What year is it?"

"2019"

"Your name?"

"Candy Payne."

"Do you have any blood in your urine?"

"No."

"Do you have a headache?"

"I feel light headed from lack of food, but no headache."

"Good. You can have your shower now."

"Thank you all for supporting me."

Candy proceeded to have her shower. Revelling in a having a clean negligee and some food to quell the growling of her empty stomach!

As Candy settled herself into bed, she noticed that the viewers were still watching. She gave them a smile.

"Good night!"

Meantime "Hoodie" had been contacted. He accepted the deal, arranging to do the job in four days.

He would be contacted with the co-ordinates to meet the traffickers on a road.

In Europe a team had been summoned for a long haul recovery mission. It was going to be challenging for everyone, especially the pilots who had to find a suitable airport in Western Australia that would be unmanned by customs during the night, but still had access to fuel. They decided to enter via Broome, for a day before heading to Jandakot.

Claude, the doctor in the team shook his head at the current condition Candy was in, and worried at how she would travel by air with her concussion and the extensive bruising. He hoped there wasn't any deep vein thrombosis hiding among the Haematomas and other bruises Candy carried.

He arranged with the pilots to keep the plane as low as Candy could tolerate, and Asian air traffic control allowed, especially in the tropics where the clouds made travel "bumpy". They also set up a cradle with extra padding to protect Candy for this part of the trip.

Candy's sister Jillian received another visit from the detectives, advising her of the plan to smuggle Candy out of the country to Europe, and that they had all the authorities on watch.

"Have you any wealthy relatives over there, by any chance?" Geoff wanted to know. "They are paying $50k just to get her out of the house, which means the traffickers expect someone to pay $1m or more for her."

"I don't think so. Not that kind of money! Our mother has family over there, but she lost touch with them after she married and came out here."

After the detectives left, Jillian Looked at the painting of her great, great grandmother, in her bedroom. Looking back at her was an image of Candy.

Aleshia sniffed as she waiting for her next customer. She had to be careful, as the police were always on the lookout for girls working the streets. Usually locking them in the scanky watchhouse; an uncomfortable den of concrete and steel, for the night. There, they had to put up with the drunks causing trouble and strife till they sobered up.

She had been on the streets for several years now, living off her wits; ever since her mother took up with her partner. The moment Aleshia set eyes on him, she knew he was trouble. It didn't take long for him to try to take advantage of her for sexual favours. When she tearfully asked her mother to stop him, she didn't believe her.

"You're imagining things! He's not that kind of bloke!"

"I will leave you to him, then. I'll go and stay with Linda."

Linda was a school friend. Aleshia didn't tell her mother that Linda had moved interstate. On her first night she had roamed the streets in the city, feeling lost and hungry until one of the homeless men noticed her and took her under his wing, showing her the best sleeping spots and where to find food.

It didn't take Aleshia long to find that the streets were similar to home, only here you could insist on being paid for the sex. When some of the punters tried to pay her in drugs, she resisted, but after trying some, she gave in. Now she needed to have it every day. Aleshia was hooked.

Barry was cruising the back streets of Northbridge. Picking Candy up at the bar had been a bad idea. Yesterday her image (and his) had been in the Newspapers and on the TV news. Luckily he had his mask on, to put them off. The clothing he had worn was now buried under the house.

In the leafy tree-lined street, Barry spotted a solitary figure lingering in the dark. He knew a street walker when he saw one. He looked around. There was no sign of a pimp. This was even better! She wouldn't be missed as quickly, maybe not at all. Barry drew up alongside her and wound down his window, giving her an encouraging smile.

"I'm Dave. Are you ready for a good time?"

"As long as you can pay." She smiled back. "I'm Aleshia."

Even in the dimmed light, Barry could see this girl had a drug habit. From his inside pocket, Barry pulled out a wad of notes and threw them on her lap.

"Will that do?"

"It will do nicely. Where are we going?"

"My place isn't far, and it's more comfy than the car. What are you using, Meth?"

"You have some?"

"Of course!"

Barry brought Aleshia into the house via the garage. He waved her to a comfy leather couch.

"What's your poison?" he asked.

"Rum and coke."

Barry brought Aleshia her drink and Meth,

making sure she had both. Once she was in a haze, he picked her up and carried her into her new home.

"What are you doing?" Aleshia mumbled.

"I'm just making you more comfy. You want that, don't you?"

Aleshia didn't answer. The cocktail Barry had given her was already working its magic.

Candy had a pleasant day, chatting to viewers who came online to see her. She tried some gentle exercise, but as soon as she started moving her head around, she became dizzy and nearly blacked out. Candy had to be content to do some walking along the floor boards. She was nervous when Barry came in with her rations of food, but he left immediately with a preoccupied look on his face.

Peace reigned until the next evening when shouting and screaming came from Aleshia's room. Candy realised that she now had company, but felt helpless to do anything to help her new housemate.

In the meantime, Hoodie and his mates cased the house, leaving cameras in the trees and bushes to check on Dave's comings and goings.

One of the helpers also had a drone, which he was to bring along on the night.

Candy woke to find that some of her viewers were watching already.

"You're awake at last! Any chance of some exercises today?"

Candy gave them a beaming smile. "I will try, but breakfast first!" She pulled the cereal out of the fridge.

"Is that all you've got?" One viewer asked.

"Yes. I have a sandwich for later. Is anyone up to making me a full English?"

"Will this do?" A viewer held up a plate laden high with his meal and pretended to feed her some.

"That was delicious thank you." Candy gave him an extra smile.

It was time to give them what they wanted to see. Candy started by limbering up. Stretching her arms and legs. Lying on her back and pretending to ride a bike proved very popular. Standing at the end of her bed, she used it as a bar, to do a few ballet exercises she remembered from her childhood. However, when she leant over to make a scooping motion, her head went into a spin. Candy had to stop for several minutes until equilibrium restored itself.

"That's all for today." She announced before settling into a lotus position for some meditation. Her viewers had to be content with her chatting to them for the rest of the day.

Aleshia woke with a start. She looked around her at the room. She remembered Dave bringing her in and putting her on the bed, but not much else. She couldn't see the money he had given her either! Where was he? She needed some more meth soon! First, she needed a pee! As Aleshia sprung out of bed, she saw the cuffs on her wrists and ankles!   She shot across to the ensuite, checking there was no easy way to get the cuffs off without a key. It was only when she was sitting on the toilet that Aleshia realised she had an audience!

"Bloody perverts!" she shouted at them, which only made them laugh. Taking a good look around the room, Aleshia realised for the first time that she was in a situation that she wouldn't get out of easily. She checked the door. Of course it was locked! Aleshia went over to the window. She had a good try at removing the slats on the window, but that wouldn't budge either.

There were encouraging comments from her audience.

"Come on! Where's your muscles?!"

"Shut the F%#*k up, unless you're coming to help me get out of here!" resulting in roars of laughter and more encouragement. She looked at the table next to the bed, moving the crockery and cutlery. Turning it up-side down, Aleshia noticed that the legs were screwed on. Grabbing the knife she started to unscrew one of the legs. After removing it, she ran over to the slats. Just as Aleshia was attempting to wedge it between two slats, the sound of a key in the door, told her that she had been caught! Aleshia faced Barry with a look of defiance.

In a couple of strides, he crossed the room and ripped it out of her hand. Twisting her arm up her back, Barry frog marched her across the room to force her face down across the bed, where he proceeded to spank her on her legs and buttocks with the leg of the table, till she was black and blue. Her screams filling the house.

When Barry turned Aleshia over to tie her arms and legs up, she shouted at him.

"What the F%&*K are you doing? Where's my meth?"

"You will get your meth when you behave yourself!" He chose to wear protection while he raped her. He had no intention of having children with this girl. Barry knew that Aleshia could be harbouring any of the sexual diseases.

"If you don't want me to wreck the place, you will get me my Meth!"

"If you would like me to tie you up in the dungeon, and never come out, just try it!"

"I go crazy without it! I need it every day! PLEASE!"

Aleshia saw that Dave couldn't be manipulated. He had a ruthlessness that she didn't want to test, in that dungeon of his. She was relieved when he left the room and came back with a small amount. She pounced on it before he changed his mind.

The take-away Chinese meals Barry gave Aleshia and Candy were now stone cold, but they didn't dare complain.

"I see you're improving." Were Barry's words to Candy when he tossed in her meal.

In Europe, the flight had departed, with its first stop for fuel in Hong Kong, then on to Singapore.

In Perth, Hoodie and his team spent a session at a rifle range, getting used to the pistols they would be given during the raid. They also parked between street trees near the house, waiting for Barry to depart from

the house. Deploying a drone, they followed him to his
unit. Once Barry was indoors, they took note of the unit
he lived in and attached a GPS transmitter to the
underneath of his car.

NELLIE'S CAPTURE

Nellie was enjoying a "seniors" lunch at the tavern with her friends from her craft group. She was glad she didn't have to cook a solitary meal for herself in the evening. It had been several months since the love of her life; Dickie had fallen off the ladder he was using to clean the gutters. He never recovered from his injuries. She was grateful that they had nearly fifty years together. Some couples didn't have one!   So far she had sorted Dickies clothes, sending them to charity. Clearing out the shed that Dickie had used for his "man cave" had been harder. In the end she invited all the neighbours in to help themselves to his treasures.

The caravan and four wheel drive were put up for sale. She was going to miss their trips away, but the extra money would come in handy for her move when she was ready.

Nellie had thought she would be in this house forever, but it now felt too big on her own, and she was feeling a little vulnerable. It was time to sort out her craft and other "treasures" too! She had seen the size of units her friends now lived in. Most of the things she had collected over the years would need to go too. Nellie picked out a few things she couldn't part with, that filled a box.

She invited her daughter around for a cuppa and told her to take everything that she wanted, as everything else of value would be sent to auction. At first her daughter was alarmed, but was reassured when Nellie explained that she was downsizing. There simply wasn't room for most of the things she had collected. Her daughter insisted on coming with Nellie when she went house hunting!   If they didn't find anything suitable, she would have a granny flat built out the back yard for her.

When Nellie approached the bar for her usual Lemon lime and bitters, she didn't realise that she was being studied. When it was time to leave, Nellie nipped into the ladies before heading outside. It was only a short walk from home, but she wanted to pick up a few groceries on the way. Nellie noticed an exit by the conveniences, but didn't think anything of it.

As she came out of the Ladies, Nellie found herself being grabbed in a bear hug that left her arms pinned to her sides. She managed to keep hold of her handbag. A hand also covered her mouth as he hustled her out the door to a nearby car where she was unceremoniously dumped in the boot.

"Be silent or I will kill you!"

Nellie was so shocked that she was speechless anyway. She had more shocks to come, however, when the car stopped. When the boot opened, a heavy set man with greyish short hair pulled her out of the boot and hustled her inside the house from the carport and sat her on a leather couch.

"We can do this the easy way or the hard way. It's up to you."

"What do you going to do with me?"

"Take all of your clothes off!"

Down the hallway Nellie could hear a girl yelling and swearing at something. From his cold impersonal tone, Nellie could tell that this man had no consideration for her feelings at all. For the first time she began to fear for her life.

Shaking, Nellie obeyed. She felt completely vulnerable once her clothes were off. Cuffs were snapped onto her wrists and ankles. Nellie found a firm hand was placed on her shoulder, to propel her down the corridor. Dave opened a door to a cupboard. He pressed a switch behind the light in the ceiling. A door opened at the back. Nellie could see steps leading down to a basement. Dave pushed her forward into the cupboard. Stumbling, Nellie made her way down the steps to the basement with Dave following close behind her.

Nellie found herself in a large space, that she recognised as a dungeon. Limestone blocks lined the sides with a door at one end. Thick poles supported the floor above. A long table stood in the centre of the space. Chains were attached to the table. A large screen was positioned both on the wall and on the ceiling above the table.

"Get on the table."

Nellie tried, but she didn't have the strength to climb up. Dave then grabbed her to lift her on, attaching the chains to the cuffs on her arms and legs. He reached underneath, and pulled a lever. Part of the table between her legs opened. As Dave was making Nellie secure on the table, the screen above them came on. Nellie was mortified to find some men were looking at her. She looked away.

Dave went upstairs, returning with some bottles of water that he placed near her hand. Her handbag and clothes that Dave had brought down with him were taken through the door to another room that seemed dark. It was only when Dave finally left the dungeon and closed the cupboard door that Nellie burst into tears. It seemed that her fears were founded. She wasn't getting out of here alive!

Above the dungeon, both Candy and Aleshia were entertaining their viewers. Dave rewarded Aleshia by throwing her some more Meth. He shook his head at Aleshia's use of the ropes from the ceiling. She had brought them down and tied them together to make a swing.

"If that breaks, I will break your neck!" Dave threatened her.

"Promises, Promises!" Aleshia retorted as she swung higher, revealing more of herself to her audience.

Candy was feeling more tired today, and a little headachy, so was doing her walking along the floorboards. She was stopped in her tracks by the sound of sobbing from beneath the floor.

She knelt down and put her ear to the floor. Yes, someone was down there!

"Who's down there?" Candy called loudly. "I can hear you crying!" Through the sobs, Candy could hear her answer.

"I'm Nellie. I've been forced to strip and I'm chained to a table. There are men looking at me too! What's going to happen to me?!"

Candy could hear the panic in her voice. "I'm so sorry this has happened to you. I wish I could help you, but I'm locked up too! Just know that You aren't alone."

"Thank you!" Nellie replied before more tears came.

Knocking then came from the wall where

Aleshia's ensuite joined Candy's.

"Hey is someone there? I heard you calling to someone."

Candy knocked back. "Yes! its Candy here." I was talking to Nellie. She is in the dungeon! And she is scared stiff."

"OMG! Really?"

"Yes! Really! I feel so sorry for her! She sounds like an older lady too!

"That's not right!   It's bad enough for us..."

The sound of the front door announced Barry's return. Aleshia and Candy quickly returned to their beds. When Barry came in to restock her fridge, he tossed some Pasta Candy's way.

"Have you got some for our new lady?" Candy asked. "If not, give her mine." Candy picked it up and held it out.

Barry glared at her. "I run this house, not you! Stop interfering!"

"It's bad enough that you are going to harm her.."

"Shut up! You will be next!" Barry growled as he took the container of food from her and stormed out the door. He was going to throw it in the bin, but changed his mind and took it down to Nellie. It wouldn't hurt to lull her into thinking she was safe for a little longer.

"Here's your dinner." Barry dumped the pasta next to the bottles of water. He noticed she had drunk one already.

"Thank you." Nellie said quietly. She hadn't expected to get any food.

"Don't thank me, thank Candy upstairs."

"I'm feeling cold. Is there any chance of a blanket?"

Barry felt Nellie's chest. It felt cool.

"You will get one after your first session that your viewers are paying for."

In Candy's room there was silence until after Barry had closed the door.

"I dunno whether you are very brave or just plain stupid!"

Candy fixed the offender with a steely gaze.

"If you were in this dungeon, and waiting to be tortured and killed, would you be happy for me to let you starve?"

She decided that she had done enough entertaining for today and settled herself down for some meditation.

After dropping off Nellie's meal, Barry returned to Aleshia's room. Undoing his trousers, he ordered her to come over to him.

"Get down and suck it!" he ordered as he forced her to kneel in front of him. Aleshia had been forced do acts like this one before, one of her pet hates! She managed to keep an impassive face, all the while imagining biting and making him a eunuch!

In Candy's room Barry found her meditating. Her viewers were still watching.

"Why aren't you entertaining your viewers?" Barry asked in a non-tolerant tone.

"I haven't been so well today. I'm feeling headachy, so I'm taking it easy."

"Make sure you're on form tomorrow! By the way, when is your period due?" Candy had been dreading this question, but had expected it.

"In about a week."

Back down in the dungeon, Nellie dreaded Barry's return, she tried not to think of what he had in store for her first session. Hearing the door open and his steps on the stairs, she was glad to see the blanket she had asked for. He came over to the table and adjusted Nellies chains so her arms were above her head and her legs were firmly held down the bottom of the table.

"Ride her cowboy!" someone called from the screen. "Yeah, saddle up!" called some others. Barry hadn't intended to have sex with her, but he wasn't going to deny the viewers what they wanted to see. Barry dropped his trousers and climbed onto the table, forcing Nellie's legs apart to stimulate her before he mounted her. He noticed she kept an impassive face during the act.

"Isn't it time for her spanking?" was the next request. Barry was ready for this one. In a drawer under the table he pulled out a whip that he obtained from another dungeon in town, where anything goes, as long the act was consentual between the participants.

The first strike of the lash tore the skin on her shin. Nellie's cries echoed through the house. Both Candy and Aleshia stopped what they were doing to listen, tears pouring down their faces. Both of them vowing with grim determination that they would try to do something to stop him from hurting her again!

When Nellie succumbed to the pain and shock of her ordeal, Barry was unable to rouse her with the cattle prod. He checked her pulse. It was still there, but thready.

"Show is over for today." He threw the blanket over her, adjusting the chains for her arms down to the side of the table.

In Broome, the team's arrival had gone without a hitch. Emmanuel the trafficker's visit here as a businessman to check out the possibility of a resort for European visitors was accepted.

Barry woke up with a yawn. It was his day off, but he was on call for any searches that needed numbers of officers. He realised that he needed to get another girl for breeding. If Candy wasn't pregnant, he definitely would send her to the dungeon. This time he would find someone a bit younger and more compliant.

In Broome, the team had enjoyed their day in the sun while Emmanuel had pretended to make enquiries about investment opportunities. They now were airborne for the business end of the trip. They reached Perth in a few hours, touching down in Jandakot and refuelled by lunch time. With the plane parked up and the hire van delivered, they set off for a pleasant afternoon in the city. A message was sent to Hoodie.

"We are ready when you are." Emmanuel gave the co-ordinates for the meeting place. "Advise us when you start."

In the house, Aleshia, Candy and Nellie had awakened to a new day. Nellie could hardly believe that she was still alive, after the beating she received the previous evening. The table was terribly uncomfortable, but she was feeling too sore to move. She wondered if her daughter knew she was missing yet. Nellie reached for the water. She was certain she wouldn't be fed today.

It was mid-morning. Nellie's daughter Karen rang her home phone for her daily chat. There was no answer. She tried her mother's mobile. When the automated reply came "This phone cannot be reached.

Please check the number." Karen knew that something was wrong. She asked her husband to keep an eye on the children while she checked on Mum.

At her mother's house, Karen knocked the door, but didn't get an answer. Using her key she opened the front door.

"Mum are you there?" Karen called, half expecting to find her on the floor. Her call was met with silence. She searched the house and garden, there was no sign of her. Her mother's car was still in the carport.

Karen knew that her mother had been out with her craft club friends the day before. She found her mother's book for phone numbers and started ringing.

"Yes," Ivy the first friend she rang confirmed. "Nellie was with us for our lunch. She went off to the Ladies at the end when we were leaving. We didn't see her after that."

Karen checked all the hospitals for patients with her mother's name. She wasn't there. Karen then knocked the door of her mother's neighbours. They hadn't seen Nellie since she went off for her lunch. Karen left her number in case her mother turned up. She went back to her mother's house, took a deep breath and dialled OOO for the police.

Several hours had gone by and Karen hadn't returned home or called. When her husband called her, Karen's voice was breaking.

"Mum's missing. I'm waiting for the police to come."

In the afternoon, Barry decided on a different scene for his next girl. He went for a drive to the Galleria shopping centre. He noticed there were lots of teenage girls in groups enjoying themselves. One particular group caught his interest. Walking around, they were admiring all the fashion. One called Emma sighed.

"I could do with a Sugar Daddy!"

"We all could!" replied another, "but who would take us all on?" and they all laughed.

Barry took his chance when they split up to go home. Emma had gone outside alone to catch a bus.

"Excuse me." Barry gave Emma his most reassuring smile. "I couldn't help hearing that you are looking for a Sugar Daddy. I have the means to be one for you."

Emma looked around anxiously.

"Are you for real?"

"I certainly am. I'm Dave by the way."

"I have to be home by tea time."

"That's not a problem. My car is over here."

"We'll be doing it in the car?"

"No. My place is much more comfortable."

"A drink first?" Emma's reply was a big smile as she settled herself on the couch after Barry led her into the house.

"What sort of money are you needing?" Barry asked as he handed Emma her drink.

"A couple of hundred." Emma replied tentatively. Barry pulled his wad of cash out of his pocket and tossed it to her.

"Will this do?"

Emma flicked through it with a smile. She then gave Barry a saucy smile as she tossed down her drink.

She grabbed the money and put it in her bag as she let Barry lead her down the corridor to the back of the house where a bed was waiting. Emma's eyes boggled as she took in the room, with the open ensuite, screen and ropes hanging off the ceiling.

"Ohhhh!!! This is different, but I like it!"

Stripping off quickly, Emma helped Barry to strip his trousers off too, pulling him onto the bed. It was only then that she noticed that the screen was turned on with viewers watching. Emma looked at Barry questioningly. He gave her a smile.

"We have company, VERY jealous company! Give them a wave!"

Emma gave them a brilliant smile and a wave, which brought cheers and whistles. As they started to have sex, Emma found she couldn't keep her eyes open. That drink was more potent than she had thought. As Barry carried on his session with the now unconscious Emma, a message came through to her phone.

"Get something for tea. We will be out till late."

Barry had changed Emma into her see-through negligee, and was about to take her clothes and bag down to the dungeon, when a call came through. He was needed for a search in the northern Wanneroo area. An elderly man with dementia had wandered away from his lodge into bushland. They hoped to find him before night set in, as rain was expected overnight.

Hoodie and his crew had been monitoring Barry's movements to the Galleria then to the house.

"He's got himself another girl." Mac commented after logging into the "Dark Sex" site to see what Barry was up to. "This one looks much younger than the others. She looks like she is under age too!."

They monitored Barry's car return to his Unit. They sent up the drone and settled it on a nearby roof to be rewarded with footage of Barry re-emerging in his sergeants uniform to drive his car to the police station at central. Seeing Barry get into a police vehicle and head north on the freeway, made them feel easier.

"We will go in as soon as it is dark. Just hope he isn't back before then."

"A news headline's on my phone. An old bloke is missing. He's probably helping search for him."

Karen was now at home, with her husband comforting her. The detectives had been and taken some time to question her about where her mother had been. They were now visiting the tavern and requesting to see the security tapes from yesterday.

As they went through the footage, their anxiety increased. They saw Nellie head towards the corridor where the conveniences were, but she never came back. A thick set man, similar to the one who took Candy Payne followed her. He didn't return either.

The detectives asked whether there was an exit from that corridor. The manager confirmed that there was and brought up the footage of the back entrance and carpark. Plain to see was the man wrestling Nellie out the door with his hand over her mouth, and dumping her in the boot of his car. They didn't get the number plate, but they did have the model and colour of his car.

They thanked the manager for the footage and headed back to base. Ringing their families to say they would be home late. It was going to be a long night while they went through the clues they had and compared them to known criminals on their data base.

Darkness finally settled over the city.   In Wanneroo the police searchers were regrouping. There was no sign of the man so far. They would start again at seven in the morning.

Hoodie sent the message. "Starting now." Which was promptly answered by "Moving into position."

His team were dressed in black, with balaclavas on their heads and gloves on their hands. Parking on the verge near the house, a rope ladder was thrown over the other side and anchored to the wall. Swiftly they shinned over the top to approach the house. There wasn't any external alarms, which they were thankful for, to slow them down. It took a minute or so to pass the heavy security door, which was propped open. A master key swiftly gave them access to the interior. Lights were already on in the house as they traversed the corridor.

They came to the first door, but heard and recognised Aleshia's voice scolding someone for their cheeky request to see "more." Grinning, they moved on to the next door, Where they knew Candy was kept. A look at the lock, showed it was a special one that would take longer to bypass.

"Up the top. Who's the tallest?" The key was swiftly produced. A couple of swift knocks before they turned the key and opened the door.

Candy had been dreading the evening visit from Barry as she knew she would be expected to "perform" so it was a surprise to hear a knock before the door was unlocked. Barry never knocked! An even bigger surprise was the entrance of four men in black.

"Candy, we are busting you out of here! Come on, before he comes back." Hoodie came to lead her out of the room.

"But there are two others. Can you get Nellie first? He is going to kill her tonight!"

"We can't make any promises, but we will try. Our mission is to get you out!" Candy found two firm hands holding her arms and hustling her out of the room and the house. The sounds of "Good luck" coming from the screen as she left.

"Do you know that he has a GPS chip in me. Once I leave the house it will go to his phone. He will be able to follow us and grab me back. Dave has promised that if I do escape he will bring me back to the dungeon and kill me."

Hoodie pulled out his pistol to show Candy.

"We are ready for him."

It took a few minutes to get everyone over the fence and into the car. They were pleased that no-one was around to witness their coming and going. They headed for the freeway south.

Barry was looking forward to the evening's activities in the dungeon. The interest so far showed he would have a record crowd. The alarm from the phone in his pocket made Barry frown. He pulled it out. Candy was out of the house! While his mind was buzzing how she escaped, the officer driving looked over at him.

"What's up? Can we help?"

Barry turned the sound off and put the phone back in his pocket with a sigh.

"No. It's just the dog has escaped again! I will go and get him when I get back to base."

There was laughter and stories of dog escapades from the other officers in the car for the rest of the journey.

Once back at base, and in his car, Barry checked his phone. He could see Candy was in a vehicle on the Kwinana Freeway. It explained how she escaped! Someone had let her out! It could only be one of the viewers! He would make them both pay! Making sure his gun was loaded, Barry set off in pursuit.

In the car, Candy could see they were heading south. "Where are we going?" She wanted to know.

"We are meeting someone who wants you for their client in Europe."

While Candy was digesting the fact that she was being smuggled out of the country, and also wondering what country and "client" she would end up with, Hoodie looked at the GPS locator on his phone. Barry's car was following them. He looked back at Candy.

"He's coming after you. Where is that GPS transmitter?"

"It is in my back where I can't reach it."

Hoodie messaged the team, who were now in Position.

"Ten minutes away. Remove GPS transmitter ASAP located in back. – being tracked!"

"Will do. What apparel being worn?"

"Just see through negligee."

"Time of last meal?"

"Sandwich at lunch time."

When they reached the meeting point, they spotted the van parked under some trees. They parked directly behind it. Immediately a woman with a large blanket exited the van, followed by a man, who was carrying a brief case.

"Jazz, Bucky, Hide behind a couple of trees in

case Barry turns up." Hoodie ordered them, before he too got out to meet the team. The two men either side of Candy promptly exited the car and melted into the shadows. By now the female had reached the car and opened the door nearest Candy.

"Good Evening and Bonjour (Hello) Candy. I am Therese your chaperone. Please come with me. You will be well taken care of."

"Bonjour Therese. Merci(Thank you)." Candy replied without thinking in the French she had learnt at her mother's knee, as she exited the car. Therese swiftly wrapped the blanket around Candy and guided her towards the van.

"Thank you." Candy farewelled Hoodie as she passed him. Hoodie now had the brief case.

"Contact Jase Burrows when your settled."

In the distance a car was approaching.

"That will be Barry." Hoodie told Emmanuel. "We will sort him"

Emmanuel swiftly returned to the van where Claude had Candy lean over the back of a seat while he located the transmitter. Yvette his nurse held a torch to give him better light.

"A sharp scratch" Claude warned Candy as he used a blade to make a small incision. Candy gripped the seat a little harder, but it didn't hurt half as much as the whip Barry has used. Using a pair of tweezers, he extracted the device.

"Put down the window." Claude ordered Emmanuel. The Device was promptly thrown into the long grass while Yvette cleaned and put a dressing on the wound.

Barry had pulled up behind Hoodie's car. He could see a figure standing in front of the car. Barry stepped out with his gun in his hand. It was the last thing he knew. A bullet lodged in the base of his brain from behind. The occupants of the van heard the single shot as they pulled away and sedately drove the short distance to Jandakot airport.

In the van, the negligee had been swopped for a clean hospital issue gown and a top to toe exam was being conducted by Claude with a set of observations done by Yvette.

"What is this?" Claude asked about the still red deep cut on Candy's arm.

"It's from a whip."

"And this?" Claude referred to the burn mark on her abdomen.

"A cattle prod." Yvette hastened to clean and apply some cream to the areas, which immediately felt better.

Candy was bemused to find a pair of long white "Ted" stockings being applied to her legs. She understood when Yvette explained that they were to prevent DVTs during the long flight to Europe.

In the front, Emmanuel had phoned the Pilots and advised them to lodge their flight plan. To be ready to leave in thirty minutes.

Claude asked if Candy had any headaches recently.

"I had one yesterday, but it is mostly gone today."

"What if you bend over or move your head

around?”

“I still feel dizzy.”

“We were going to feed you, but to be on the safe side, we will start you on a drip of glucose.”

“What part of Europe are we going to?” Candy wanted to know.

Therese had been sitting next to Candy thoughout proceedings now replied. “We are taking you to a clinic in Switzerland first, till you are fully recovered from your injuries. Then when you are ready, you will be delivered to your benefactor.”

“Is there anything else you need to tell us from your experience in captivity?” Yvette asked.

“I may be pregnant. He was wanting children for his paedophile clients.”

“If you are pregnant, do you want an abortion? It can be arranged.”

Candy thought for a minute. “No. I will welcome the child regardless of how it was conceived.”

“What if your benefactor doesn’t want to provide for a child that isn’t his?” Therese asked with some concern.

“I certainly don’t expect any benefactor to support my child. I intend to be financially independent as soon as circumstances allow.” Candy looked at Therese with determination. “I have had an independent life with a successful career. I intend to do so again.”

Their conversation was curtailed by their arrival at the hangar at Jandakot, where Candy and the team transferred to the jet. Candy was surprised at how big it was. She was escorted to her seat – a plush leather chair, which was capable of lying flat, and was shown the belt for fastening.

Claude inserted an intravenous cannula into Candy's arm while Yvette set up the bag of glucose and the line to connect it to the cannula. Candy shivered as she was feeling cold. She didn't know whether it was from lack of food or from the air-conditioning in here! Therese pulled the rug over Candy again while Yvette took her blood sugar level.

"It's a little low. Your shivering should stop soon."

The pilot asked everyone to take their seats as they were beginning their departure. In five minutes they were in the air. Candy looked out the window at the carpet of lights below them, biding a silent farewell to her sister and her family and wondered if she would ever return.

In the cockpit, the pilots were giving a sigh of relief as they had to answer some awkward questions from the tower as to why they were leaving at such short notice instead of the planned departure in the morning. The excuse that there was a family emergency for Emmanuel to return to Europe asap seemed to be accepted. However, the police were contacted, with Interpol and authorities in Europe put on alert.

Candy noticed that the plane levelled out at much lower altitude than the airlines, but her attention was diverted by a clipboard full of forms that Therese gave her to fill in. Among all the data wanted, of her family history and that of her own life history, was a form for ID.

Therese took a quick look through all the details Candy had submitted, and gave a little smile as she passed the information over to Emmanuel. Their passenger was indeed a valuable one. Her mother was member of French nobility no less.

Candy could smell coffee and food being prepared in the galley behind them, but had to ignore her stomach grumblings that the smells triggered. While the others went to the dining area, Yvette drew a curtain around Candy's area and placed a catheter pack on the table in front of them.

"Claude doesn't want you walking around the cabin if possible, so I will put in a catheter for you for the journey." Candy was happy to have this done, as she felt the need for relief soon.

"We may have to fly at higher altitude when we reach the tropics, so please let us know straight away if you get any headaches or pains anywhere."

Candy looked at the padded cradle lying nearby. "Is that for me?"

"Yes." Yvette smiled. "If it gets extra bumpy we will pop you in there."

Despite all the questions running through her head, Candy found herself nodding off to sleep, only to find Yvette calling her name and giving her a gentle shake.

"The pilot has detected turbulence up ahead. Can you stand up for us while we arrange the cradle?"

Despite the comfort of the chair, Candy was relieved to stand up for a few minutes while they strapped it in place on her chair which was now flat. Once Candy was installed and strapped in the cocoon,

Claude came and injected medication into her canula.

"We are putting you to sleep for a while."

Yvette attached Candy to a monitor for her observations. By the time Yvette had finished, Candy was oblivious to everything around her. An airway and oxygen were also applied, before Yvette settled on the bed she had made up for herself next to Candy. Therese had already retreated to the sleeping area down the back of the plane.

Candy had no idea what time it was, when she came round. She went to stretch, but was reminded by the straps that she was still in the cocoon. Another bag of fluid was keeping her hydrated. She looked over at Yvette who smiled to see Candy awake at last.

"Are you ready to get out of there yet?"

"It's very comfy in here, but yes!"

Therese bustled forward to help support Candy as she stood up while Yvette removed the cradle and restored the seat to the upright position.

"Where are we?" Candy wanted to know. She could see lakes, fields and towns passing below.

"We are over Europe. We land in a few hours. You don't feel dizzy at all?"

"No." Candy gave her a big smile. She was feeling better than she had for several days.

"Are you ready for a shower? I will remove the catheter too."

"Lead me to it!" Candy grinned. Yvette stayed with her while she showered.

"This is so nice!" Candy commented, "not having men looking at me while I'm in the bathroom!"

"Surely not on the toilet too?!" Yvette was

shocked.

"Nothing was private! The ensuite was completely open to the room. They could see everything in the room." Yvette shook her head at the thought.

"How long were you in there?" Yvette wanted to know.

"A week. I am extremely grateful that your team has removed me from the country. You have saved my life."

"What do you mean?"

"I had another week to prove that I was pregnant. If I wasn't, I was to be sent into his dungeon to be tortured and killed. If I survived till delivery, I would have been killed afterwards. The day before I was rescued Aleshia and I had to listen to him torturing an elderly lady called Nellie. He was intending to kill her the evening I was rescued."

"I believe you have grounds to apply for asylum!"

For a few seconds Hoodie and his friends stood looking at the van as it drove into the darkness. They would miss her! Hoodie broke the mood by flinging the briefcase into their car.

"Come on, we have lots to do. I'm not sure how much time we've got."

It took the four of them to lift Barry's body into the boot of his car. They then went through all of his pockets, finding both of his phones, and keys to both of the properties. The police phone was turned off.

It was agreed that Hoodie and Bucky would go to the house, free the girls and look for a suitable place to bury Barry. Mac and Jazz would go to Barry's unit to have a check for anything of value they could liquidate. Barry's phone would be left there. They knew the police would check there eventually, along with the house he had been using.

At the house, Nellie was feeling very sore! She had been on this table for over thirty hours. Her water had run out and she tried not to think of how hungry she was. Nellie reminded herself that she wouldn't be needing any food shortly. She had comforted herself during the long day that very soon she would be reunited with her Dickie. Large numbers of men were now looking at Nellie and telling her to take her blanket off. Nellie happily ignored them.

In Aleshia's room, she was starting to feel jittery. Barry was late coming to give her, her fix of Meth. She was also starving hungry! She also noticed that more men were looking at her than usual.   She went over to the Ensuite and knocked on the wall next to Candy's room.

"Candy!"

"It's no use calling her," came calls from the screen. "She's gone."

"What do you mean, she's gone?"

"Someone came and took her away."

"It wasn't Dave who runs this place, was it?"

"No. It wasn't him. They had masks on."

For the first time since she had come here, Aleshia began to have hope that she might get out of here! She got on her rope swing and began to propel herself higher and higher – she had a feeling this would be her last performance for them, so she might as well make it a good one.

In Emma's room, she was starting to wake up. She felt guilt and fear! It was dark and she was supposed to be home by now!   Emma looked around for her handbag. It was missing! What had Dave done with it? She went to the door. It was locked! For the first time Emma noticed that she had a see-through negligee on and she had cuffs on her wrists and ankles. Where were her clothes? She started to panic. Men were looking at her again and asking her to show them her privates. Emma turned her back and tried not to cry. It had seemed fun this afternoon while Dave was here, but it wasn't anymore. She just wanted to go home!

The sound of the front door drew both hope and fear in the house occupants. Aleshia's door was the first to be opened. She was already down from her swing. Hoodie took the extra precaution to wear a cap as well as his balaclava in case the police were in the crowd watching. Bucky came forward to release her from her cuffs while Hoodie addressed the crowd.

"This show is being shut down. If it does restart, it will be under new management and with girls that are not only free, but want to be here."

"What about our money?"

"Sort it with your bank."

"Where's previous management?"

Hoodie didn't look at the viewer asking the question. He knew it would be the police.

"He's where he belongs! – in the grave he intended these girls to be in. Come on," he addressed Aleshia. "We have some pizza for you."

"What about Nellie in the dungeon? She won't have had anything to eat all day!"

Down the hall they could hear yelling and banging on a door. Aleshia went with them. On opening the door, a tearful Emma came out. She saw the men in black and with balaclavas. She became silent, not knowing what to expect next.

"What's your name?" Aleshia asked her, shocked at how young this girl was.

"I'm Emma. Where's Dave? And where's my things?"

"One thing at a time." Hoodie spoke firmly. "You won't be seeing Dave again. You've had a very lucky escape! We will look for your things and once those cuffs are off, there is some pizza in the front room."

Aleshia Hoodie and Bucky went through the rooms in the house, but couldn't find the entrance to the dungeon. So Aleshia put her head to the floor and called out to Nellie.

"Nellie! Nellie, it is Aleshia! Can you hear me?"

"Yes, I can hear you."

"How did you get into the dungeon?"

"There's a cupboard in the hallway. Behind the light there is a switch that opens the door."

Aleshia looked at Hoodie. "Behind the light in the hallway cupboard."

"We would never have found it!" Hoodie muttered as the door opened.

Aleshia led the way down the stairs to the figure laid out on the table with only a blanket for comfort.

"You can all bugger off! No snuff happening here!" Hoodie growled at them as Bucky released Nellie from the Cuffs.

"We are getting you out of here!" Hoodie promised her, but there is something I have to do first!'

He sprinted back up the stairs to search for the computer he thought he saw on the way in. Finding it, there was of course a password to get past. He tried "Dark sex" and to his delight gained entry to the system showing all the rooms in the house. One by one he shut down all the cameras in every room, starting with the dungeon.

Both Nellie and Aleshia saw the screens go blank and smiled at each other. Bucky took his balaclava off.

"He took my clothes and bag through that door." Nellie looked at the door at the end of the room. "Can you get them for me?"

Bucky led Aleshia over to the door. When he opened it, a pitch black space confronted them, the smell of soil was in the air. They eventually found the light switch inside the door. When turned on, light flooded the space to reveal four graves. It was obvious there were plans to create many more, by the markings Barry had made. Bucky turned to Aleshia.

"I don't think you should be looking at this!"

"I know these are supposed to be our graves! – He threatened it often enough. Right now, we need to find Nellie's things! I bet they are in one of the graves. My bag is probably in there too, along with Candy and Emma's things."

When Hoodie came back down stairs, he had Mac and Jazz with him.

"They are getting my things." Nellie explained when Hoodie found her alone. He could hear voices from the room at the end of the dungeon.

When they looked in, they were stunned into silence. Bucky had jumped into a grave and was handing out clothes and a bag to Aleshia. She helped to pull him out after he retrieved items from each one.

Hoodie turned to Mac and Jazz. "Get a couple of sheets from one of the rooms. We will wrap him in them. This solves the problem of where to put him."

Nellie beamed when she saw her clothes and bag. By now Emma had joined them and was happy to have her clothes and bag returned to her too. While the men went outside to attend to Barry, Aleshia and Emma dressed before helping Nellie into her clothes. They were helping Nellie off the table when the wrapped body came skidding down the stairs, with the men following behind.

"Do you think you can get up these stairs?" Aleshia asked Nellie ignoring the nearby body.

"With your help I can."

Her handbag firmly tucked under her arm, and with Aleshia and Emma each side of her, Nellie slowly made it up the stairs to sit in the comfort of the couch. Half cold pizza was waiting, but neither Nellie nor Aleshia cared.   They looked through their handbags. Their cards were there, but their cash was gone. When the men came back, Aleshia had a small safe sitting on the table in front of them.

"Can anyone crack this?"

"Allow me!" Bucky replied with a smile.

Within a minute, the door was open. Inside was a stash of cash and some small packets of pills that she recognised as Meth. She looked at Hoodie.

"It's up to you, but I think you should go into rehab and give yourself a new start."

"Back on the streets isn't a new start."

"You can always come and share my house with me. I need someone to keep it nice."

"I will have my own room?"

"Yes, and your own bathroom."

"It's a deal." She looked at the money.   "He took all our money off us."

"Nellie, how much are you missing?"

"$300."

Hoodie peeled off $500 and handed it to her. He also handed Aleshia $500, but she handed it back.

"Hang on to it till I get out." Aleshia could no longer hide the trembling and agitation she was feeling.

"Can someone take me to the hospital?"

"$200 for me please. And, can someone take me home?" Emma asked. She had seen the message her parents had sent. She just might get home before them!

"When you've sorted the girls, I would love a lift home." Nellie added.

"I will take Aleshia and Emma." Bucky offered.

Hoodie gave Aleshia a card with his phone number.

"Call me. I will pick you up when you're well."

Hoodie then rang a mate with contacts.

"I have a car that needs to disappear. How soon can it be collected? Half an hour? Sweet."

When the tow truck driver came and saw the car, he nodded his approval.

"Is it drivable? Good. You will get a good price for it." Within five minutes, it was driven onto the back of the tray and off to its new future.

While Hoodie was waiting for Bucky to return, they did a sweep of the house, removing anything they could use.

Nellie had a little nap while she waited. She was extremely tired after her ordeal, but happy to be alive and being looked after.

"Nellie!" a gentle shake woke her up. "It's time to take you home. You've done so well after everything you've been through."

"Thank you." Nellie gave him her best smile. "I'm looking forward to getting into my own bed at last!"

Hoodie pulled up outside Nellie's house as quietly as he could. All the houses around them had their lights out. He whispered to Nellie when he helped her out of the car and into her house.

"Are you sure you will be alright?"

"I will be fine, thank you very much."

Nellie gave him a quick hug, before she shut the door and turned on the light inside. A nice cup of tea was called for!

Hoodie's quiet exit was heard by her neighbour across the road who saw that Nellie's light was on. She immediately rang Nellie's daughter Karen. Karen looked at the time. It was nearly midnight! She called Nellie's home phone and was relieved to hear her mother's voice answer her.

"Mum! What happened to you? Are you alright?"

"Nothing that a nice cup of tea and a shower won't fix."

"I'm coming over!"

Before Nellie could reply, Karen had rung off. She then rang the detectives who were still at the office.

"Mum's just got home!" I'm about to go over."

"Tell her we will come and talk to her in the morning."

When Karen let herself into her mother's house, Nellie was in the shower, with her back to her. Karen took one look at all the whip marks and the pressure marks on her mother's body, and had to take herself into

the other room for a good cry. It was obvious she had
been abused.

When Nellie eventually turned the water off,
Karen had composed herself enough to go in to help her
dry off, put some dressings on the pressure areas and
some soothing cream on her wounds.

"Do you want to come and stay with us for the rest
of the night?" Karen offered her mother. "You may get
some flashbacks that may be hard to deal with on your
own."

Nellie was hesitant, but Karen was right!

"I was looking forward to being in my own bed,
but just now I didn't want to go to bed because I'm
thinking about everything that happened! Can I bring
my foam underlay?"

"Of course you can!"

She gave her mother a big cuddle, which
prompted her to burst into tears. She had been strong
for so long and now all the misery she had suffered
during her ordeal was coming to the surface. As she held
her mother, the home phone rang, but she ignored it.
Shortly afterward there was a knock at the door. The
neighbour let themselves in. Seeing Nellie crying in
Karen's arms, she came over to comfort her too.

"Is there anything I can do?"

"Can you keep an eye on the place?" I am taking
her home when she is up to it."

When Nellie had calmed a little, the neighbour sat
with Nellie while Karen loaded her car with her mother's
bedding, some clothes and her toiletries. She then rang
her husband to say she would need some help when she

brought her mother back.

The neighbour promised to visit her in the afternoon.

After Bucky dropped Aleshia off at A & E, the triage nurse told her to take a seat.

"It may be a while before we can take you in, and we may have to sedate you."

Aleshia nodded her agreement. She was feeling so agitated, she had to stop herself from punching the nurse, crossing her arms extra tight.

"Why are you doing that with your arms?"

"I'm trying not to punch someone! I need rehab. Can that be arranged while I'm in here?"

"Are you sure that is what you want?"

"Yes!"

The nurse made a call to psych for a nurse to review her.

"Do you object to a straight-jacket and a padded room?."

"I won't be able to hurt anyone?"

"No."

"Good! I can't control my arms for much longer!"

The nurse nodded to some security guards who came to restrain her while the jacket was put in place and took Aleshia to her new home while she recovered from her withdrawals.

Bucky looked at Emma who was now silent and looking very pensive as he drove her home.

"Emma, are you on the pill?"

There was silence for a few seconds.

"No. Why?"

"If you are going to have sex with blokes, you need

to be on it. You know you could be pregnant?"

"You mean I could be after that one time?"

"That's all it takes. Do you know the date when your last period was and when your next one is due?"

Emma thought for a minute or two.

"It's in about a fortnight."

"Then you need to see a doctor in the morning for the morning after pill, to stop you getting pregnant. Do you have a doctor you can trust, to see?"

Emma was silent again. She didn't have a doctor she visited on her own. Her mother usually took her.

"How old are you Emma? Thirteen?"

"I'm twelve." Her reply was extra quiet.

"Do you know that any blokes that have sex with you can go to jail?"

"Why? What's wrong if we both want it?"

"Because you are under age until you are sixteen. It's the law."

When Emma's parents came home, her mother went to check on her. Emma usually had some music on, but tonight there was silence and she thought she could hear Emma crying. She knocked on Emma's door and went in. Emma was huddled in her bedclothes, tears streaming down her face. Going over to cuddle her, she asked.

"What's up? Whatever it is, you can tell me about it."

Emma gulped. "I met someone." She took a deep breath. "I think I'm in trouble."

"You need to see a doctor?"

Emma nodded.

"I will take you in the morning. Whatever

happens, I will help you through this. Okay?"

Emma nodded. They stayed cuddled for a while as both Emma and her mother came to terms with what may be. Her mother gave an internal sigh. She hadn't expected this for a few years yet!

SOLVING THE PUZZLE

When the police gathered the following morning to search for the missing man, Barry was absent. A call was made to his phone, but it went to message bank. They thought it was strange, but carried on without him.

Afterwards, officers were sent to his unit, in case Barry was ill and unable to contact anyone. Inside, they found it empty, but his phone was there. It was obvious though that someone had been in to clear out any valuable items. Barry's television and computer were missing, along with his car. Forensic testing found no traces. They asked Telecom to give them a record of where Barry had been before his phone had been turned off.

A message was waiting for Geoff and Ken when they came in to their office in the morning, to say that Nellie was staying at her daughters and that she would be up late after having a bad night.

The detectives interviewed Nellie in the afternoon. They found that Nellie had been kept in a house, along with some others, including one called Candy. It could only be Candy Payne that was now in Europe. She also mentioned a girl called Aleshia who was unwell. She had been taken to hospital and a much younger girl, Emma.

The detectives were thankful they brought a female police officer with them as Nellie found the abuse she received difficult to talk about; though she had nothing but praise for the four masked men who rescued her and the other girls from the house. The female police officer was able to persuade Nellie to show her the injuries she had sustained and also recommended to Karen to take her to the doctor in the morning for a check-up.

When the detectives returned to their office, a message had come from Interpol. They had interviewed Candy Payne on her arrival at Lucerne in Switzerland. The man who abducted her had called himself "Dave" but his real name was Barry and he was a policeman.

Geoff and Ken looked at each other. Up till now they hadn't connected the abductions of Candy and the other females with Barry's disappearance. This now needed to be dealt with by internal affairs. Geoff made a call to the commissioner. Could they have a photo of Barry to compare with the man who had abducted the females?

The information from Telecom had come in. There was a property near Barry's home that needed investigation, also the area where Barry's phone had been turned off. They also needed to locate Aleshia and Emma and interview them.

When the team from Internal affairs came for a briefing, there were shocked faces at the enormity of the task ahead of them. When they left work, Geoff and Ken were given a couple of days off before they were allocated to new cases to solve.

The new team's first priority was an interview with Aleshia, but they had to wait a few days while she recovered sufficiently for the interview.

She agreed to do the interview as long as a nurse was with her. If it became too much, they had the authority to stop the questioning. The detectives also had a female officer lead Aleshia through their questions. With gentle probing, Aleshia was led through her experience, from the time "Dave" picked her up, through to when she and Bucky found the graves with their possessions inside. At the time, Aleshia had been more concerned about getting Nellie's clothes and bag for her, and had been delighted to have her clothes and bag returned. But now it hit home, that "Dave" had really intended to murder her! – He had intended to murder them all! Aleshia couldn't continue.

The police now had an idea where Barry's body was, but how to find it. They searched high and low for the entrance to the Dungeon that they had been told about, with no success. They had to half demolish the interior walls in the house to find it. It was only when they chain-sawed the back wall of the hall cupboard, that the stairs to the dungeon revealed themselves.

Down in the Dungeon, they found the table where Nellie had to endure her abuse. They also found the whip he used. Tests detected Barry's DNA on the handle and Nellie's DNA on the lash end.

Finding Barry's body was much harder than they had expected. The door was no longer in place. In fact, the blocks fitted together so well, it was almost impossible to know that another room existed beyond this one. They had to go outside and walk around the building, before they deduced that the graves had to be under the back patio area.

Having another look at the wall, they gave all the bricks a good push. Eventually they found one that moved. Once in the grave yard, they found the door and three of the graves. They had to bring in a cadaver dog to locate him. Barry's gun was still in his hand. In the grave they also found the mask that "Dave" had been wearing. The bullet hole in the mask matched the bullet entry wound in Barry's head. Barry's DNA was also found in the blood on the inside of the mask.

The team also wanted to interview Emma, but apart from footage of him following a group of young girls around the Galleria, there weren't any cameras of him picking any of them up. There hadn't been any complaints of girls being assaulted either. The team did keep photos of the girls on file just in case more evidence came up later.

The team also tried to find "Hoodie" but he had disappeared without trace. Even though Barry had broken the law, killing a policeman was also an offence.

Aleshia woke up in the female room of the psychiatric ward. It was early yet, with the soft light of early morning coming through the curtains. She had come so far since the night she had been admitted, when her withdrawal from Meth had caused her to be out of control.   Aleshia never wanted to visit that painful place ever again. The counselling sessions she had received, had helped her to accept and move on from the life she had been forced to live, first with her abusive stepfather, then on the streets, and finally her time in captivity.

Aleshia's recovery had been progressing well, until the police visit for information about her time in captivity; but now she broke down. Even though she had been told that "Dave" could no longer harm her, it took some time for her to feel safe and fully recover.

The day finally came when Aleshia was ready for discharge. When she called the number that Hoodie had given her, it went to message bank, so she left him this message.

"It's Aleshia, ready to escape! I will be out the front. If you aren't here in an hour, you will have to search for me!"

Jase had been up late, sorting things he didn't need. He had a yearning to hit the road to see the country. Given the cash he now had, if he picked up the odd job here and there, fine, but it wasn't essential.

He heard the phone ring among the clutter on the

floor. By the time Jase found the phone, Aleshia had left her message. He grinned as he quickly dressed. He would see whether she was up for a road trip. Within half an hour his Toyota drew up beside her. Aleshia recognised him despite the hat, hood and sunglasses and quickly piled into his car. Jase gave Aleshia a big grin.

"It's great to see you looking so good!" then concentrated on driving in the heavy traffic. He took another look at her while they waited at the lights. This was a completely different Aleshia to the drug affected girl they had rescued. She grinned back at him. "I know I look much better! I'm feeling it too! It's been a long hard road though, but I'm not going back there!"

"Good! What do you think about going on a road trip? We can look for the odd job on the way round, but the world won't end if we don't find one?"

"Where are you thinking of going?" She wasn't sure about this change of plan, but didn't show it.

"We will head up the north west to begin with. There are plenty of spots to throw a line in and there are lots of country towns where we can get casual jobs in the Pubs or on farms."

"So you don't need me to sort your house out for you?"

Jase grinned. "Actually I do! It's still a mess! If we can get it sorted, I will rent it while we are away. I don't want to leave it empty."

Aleshia felt better that they were coming back some time.

"I hope they don't trash it on you!"

"They shouldn't do. It's Bucky and Jazz."

"That sounds like a plan! You know I've never travelled, and never thought I would get the chance to do it." She thought for a minute. "Would you still be going if I hadn't come out?"

"Yeah, though I would be doing it on my own, which isn't as much fun. I would have left Bucky's number at the hospital if I had gone alone."

It took several weeks to make the house habitable for someone else to live in and "declutter" all the gear that wouldn't be needed when they came back. It was decided to put all Jase's gear he wanted to keep, in storage. Aleshia also persuaded Jase to get a "Jim's mowing" contractor to look after the garden and a cleaning lady, to look after the house once a month. This was much appreciated by both Jazz and Bucky when they moved in.

In the meantime, Aleshia revelled in having her own room and bathroom as promised.   She knew things would change when they were on the road, but she would take things as they came. One thing Aleshia was sure of, that Jase wouldn't mistreat or take advantage of her.

They were having dinner one evening, when a new message came through on Jase's phone. He took a quick look, scanning through the message before grinning at Aleshia.

"Guess who's just got in touch? It's Candy!"

"Candy!" Where on earth is she? Does she say how she is?"

"She is in Switzerland, and listen to this! – she's having twins! Also she's heading to France soon!"

"OMG! Do you know who's kids they are?"

Jase nodded. Aleshia looked at Jase with both pain and admiration in her eyes.

"I'm so glad you rescued us all when you did. It isn't worth thinking about, what he would have done to her and those kids."

Aleshia's face crumbled. She was still vulnerable. Jase came and took her in his arms to comfort her.

"No, he isn't worth thinking about, and you must remember he can't hurt any of you ever again!"

Nellie was pottering in the garden, though it was a different garden to the one she used to have. Her stay at Karen's ended up being permanent. Her old home she had shared with Dickie now had a new family living in it. After the sale went through, it took another six months for her new home to be built in Karen's back yard, with a small patio area for her to sit outside. Karen made a border garden bed for her around it and took her to the nursery for some plants that she helped her to plant.

Nellie now had a weekly "Ladies lunch" at her place, to catch up with her friends. She also had a regular visit from her neighbours by her old house, who kept her up to date with happenings in the street. Her days of going to the tavern for lunch were over. Karen now took her out shopping whenever she wanted. Nellie's new world was a much smaller one than the one she had, but she was content and more importantly she felt safe.

Emma and her mother sat in the waiting room of the medical centre. She had tried to dress more "grown up" for this appointment and hoped that the doctor would be understanding. When they heard that the female doctor was off sick and that a male doctor was available, Emma wanted to turn round and go home, but her mother had squeezed her hand, and reassured her, that everything would be okay.

When they sat down in the doctor's office, Emma was pleased that her mother had offered to do the talking. His manner seemed to be abrupt. Maybe he had too many patients to see.

"When Emma was out with her friends yesterday, she met someone. They ended up having sex. Can you give her a script for the morning after pill please?

The doctor looked at Emma's date of birth and frowned. "She's too young! What do you.."

"She's too young to be having a baby!" Emma's mother cut in. "We didn't come here for a lecture, we want help. If you won't help us we will go elsewhere!"

In stony silence the doctor typed up a script and printed it out.

"This is a once only treatment." The doctor commented as he handed the script to Emma. You will experience a period and maybe some cramping within the next twenty four hours.

"Thank you." Emma replied just as gravely as she accepted it.

"Are you on the pill?" the doctor asked, reaching for the blood pressure cuff to put it on her arm.

"No. I wasn't expecting it to happen." The doctor allowed himself a glimmer of a smile.

"Many people aren't the first time."

"Are your periods regular?"

"They are."

He also typed out a script for the pill, telling her about their expected side effects.

"You will also need to have regular pap smears too. We will put you on our data base to be called up when it's due." He also gave her a sick note for a couple of days off school.

"Are you okay?" Emma's mother asked when they were out of the office. Emma nodded.

"Thanks Mum."

On the way home Emma was unusually quiet.

"Have you decided what you want to do with your time off? Do you want to visit the shopping centre for a browse?"

"Actually, I might do some study and try to catch up with some of my school work."

Her mother couldn't help looking at Emma with surprise. Up to now, Emma had hated school as she couldn't see any point in studying things she wouldn't use when she left. She grinned at her mother's expression.

"That doctor's bad manner has just shown me what I need to be! - a GP!"

"Well, you will need to aim for top marks in your English, Maths, and science – especially biology. And you will have at least eight years of training before you can be a GP. Are you up for it?"

"Why top marks in those subjects Mum?"

"You need English for accurate writing of reports, not to mention scripts. With Maths, accurate calculations of dosages of meds you are prescribing or giving patients. You don't want to overdose or poison anyone! With science, you need to know what the substances are you are prescribing and in biology you will need to know all the systems of the body, how they work and all the common diseases that occur. Not to mention how to treat injuries."

True to her word, when they arrived home, Emma brought out her school books and started to go through the work she had been neglecting. It didn't take long for her to sigh.

"You need help with something?"

"I'm finding some of these words hard to figure out."

Emma's mother was shocked to find that Emma didn't know how to sound words out and didn't really know all the letters in the alphabet. She didn't know her times table either.

"I think we should forget the school work for today and concentrate on knowing how to read. Everything will be much easier when you know how."

When Emma went back to school, her teacher was surprised that her knowledge was much better than she had all term.

"Did you have a private tutor on your days off?" the teacher joked to her.

"No. Mum showed me how to read. We are doing the times table next."

The students around her made jokes about her reading and times table, but Emma didn't care. She now had a purpose to her studies.

CANDY'S

FRENCH

CONNECTION

Candy could see the large lake below, surrounded by mountains as the plane descended towards the Lucerne airport. Some villas dotted the lakefront, separate to the township. A road weaved it's way along the shoreline, disappearing at intervals into tunnels in the mountainside.

She had enjoyed a cooked breakfast in the dining area with the team. While there was talk by the crew of their plans on their days off, Candy wondered what sort of reception she would receive by immigration, arriving with no passport! She had visions of being thrown in prison!

After a smooth landing, the plane taxied to a spot reserved for them, separate from the airlines. Candy noticed two officials approach the aircraft. One had a wheelchair and rug with him. Coming on board, the passports of all the crew were examined. When he came to Candy, Therese handed him the clipboard of the information Candy had given her.

"What is the purpose of your arrival, Mademoiselle?"

"To immigrate. I apologise for the absence of my passport, but I was in captivity at the time I was rescued and brought here." I have the skills to set up a business and to provide my own income."

"What means do you have at present to support yourself?"

"A benefactor is being arranged to give me financial support until I am able to be financially independent.”

“Where are you staying while you are in Switzerland?”

“I will be attending a clinic. Therese will be able to give you the details.”

“You mentioned you have been in captivity, what was the name of the institution you were incarcerated in?”

“It was a suburban house, where the owner took women he had drugged and captured, to use and abuse to broadcast to the dark web.”

The official could see that this passenger was fragile. There was a haunted look in her eyes that shouldn’t be there and he detected a bruise on her chin. She also displayed a thinness that wasn’t natural either. He had noted that she was related to a leading French family and that her French was faultless.

“Welcome to Europe, Candy. Are you well enough for an interview? Interpol would like a chat.”

“Yes, certainly.”

Candy was helped out of the aircraft and into the wheelchair, which Therese wheeled to the terminal. There, they were escorted to an interview room. Therese was asked to wait outside. Two men in suits were waiting. She noticed the familiar camera in the ceiling, giving a wry smile.

The police introduced themselves and showed their badges. Before asking whether she had any objections to the interview being filmed.

“No.” Candy looked at the camera again. “I’ve been living with one of these from the time I was captured to the moment I was rescued.”

"Can you take us through the experience you have had? We especially would like any information you can tell us about the man that captured you."

"That is easy. He called himself Dave, but his real name is Barry and he is a policeman."

"Are you sure of that?"

"Yes. On one of the occasions he was raping me, a phone call came through. I could hear the person on the other end of the phone call him Barry. They wanted him to come in to help search for an escaped prisoner."

One of the officers stood up and told the other officer to carry on with the interview while he left the room. Candy wasn't sure how long the interviewer took to debrief her about her experience, but at the end she was asked whether she wished to return to Australia.

"No. I feel safer here, besides I'm not sure the flat I rented will still be available to me, or my job will have been given to someone else. I have family in France I haven't met yet. I wish to start afresh here."

"The names and relationship of your family here?"

"Celeste and Henri De La Court. Celeste is my mother's sister."

"We will advise them that you are here. One final thing, would you be able to show your injuries to the camera? We will get a female officer to help you with that."

"Thank you."

The female officer came in and pulled down a white screen which Candy stood in front of. The officer asked her about all the marks she could see – the bruising was still obvious, as was the whip and cattle prod marks.

"Is there anything else you need to tell us about?"

"I am still suffering from concussion, and I may be pregnant. – he wanted children for his paedophile clients. I will be tested at the clinic."

"Thank you for your co-operation. I will fetch your chaperone now. We will arrange your residency documentation."

Therese looked at Candy with concern when she came in.

"Are you alright? That is the longest interview I have seen them give!"

Candy smiled. "I knew it would be an ordeal, so I decided to get it over with, so I can now relax. There was a great deal to debrief to them, about the time I was in captivity."

"Was that all?"

"No. They asked whether I wanted to return to Australia. I advised them that I am choosing a fresh start here. They also asked the names of my relatives in France. Interpol will be contacting them to advise them that I am here. They also wanted to see my injures. A police woman helped me with that."

"They didn't ask about you going to a benefactor?"

"No. I had already advised the official on the plane that a benefactor was being arranged. I fully expect that they will be comparing notes. They are arranging my residency documents."

The immigration official came to give Candy a document with a passport photo of her in the corner, stating that she had a permit to enter and reside in the European Union.

"If you are ever reunited with your passport, this form is to be attached."

Therese gave a little smile as she wheeled Candy to the waiting van.

"You have more than earned a rest at the clinic!"

In the coming weeks, Candy settled into a routine of having checks, physio, treatments and rests in between. One morning the physician came on his round.

"I have some good news for you. You have finally recovered from your concussion. All the bruising and other marks are nearly gone too." He paused. "You are also pregnant. May I congratulate you? An ultra sound will be organised for this afternoon. You will be ready for discharge in a few days."

"Thank you. You may!" Candy beamed back at him.

While Candy was in the clinic, Therese made daily calls to see how she was progressing. When she advised Therese of her pregnancy and of her impending discharge, Therese was delighted.

"We will be ready to take you to your benefactor by then. I will come in tomorrow to take your measurements for your wardrobe."

Candy's rest period was near its end that afternoon, when there was a small commotion in the hallway.

"I'm sure a few minutes won't make any difference to her recovery!" Candy's door was opened by a younger version of her mother! Candy couldn't help showing her delight.

"Aunty Celeste?" Candy put her arms out to welcome her. Celeste couldn't help showing her shock and amazement at the figure in front of her. As she came to give Candy a hug she exclaimed.

"My goodness! you are the image of Antoinette!"

"Our great grandmother?"

"Oui! (yes) I am so glad I was able to meet you. It was so sad when your mother left and.. and lost touch with us all. How long are you here?"

"I will be discharged in a few days. I don't know my destination yet, but I will be living in Europe."

"I am making sure we don't lose touch this time! Here is a phone. It has my number in it. Please call me when you arrive, so we can arrange a proper meeting."

"I certainly shall!" Candy beamed back at her. Just then an aide came in.

"It is time for your scan, mademoiselle."

"Is everything alright?" Celeste asked as Candy sat in the waiting wheelchair.

"Would you like to come with me, to see your new great niece or nephew?" Candy saw the shocked look on her aunt's face. "I have much to tell you, but this child will be much loved, despite the way it was conceived."

Outside the door, Celeste's husband was waiting.

"We won't be long." Celeste told him. "Candy wants me to be with her for her scan."

As the technician ran the probe over Candy's lower abdomen they could see a little blob. The sound of a heart beat could be heard in the room. Then they heard a second one. The technician turned to Candy with a smile. It's a little early to see what sex they are, but you are having twins! Congratulations!"

"Thank you!"

This news made Candy more determined than ever to make sure that her children lived!

"What are you going to do?" Celeste asked with a worried look, when they exited the room. "I can't see any benefactor paying to bring up someone else's child.

"They won't be! I have my own savings that I was intending to use for a deposit for my own home. I intend to restart my career as soon as I can."

Introductions to Henri were made on their return Candy's room.

"Are you well?" Henri asked with concern. They had been told about the circumstances that led Candy to be in Europe.

"I am much better now, thank you!" I will hear tomorrow where I will be moved to, on discharge. I also thank you for the phone. I will be able to contact my sister Jillian now."

"What about Camille and your father?"

"They are in a remote part of Papua New Guinea at present with Dad's job. We will have to wait for them to come down to Port Moresby. They usually contact us when they are in town."

FAMILY REUNION

Camille looked down on the city as their Cessna prepared to land at Port Moresby. She smiled at Jack. He too was looking forward to some comfort for a few days on his week off from the rigors of work on the mine site, in the forested interior.

As they walked through the terminal for the taxi to their hotel, Jack picked up a copy of "The Australian" newspaper and stuffed it into his backpack. It was their means of catching up on things back home.

At their hotel, Camille had a shower before they went downstairs to the hotel restaurant. While Jack was waiting for his turn for the shower, he opened the paper. His heart nearly stopped when he saw a photo of Candy on the front page! Reading on, he was shocked to read that she was missing and fears were held for her safety after she was seen leaving a tavern with a man. Jack reached for Camille's bag and searched for her phone just as Camille came out of the bathroom.

Camille was shocked at the anguished look on Jack's face as he searched through her bag, something he never did!

"What's up?"

"Where's your phone? We have to ring Jillian!" He thrust the paper at Camille. After a long call to Jillian, who tearfully filled them in on the details that the police had given, they looked at each other. They both knew that their life here was over.

Calls to his boss and to the airlines were made. There was little sleep that night. They were relieved when morning came. With it, a flight to Brisbane, then a connection to Perth, where Jillian and Eliza were there to meet them.

Eliza wasn't sure about these strangers, when she was passed to Jack, but he had a toy with him to distract her from the tears that flowed when Camille and Jillian embraced. They were at Jillian's home for a few days, when the police came to the door; giving them the news that Candy had been rescued, but she was now on her way to Switzerland. They would be in touch when further information came through.

Camille managed to act normally, but internally all the pain of her departure from France so many years before, had come back to her.

Her parents had been adamant that she should marry a man who had been recommended through their network of contacts. Camille had been equally adamant that she would choose her own partner. If she accepted her parents recommendation, she would have to put up with a mistress in his life as well!

Packing as light as she could, Camille left a note with her farewell to her family, before catching a train to Paris and a flight to Australia, which was almost as far as one could get from Europe. On the flight she was placed next to Jack, who was on his way back to Perth after a Contiki tour of Europe. When they disembarked from the plane, Camille had Jack's phone number safely in her bag.

At their wedding, all the guests were either their friends or from Jack's family. The only contact with her own family was through her sister Celeste, with infrequent letters that petered out when Jack's work took him to distant places. Caring for her two girls as they were growing up and supporting Jack, took most of Camille's time.

Camille took a deep breath. It was time to get in touch with Celeste. She dialled the number of the chateau. Celeste was passing the phone when it began to ring. She looked at the number calling. It was from Australia! She picked up the phone.

"Bonjour, Camille?"

CANDY MEETS HER NEW FAMILY

The door to the Mercedes was opened for Candy to step inside. In the last few days Therese had taken her measurements, then arrived with two cases with an extensive wardrobe for Candy to try. Candy noticed there wasn't any casual comfortable clothing among the garments, which she would have to rectify at the first opportunity.

Candy had been given a dossier on the new family she was joining. Corbin Blanchet was the CEO of a pharmaceutical company. He had a wife Fleur and a son Andre. Their home was in Paris, but she was meeting him at their holiday home at Chambery in the French Alps.

After a long but scenic drive from Lucerne, they arrived in Chambery. Candy liked the look of the town, with its Heritage buildings and outdoor dining, though the tables were empty, with patrons preferring to dine indoors. Being February, the tourist season was some months away yet. Some snow from the previous day was still lying on the pavement.

The building they drew up outside had four floors. Candy hoped it had a lift. She didn't fancy lugging her cases up to the top floor where Corbin was waiting. Therese showed Candy where the foyer was and gave her the number of the apartment, before getting back into the car. Emmanuel sent a text to Corbin that Candy had arrived as they pulled away.

Andre Blanchet was also been delivered to the apartment by the family chauffeur. It was his thirtieth birthday. His father had said on the phone that he a special surprise for him. As he came to the lift, it was already open.   A striking red haired female was arranging her suitcases. Immaculately dressed and made up, she moved to the back as Andre entered the lift. He automatically pressed the button for the top floor without noticing that it was already pressed.

As the door opened at their floor, a blazing row could be heard from his parents apartment. They were arguing about a female! His mother could be heard with anger in her voice, asking where he had got her from! Andre stepped out of the lift. Something made him look around at the female he had shared the lift with.

He registered a look of shock and horror before the doors closed and the lift descended back to the ground again.

Candy was now glad she had organised a plan B in case the meeting had been a disaster. Having to meet an angry wife was as disastrous as you could get! She immediately turned off the phone that Therese had given her from her new benefactor and pulled out the street map of the town she had been given from the hospital receptionist.

Andre pulled out his key and opened the door of the apartment. Immediately, the arguing stopped. He went through to the living area from the foyer. His father came to meet him, looking behind Andre to see whether anyone else was there. He had just received the message that Candy was here.

"Don't tell me that the ravishing red head was my surprise!"

"She is! Where is she?"

"She came up in the lift with me, but she was horrified by the argument you two were having and fled!"

By now they had been joined by his mother, who had the grace to look ashamed that a suitable suitor had been scared off. Corbin tried to call her, but the phone was turned off. Andre pulled out his phone and called Jean the chauffeur, who was covering the car.

"Jean, can you see a red head with two suitcases walking down the street?"

"Oui monsieur."

"Can you follow her and find out where she goes?"

"Certainly monsieur!" Jean was happy to obey this order. It wasn't every day he had to track an attractive mademoiselle like this one!

At the next street corner, Candy had stopped. With her map out she was looking for the street sign so she could find her way to the hotel she had booked for the night – just in case!

"Bonjour Mademoiselle! Can I help you?"

Candy looked at the friendly twinkling eyes and was reassured. She gave Jean a welcoming smile.

"Can you tell me the name of this street? I am trying to find my way to my hotel."

Jean looked at the hotel marked on the map.

"I know where that is. May I escort you there? Some of the paths are quite slippery this time of year."

"Thank you!" Candy replied with gratitude.

Jean grabbed one of Candy's suitcases and put his arm out for her to tuck her arm in his while she wheeled her other case. As they walked and introduced themselves, Candy couldn't help shivering. By now the mohair shawl Candy had been wearing round her neck was wrapped around her shoulders. She definitely needed a warm coat! – and some boots!

"You need some warmer clothes Candy!" Jean commented.

"I certainly do! Will we be passing any clothing shops on the way?"

"I can make sure we do!"

On the way, they passed a café with a sign outside wanting some casual help.

"Excuse me, Jean, I need a job while I establish myself. Do you mind if I pop in here and enquire about this position?"

Jean just smiled and waved her in. Within ten minutes, she was out again, with a big smile on her face.

"I start at seven in the morning. Their regular waitress is off sick this week."

While Candy was in the café, Jean received a text from Andre.

"How are you getting on?"

"I'm escorting her to her hotel. – just waiting while she's applying for a job."

Wordlessly, Andre showed Jean's reply to his parents.

Much later, after some shopping for a suitable coat, boots and a bag of "essentials" which Candy insisted on carrying, she was safely delivered to her hotel.

"Thank you so much Jean, for all of your help!"

"It has been my pleasure!"

When Candy extended her hand to shake his, He brought it to his mouth and kissed it, which brought a big smile to her face. She hadn't quite expected such gallantry, but she was in France now, she reminded herself.

Corbin had intended to take the family and their new arrival out to dinner, but Jean had taken so long to return, they ate a quickly prepared meal at the apartment instead.

At the hotel, Candy had the room heater on, and had exchanged the outfit she had worn all day for comfortable lounge wear. Her outfit for work was sitting ready on the chair. She also trimmed her hair to a more manageable length at her shoulders. Her hair would be a mass of ringlets she would have to tie up in the morning. Candy had just removed all her make-up when the room phone rang. It was reception.

"Mademoiselle Candy, can you come to reception? Monsieur Corbin Blanchet and his family are here to see you."

"Thank you. I will be there shortly."

With a sigh, Candy put on a different outfit, The mohair shawl slung over her shoulders, and her boots to keep her legs warm. As she exited the lift, a video call came through from Celeste. Her parents were with her!"

"Bonjour Celeste! Mum! Dad! You are here! I can't wait to see you!

"Where are you?" Celeste asked. "Are you free on the weekend to come to the Chateau and what is your new benefactor like?"

"I'm at Hotel Mecure, and the weekend should be fine." Candy looked around to see Corbin and his family looking at her. "I'm just about to meet them."

"Can we listen in, to make sure all will be well?"

Candy smiled before she put the phone in her pocket. She then took a deep breath before composing herself to meet her new "family." As she approached them, Candy chose to look at Fleur and gave her a smile, which was answered by one of her own. Only then did Candy look at Corbin, who along with Fleur and Andre had risen to meet her.

"Bonjour." Candy greeted them. She put out her hand for a handshake, but Corbin wasn't having any stiff English handshake! She was grabbed by the shoulders and given a thorough kiss on both cheeks, which made her blush!

"Bonjour Candy!" Corbin grinned. He could see she was even more beautiful than the haunted creature he had seen on the video clips during her capture. Fleur came to give her the customary kiss on both cheeks. She also gave Candy an extra hug.

"I am so sorry you came when we were having our little discussion! Corbin sprung his little surprise on me just before you came! That's men for you!" Candy nodded.

"If I was in your position, I would be more than a little cross too! I heard you arguing about me, so I was horrified that I was coming between a man and his wife, which I had no intention of doing. I know that many French men have a mistress, which is not the normal thing to do in Australia."

Fleur laughed. "The surprise was for Andre! He was quite put out! He hasn't had anyone flee before!"

Candy turned to face Andre who took her proffered hand to kiss it, while looking at her intensely.

97

Candy noticed that his black hair was as curly as her own.

"Are you usually so impulsive? And why have you cut your hair!? Andre saw a flash of annoyance in Candy's expression before she concealed it.

"There was nothing impulsive in my actions, Andre." Candy replied coolly. "I had come from an unpleasant situation, to be confronted with another one. I was merely implementing my plan B! I trimmed my hair as I have taken a temporary position as a waitress. It was only sensible to make sure my hair didn't end up in customers food or drink!"

Not waiting for his reply Candy turned to Corbin. "I express my gratitude to you for providing the means for me to be brought to Europe. It not only saved my life from a situation where I would have been killed sooner or later, I have been able to be reunited with our family over here too." She looked at both Corbin and Fleur. "I thank you too, for welcoming me as an unofficial member of your family."

"What does it take to be official?" Andre cut in.

"Either birth or marriage, as you should know!"

"That's easy to arrange!"

"I will not be marrying without consent! At this point you don't have my consent! Candy's obvious annoyance didn't deter Andre.

"You won't be needing your waitress job! You will be given an allowance and I will be taking you back to Paris with me tomorrow." Andre's tone allowed no argument.

Candy's eyes were glacial and her tone matched

his as she faced him.

"You will NOT be taking me back to Paris tomorrow! I neither want nor need your money! Before I was abducted three weeks ago, I had an independent life with a good income, which I will return to as soon as I can manage it. I have already arranged for my own savings to be transferred here.

During my time in captivity, I had no control over the abuse that was done to me, resulting in my pregnancy. As of now, I am retaking control of my life and my body! If you want to have any type of relationship with me Andre, you can stop expecting me to comply with your demands and start by asking whether it suits me to do so! I intend to carry out my job, as it is only for this week while I organise myself."

"You can get an abortion."

"If I wanted one, I would already have had it done." Candy looked at the gold cross around Andre's neck. "As a Christian man, you know as well as I do, that it is not for me or you to destroy the life that god has given me. If I can accept it, so can you!" There was silence while Andre digested this.

"How are you going to manage your career and your child?"

"I will employ a nanny of course!"

"Of course!"

"Seeing you are busy this week, can I pick you up to spend the weekend together?"

"Um...For the first time Candy was hesitant. "I have already promised my Aunt and my parents that I would visit them this coming weekend."

A loud voice came from Candy's pocket.

"Bring them with you!"

Candy grinned as she brought her phone out of her pocket. "I apologise for the eavesdropping, but they insisted on listening to make sure I would be safe."

Candy showed the screen with three beaming faces to Andre. "Please meet my parents, Camille and Jack, and Aunty Celeste, Andre."

"Bonjour Andre! Are you and your parents free from Friday evening through to Sunday afternoon?"

Andre grinned. "I'm free! Mum? Dad?"

Candy turned the phone to Corbin and Fleur who were already smiling broadly.

"We will be delighted to accept your invitation, and look forward to meeting you!" Fleur replied for them both. Arrangements were made for them to arrive before dinner.

After the call ended, Corbin and Fleur elected to return to Paris in the morning. Andre was to remain in Chambery with Candy. He would come to collect her luggage before she started work in the morning. Jean the chauffeur would bring Andre's car from Paris for them. At the mention of Jean's name, Candy now knew how the family knew where she was staying! They had sent Jean to follow her! Andre saw the little smile on Candy's face.

"What's up?"

"Jean has multiple talents, hasn't he? I've just found out how you knew where I had gone."

It was Andre's turn to smile.

"Well you had turned your phone off! Speaking of which, please leave it on, unless you give us your other phone number." He looked pointedly at the phone

Candy was carrying.

"I will give you this number which I will keep for personal calls. I'm going to need a separate phone for my business, so I may use the one that the team gave me for that. I will of course take over the cost of the phone plan."

"That won't be necessary." Corbin interjected.

"That's kind of you to offer." Candy's tone was gentle, "but I don't expect you to subsidise my business expenses. I will make more than enough to pay for them."

Corbin shook his head with a smile. "I have never met such an independent woman! Is this normal for you?"

"It certainly is!" Candy replied with a beaming smile. "It is an Aussie thing. Women in our part of the world appreciate the freedom that our independence gives us."

Candy noticed that both Corbin and Andre were very thoughtful following her little speech. After she bade them goodnight and retreated upstairs, Corbin called Jean to collect them.

"That is some surprise you've given me!"

Corbin couldn't help grinning. "I thought you might enjoy the challenge of this one! When I consider all the ones that have thrown themselves at you over the years, and none of them have lasted."

"How did you find her? She mentioned something about being abused!"

"Word got about at my gentlemen's club that a "gem" was coming onto the market. I made enquiries and was given a dossier of her history, also some of the footage of her time in captivity." Corbin looked at Andre with stricken eyes. "I have never seen such dignity, spirit and courage in anyone, despite what he was doing to her! I knew I had to rescue her, and I did! - If it doesn't work out between you, I will find a place for her in our advertising department and set her up."

"I will be making sure it works!" Andre had a determination in his voice that neither his mother or father had heard before.

Back in her room, Candy had some heart searching to do. She had fully expected to continue her independent life as Corbin's mistress. To be the wife of his son, Andre was another matter.

Candy knew Andre was attracted to her, but she had no intention of allowing him to push her into an arrangement that didn't suit her. She also had felt an attraction to Andre when they met, leaving her feeling vulnerable. Candy managed to hide it, especially when he tried to dictate how her life would now be. Candy needed to know he was committed to her, before she revealed her feelings.

Living in Paris with the knowledge that other women would be competing with her for Andre's attention and his body, didn't appeal at all!

She pulled out her phone to check the real estate pages for the Loire Valley. One property in particular caught Candy's attention. She was able to afford it too! A message was sent off to the real estate agent

"Mr Andre Blanchet is waiting for you." The call came through from reception. Candy looked at her bedside clock. Just as well she had risen early to shower and had just finished packing. She made a mental note to get another watch! She was missing it already.

"I'm on my way."

Candy put on her coat over her long pinafore and jumper that she knew she would be needing outside. When she reached the ground floor, both Andre and Jean were waiting for the lift. Jean came forward to collect her cases. She noticed they were wearing beanies.

"Morning to you both!" Candy smiled. "I will just return my key."

"You slept well?" Andre asked, looking into her eyes with a searching look. He noticed she had changed the style of her hair again as he came forward to plant a kiss on her forehead. It was now pulled back, with a mass of ringlets at the back. He noticed that she didn't withdraw when he kissed her, a good sign. He wondered how she would react when he attempted to be more intimate. He might have to take things more slowly than he wanted, and maybe get some therapy for her, but he would cross that bridge when they came to it. Andre was pleased they had this week to themselves to get to know each other properly.

"I have thank you! The bed was nice and comfortable. I take it that it is fresh outside?"

"Andre gave her a grin. "To put it mildly! Where's

that mohair shawl of yours?”

“I packed it!”

Candy quickly returned the key to the desk before meeting Andre at the entrance. Jean was already waiting with the motor running. When the door opened, Candy couldn’t help gasping at the blast of cold air that met them when they ducked out to the car. Inside the car was warm. She didn’t relish getting out again, but knew she must.

“I take it you don’t have snow at home?” Andre asked. “Have you skied at all?”

Candy shook her head. “We don’t get snow in Perth, so I haven’t been skiing, but I’m happy to learn!” she smiled at Andre, realising she would be adjusting to a completely different lifestyle. “All of our ski fields are on the other side of the country, several thousand kilometres away.”

By now they had drawn up outside the apartment. Andre noticed with amusement, that Candy didn’t wait for the door to be opened for her, but quickly stepped out and went to the back of the car, opening the boot to pull one of the cases out, before Jean came running over with alarm, to move her gently out of the way.

“I will get these!”

Andre came and put his arm around her and led her inside.

“You don’t have to be super independent anymore, you know!”

“Sorry!” Candy couldn’t help grinning, which spoilt the effect of her words. “I’m so used to having to do everything for myself!”

Andre kept his arm around Candy as they travelled in the lift up to the apartment.

"Are you making sure I don't escape again?" she teased him. Andre looked at the twinkle in her eyes and kissed her forehead again.

"If you do escape, I will be coming with you!"

Candy laughed outright at this suggestion.

In the apartment, she was surprised at how spacious it was. A large foyer for the depositing of coats and boots, had a door to a separate area for Jean. A corridor led through to a large living area with big windows. It was still dark, but she knew there would be nice views once daylight came. Andre showed her to a large bedroom with its own ensuite. Jean came down the corridor with her suitcases, putting them in her room.

"Thank you Jean. Are you able to drop me at the café?" She looked at her wrist again, before reaching for her phone to get the time. She had twenty minutes before she had to start. Andre noticed her looking for her watch, which she didn't have. He had a fair idea what happened to it.

"Jean will take us both over before he heads to Paris with Mum and Dad."

At the café, Candy was shown the coffee machine. Luckily she had used one before, in her waitressing job while she was a student. Within five minutes the first coffees were being dispensed. Once the first rush was over she looked over at Andre who had parked himself in a corner near the window. He pointed to the board above her and indicated he wanted number three – a flat white. When she delivered it to him, he eyed her with new respect.

"You've done this before!"

"I waitressed in a café when I was a uni student."

Just then, her phone pinged with a message. It was from the real estate agent in the Loire Valley, with details of the property that she was interested in, along with details of a few others she might like to have a look at. After taking a quick look, she put it in her pocket. More customers were coming in.

"I've got something for you to look at later." Before leaving to attend to the other customers. The old independent Candy would have just made arrangements to view and buy the house, but Andre had made it clear he was in her life to stay, so she now had to include him in any major decisions. Buying a house for her family was a major decision! Andre was intrigued, but had to be patient till she was ready to share what she had to show him. He was reading a paper, when she returned to him.

"Have you had breakfast yet?"

"Not yet!" He accepted the menu that Candy offered him. After he ordered, Andre had to ask. "Any clues what you want to show me?"

"Its Real Estate." And swept away to organise his meal.

"Where abouts?" he asked when Candy returned with his cutlery.

"The Loire valley. Only two hours from Paris and half an hour from my Aunty. Its near Beaugency."

By now Andre had abandoned the paper and had his phone out. Although Andre and his father were usually at head office in Paris, he realised that their factory was close by.

"What price range?"

"€20-30K. My favourite is this one. I do have the funds to pay for it."

Candy pointed to a four story mansion, obviously in need of restoration. While Candy went off to attend other customers, Andre read the blurb on the property.

On the edge of town, on an acre of land, and surrounded by a row of conifer trees to give privacy. The house was habitable, but needed work. After years of neglect, the grounds had reverted to a large grass meadow. Photos of the inside showed a very basic kitchen and bathroom, though the saloon had some vintage features worth preserving. The staircase in the centre of the home had a large stained glass skylight above it.

When Candy returned with his breakfast, he had quizzical look on his face.

"I see you are proposing a nice challenge for us! I take it you aren't interested in living in the city?"

"I feel a home in the country will be more appropriate for our family. I had a wonderful childhood, running round and playing outdoors. I want the same for our children. Also I want space for our families to be able to visit or live with us, if necessary." She pointed to the ground floor with double doors for storing cars.

The area on one side could be Jean's accommodation, with office space on the other side. I would also put a lift in to access all floors. If you prefer apartment living we can use the first floor, leaving the other floors for members of the family. I'm sure your parents will want their own floor too; or we could have the top floor with all the views." She showed Andre a photo of the back yard. "I want an orchard and a vegetable garden too."

"That tree should go." Andre indicated an old oak tree near the house.

"I would like it to stay. We can put a swing and a cubby in it for the children. Also it will be a nice shady spot to sit under in the summer."

"What is a cubby?"

"A tree house." Candy grinned at him.

All of a sudden, Andre was feeling very jealous of the children they were going to have.

"Okay, you've sold it to me! Have you got the number of the agent?"

She handed Andre her phone with the message from the agent.

"Don't forget your breakfast!" Candy reminded him as she went off to clear some tables. She saw Andre make a long phone call as she went about her duties, before he continued reading his paper. He nodded when she pointed to the coffee menu on the board.

"What time is your lunch break?" Andre wanted to know when she brought him his coffee.

"It's early, at eleven o'clock."

"Do you want any shopping done before then?"

"Can you get some fruit and something for dinner at the supermarket? – some vegetables and meat."

"You don't fancy a takeaway?"

"Not yet. I had a week of takeaways while I was in captivity. Half the time it was cold, or had it thrown at me on the floor." Candy's face was impassive as she spoke.

"I will do the honours and cook tonight." Andre offered.

"I will do the honours tomorrow night then."

After Andre left the café, the owner came to have a chat. "Do you know that gentleman?"

Candy gave him a smile. "He is my fiancé." She saw him look at her hand. "It's unofficial at the moment."

"Congratulations! He's quite a catch!" Andre's family were regular visitors to the town and everyone knew them.

"Actually, I'm the one that's been caught!" Candy grinned at him. "I had intentions of being a "career girl." Marriage and children were the last thing on my mind!"

The café owner chuckled as he went back to the kitchen to prepare for the lunch crowd. Candy also busied herself, making sure all the tables were clean, condiments stocked up and stacks of plates, and cutlery were on hand.

When Andre came back for her, Candy was ready to leave, with her coat on and the collar turned up. He handed her a beanie, woollen scarf and gloves.

"You will need these!"

Candy noticed that Andre also had a scarf and gloves on too. He also brought a box out of his pocket, and opened it, to bring out a watch that was swiftly snapped onto Candy's wrist. A brief glimpse of pearls and diamonds around the face, told Candy this wasn't an item from a cheap production line!

"Thank you! I have missed mine!"

"Another thing he took from you?"

Candy nodded and changed the subject. "How did you get on with the agent?"

Andre grinned at her. "I've put in an offer and paid a deposit, so we just have to wait for the owner to accept it."

Candy stopped and gasped at Andre with delight. "That was quick!"

"I'm not quite as quick as you!, but I'm learning!"

Outside, a flurry of snow-flakes swirled around them. Andre put his arm around Candy as they walked. He steered her into a restaurant.

"Some soup?"

"Perfect!"

Andre put Candy's phone on the table.

"Sorry I didn't give this back before I left. I have taken the liberty of putting our numbers in your contact list. What is your number, so I can put it in mine?"

He pulled his phone out to add her number. He had just finished when his phone rang. It was the agent.

"She's here with me. I will give her the news. Are you able to email the paperwork for us to sign?"

The gleam in Andre's eyes told Candy before he spoke. "We've just bought ourselves our first home."

"This calls for a celebratory drink!"

The waitress was at their table to take their order. After choosing their soup, they also ordered a drink.

'Do you have some "Blue Nun?" – I have to work this afternoon!" The waitress smiled. "We do."

Andre ordered some shiraz.

"To us!"

"Are you an only child, Andre?" Candy wanted to

know.

"I have a brother, Pierre. He is a priest. When you are ready, I will get him to marry us."

"That will be lovely.   Where is his parish?"

"He is in Paris, but we don't have to marry there."

Their soup and a large plate of fresh crusty bread arrived, which stopped conversation for a little while. Candy realised how hungry she was – she had missed breakfast! She would make sure she ate before work tomorrow morning!

Candy was telling Andre about her family – her parents life in Papua New Guinea and her sister Jillian in Perth, with her FIFO partner Mark and their little daughter Eliza, when the phone rang with a video call from her mother.

"Hi Mum! We are just having some lunch!" Candy showed the phone to Andre who waved and called "Bonjour Camille!" before facing the screen again. With her was Jillian, Mark and Eliza, who was trying to smack the screen! Laughing, Candy greeted her sister and her family. Jillian had good news. She had brought Candy's computer with her. They had much to catch up on at the weekend.

On their way back to the café, they passed a boutique. The dress in the window stopped Candy in her tracks. Andre took a look at Candy's face and the dress in the window, and steered her inside. He knew what she had in mind!

"I haven't time to try it on now. Can I pay a deposit and come back after four when I finish work?"

"If you pay for it now, you can take it home. You can bring it back tomorrow if any alterations need to be done."

When Candy returned to the café, the owner was glad to see her. The lunch crowd was here already.

"I have a few things to do." Andre told Candy at the doorstep. "I will take your dress home and be back before four to collect you."

Given that they had an interested audience at the café, Andre contented himself with giving her a quick hug and brushed her lips with his before heading off down the street.

Inside the café, the owner had a big grin on his face, and most of the patrons were looking at her with big smiles. It seemed that he had been spreading the news to the locals.

"Please don't be telling everyone of our news just yet!" Candy pleaded with him. "We don't want the media chasing after us! This is a special time for us to appreciate being together."

"I understand!" he said, turning to the diners who were watching their conversation, and indicated for them to keep their knowledge quiet.

"You will have to send us a photo!" he insisted.

"It will be my pleasure!" Candy promised.

The next few hours went quickly as the lunch time diners were served, then others came in for their afternoon tea. There were grumbles as people came in that they might get snowed in again!

Candy looked out the window. Snow was indeed piling up outside! Before closing time, Andre came in, with both a shovel and a couple of bags of groceries. The café owner looked at Candy's stare of amazement and nodded.

"I've checked the forecast. We are going to be snowed in for a few days. You are let off duties for the rest of the week."

He handed Candy an envelope with her day's wages. "Do come and visit us when you are next here!"

"We shall! I've really enjoyed my day with you."

Candy insisted on carrying the bags of shopping.

"You have the shovel you will be needing to use! You can't carry bags as well."

Even so, Andre kept a very firm arm around Candy's shoulder as they walked, which was just as well, as the footpath was now quite slippery from ice.

At the apartment building, their car park was empty.

"Jean couldn't get through. He had to go back to Paris."

"What if we are still snowed in on Friday?"

"I have a plan B." Andre smiled.

Inside the apartment, Candy was pleased that it was centrally heated. She just hoped the snow didn't affect the heating source.

"Out of interest," Candy asked, as they put away the groceries. "What is your source of heating for this building?"

"It is heated by gas."

"So, it isn't affected by power cuts?"

"Not yet!" Andre grinned at her.

"I was having visions of maybe having to rug up indoors!"

He came to give her a cuddle. "I'm sure we will manage if we do!"

Candy put her arms round his body and brought him close, smiling into his eyes as his mouth claimed hers. It was Andre who broke away reluctantly. The lights were flickering, indicating that a power cut was probable.

"Do we have torches and candles?" Candy asked. Andre led her by the hand to the cupboard where they were kept. He started handing out all the supplies they had on hand for such occasions.

"Torches for the bedroom and bathroom, and these for the living areas." He handed her candelabra.

Once everything was in place, they prepared their dinner together, chopping the vegetables and meat, braising it in a pan before adding a meal base for flavour. Candy found the cutlery, setting the table and put their plates handy for serving. They were sitting down at the table when the lights went out.

"That was good timing!" Candy commented, using matches to light the candelabra.

"Here's to us!" Candy raised her glass. "Our first romantic dinner together!"

"May we have many more!" Andre clinked his glass with hers, giving her a look that left her in no doubt what his feelings were. Candy put her hand across to his to caress it. Andre lifted her hand to kiss it.

"I'm looking forward to kissing everything else!" he said, feeling passion rising within him.

"And I'm looking forward to kissing and caressing everything else too!" She gave a little sigh. "I suppose we should eat this before we get too side-tracked!"

Andre chuckled. "Getting side-tracked sounds good to me!" His phone started to ring. It was his parents with a video call.

"Bonjour to you both! Are you having any snow in Paris?"

"Bonjour! Not yet! It's looking dim in there!"

"We are having a romantic dinner with candles!"

"We are having a power cut!" Candy called out.

Andre turned the phone round to Candy. Her eyes sparkled as she raised her glass and greeted them. They could see there was complete darkness behind her too.

"It looks like we will be snowed in for a few days."

"What if you are still snowed in on Friday?" Fleur asked with concern.

"Andre has a plan B ready."

When the call ended, Corbin turned to Fleur with a smile.

"I would have liked to be a fly on the wall at that café this morning!" When she raised her eyebrows, he explained. "Didn't you spot the Cartier watch on Candy's wrist just now? Andre wouldn't have given her a gift like that unless he was completely sure of her! It also explains why Pierre said "I'll see you Saturday" when he finished his call earlier. I would bet my last Euro that we have a wedding to attend this weekend!"

"Oh! I had better get myself organised! You had better take a look through Andre's wardrobe too, and see if he has anything suitable for us to take for him!" They both went off to their wardrobes.

As Andre ate their dinner, he broached the subject of getting married. "Seeing you have got your dress organised, what do you say to getting married on the weekend? All the family will be there."

"That's a wonderful idea! We don't know when everyone will be together again like this." She paused with a grin. "It's amazing how things can change in twenty four hours!" Andre laughed, as he remembered Candy saying he didn't have her consent! He couldn't help teasing her.

"I take it I do have your consent?"

"Yes, of course you do!" She gave him a loving smile. "I'm thinking, I will call Aunty Celeste and give her the good news tomorrow."

"What about now? We don't know whether the phones will still be working then."

Candy scrolled through her phone to call Celeste, who was wondering who was calling at this time of night. When she saw Candy's name, she immediately answered.

"Bonjour Candy! Is everything alright?"

"Everything is fine, thank you. I have some lovely news for you! Andre and I are getting married! We would like to have our ceremony at your place on Saturday, while everyone is there. Is that okay with you?" Candy heard her gasp.

"Of course it is okay! Oh how wonderful! We haven't had a wedding here for years! I take it you want it indoors? And do you have someone to officiate?"

"Yes please, for indoors! And yes, Andre's brother Pierre is a priest. He will be conducting the ceremony.

"What about flowers? Any particular colour?"

"I have a cream dress, so anything that goes with cream. Can you ask Jillian if she will be my Matron of Honour? I would ask her myself, but the power is out here from the snow. I don't know how long our phones will last, so am calling while we still have battery power."

"I understand! Oh this is so exciting! Take care! Au Revoir!"

When Celeste got off the phone, both Henri and Camille had come to see what she was so excited about. She turned to them with a beaming smile.

"We have a wedding to prepare for on Saturday!"

"Well! That's a complete turnaround since yesterday! They must be getting on better than anyone expected!"

While Candy was on the phone, Andre cleared the table and rinsed the dishes. He remembered the forms that they both needed to sign and send back to the agent.

"I'm just going to get our generator." Andre told Candy when she finished her call. "The Agent was sending us the forms to sign for our house. Do you want to try on your dress while I'm organising things? You will find some shoes with it."

Candy gave Andre a grateful look before taking a torch to the bedroom, where the bag with her shoes was waiting on the bed. She looked in the wardrobe to find her dress hanging up. Candy quickly slipped on the dress, which fitted perfectly. It was a little long, but once she put on the cream satin shoes Andre had bought, the length was fine. She heard the generator fire up as she returned to the living area. Andre came in from the balcony to see a vision in cream lace waiting for him.

"Will this do?"

"It certainly will do! I'm looking forward to having a proper look at it on Saturday!"

Even in the dim light he could see how the dress accented her figure, flaring out from above the knee. Satisfied, Candy returned to change back to her normal clothes. She chose the comfy lounge suit, which was warmer than the pinafore she had been wearing. She saw her cases still waiting to be unpacked, but decided to leave them till the morning. The shoes were stowed in the wardrobe with the dress. Candy noticed a warm rug in the top of the wardrobe and brought it out and put it on the couch.

Back in the living area Andre was beginning to print out the forms. The balcony door was cracked open a little for the power cord to pass through. The freezing air making a difference in the room. Andre looked at Candy's suit with envy. He was feeling cold after being out on the balcony.

"You will have to get one of those for me!" he commented.

"Tomorrow, if the weather allows!" she promised.

Candy gathered the papers and put them in order for them to sign as they came off the printer.

"Do we have to send everything back again?"

"No. Just the pages we have signed."

In ten minutes, they had signed, copied and sent the pages back to the agent. Within minutes, they received a reply confirming receipt of the completed forms. Andre swiftly shut down the computer and printer before heading out to shut down the generator and bring it indoors.

Candy found the kettle and put it on the gas hob.

"Do you want coffee or chocolate?" she asked.

"Chocolate!" He grinned. It had been many years since he had chocolate before bedtime! He was delighted that she enjoyed this treat as well. They retreated to the couch where they both snuggled up with the rug over them. Andre was liking this touch too!

"It's been quite a day!" Candy began as Andre put his arm around her.

"It certainly has!" Andre agreed. "It's not every day that we buy a house AND organise a wedding!"

"I take it, that it will be several weeks for the sale to be completed?"

"She said about three weeks. If we want to take a look through before then, to assess what tradesmen to organise once completion is done, we are just to give her a call."

By now they had finished their chocolate.

"Time to be side-tracked?" he asked.

Candy's answer was to snuggle into his body. His lips reaching for hers. Candy pulled away as their kiss deepened.

"It's time to get comfortable." She murmured.

"I won't argue with that!" Andre stood up with her, blowing out all the candles, using the torch to retreat to their room.

They helped to undress each other, caressing as they removed each garment, then swiftly slipped under the bedclothes, coming together again.

"Are you sure?" Andre asked.

"I'm completely sure!" Candy reassured him, holding his body against hers. "What we have is completely different to what I've been through. With him, it was all take. He was brutal, expecting unquestioning compliance with no tenderness, or consideration. And there was definitely no love! The only reason I was there, was to produce a baby for him to..." she paused. "He wanted them for his paedophile viewers. I'm just so glad that they will never know what was intended for them. I am putting it behind me!"

"If you can do it, so can I!"

She started to caress him again. Seeing that he was ready, Candy placed her body on top of his. It caught Andre by surprise as none of his girl friends had been this adventurous! He grabbed her and spun her over, so Candy caressed Andrea down to the base of his spine. Andre found himself driven to climax.

"Ah! I've found your sweet spot!" Candy grinned. "Where's yours?"

She showed him how she liked to be massaged. When she reached her climax, the soft noises of pleasure she had been making suddenly silenced for several seconds before she gasped and started panting.

"What was that you just did?" Andre wanted to know. There was laughter in her voice as she replied.

"That" was a silent scream when I climaxed! You didn't want me to disturb the neighbours, did you?"

His laugh was loud enough to be heard by their neighbour on their floor!

They settled to sleep together, only to be disturbed by a rumbling sound which sounded like approaching thunder, shaking the building to its foundations. Andre instinctively sheltered Candy in his arms. He knew what that rumbling meant! They were in an avalanche! When it stopped. He turned on a torch, looking at Candy with troubled eyes.

"That was an avalanche, wasn't it?"

He nodded. "We need to get dressed! If we can, we will leave. It isn't safe to stay here."

"If we can't leave?"

"We will have to wait to be rescued."

Candy put on her lounge suit. It was warmer than everything else she had. Andre went out to the living area. He shone his torch through the windows. There was a wall of snow in front of him. He returned to the bedroom where Candy had her two suitcases out. Her wedding dress and shoes were already in one, and was sorting through what else she was going to take.

"Do you have a suitcase here?"

"No, I don't." He added. "It isn't looking good! There is a wall of snow outside the windows."

"Do you think the roof is covered too?"

"I will check!"

"When you come back, are there any items here

of value that your parents wouldn't want to lose? Clothes can be replaced, but family treasures usually can't be."

"Good idea!" Andre nodded, before putting on his coat beanie and gloves and collected his shovel.

When Andre left the apartment, his neighbour was already in the foyer. He had the same idea. Together they took the stairway up to the roof terrace. At first the terrace door wouldn't budge at all, but with two of them shoving against it, they opened it enough to see that the snow was three quarters of the way up. It took some time, but with the shovel, they were able to move enough snow to open the door and make some steps up on top of the snow. Worryingly, it was still snowing.

"Do you know how many others are in the building?" Andre asked. "We have to let them know that they need to leave."

Together, they went to all the levels. Some of the residents didn't want to leave, but when Andre told them that the roof was in danger of collapse from the weight of snow, they finally agreed. Some of them came up to the roof to see for themselves, returning to their apartments with shocked faces.

While Andre was away, Candy went through all the foyer cupboards. A sled and some sets of skis were pulled out along with some overnight bags to carry items. She found the candelabra had hallmarks, so they were first to be placed into a bag.

When Andre returned, he was impressed to see the sled and skis out, and two bags of valuables all ready to go. Candy had also emptied the fridge and was going through the cupboards.

"The only rooms I haven't been through, are the other bedrooms."

Andre fetched another couple of bags, to scour his parents and brother's rooms for items he knew they wanted. These bags too, were full when they joined the other bags.

Andre's computer was in a suitcase when he joined Candy in the bedroom. He also had found some thermal underwear and tossed a set to Candy.

"Pop these on under your clothes. You will freeze without them."

As she peeled off her top, Andre saw a surgical mark on her back.

"What's that from?" Andre wanted to know.

"The doctor from the retrieval team had to remove the GPS locator that he had implanted in my back. The house we were in was locked like fort Knox, but he put it in, in case I escaped. He promised that no matter where I went, he would find me and bring me back to the dungeon to be eliminated. – after some torture for his viewers to enjoy."

"He came after you?"

"He did, but the men that rescued me were ready for him. I heard the one shot as this was being removed."

"So he can't come after you again?"

"No. He's in the grave he made for me."

Andre came over to give her a cuddle. Creaking above them, reminded Andre they had limited time left to leave in safety.

"Time we got out of here."

Swiftly they dressed as warmly as they could, with

as many layers as they could manage, and packed their bags. In their pockets were some energy bars.

"I know we have food with us, but we will need these if we are out in the cold for any length of time."

They joined the other residents who were similarly dressed and had their bags packed too. Up on the snow, the sled was loaded and secured. Candy didn't like how she sank in the snow in her boots. She felt much better when Andre showed her how to slide her boots into the binders of the skis. He also gave her a pair of snow goggles along with the sticks.

In the darkness she could see light from torches, as word got around that people were trapped. Slowly they set off towards the lights. Among the searchers was the local police, who took their details and their phone numbers. They asked where the nearest safe place was.

"Out of this valley!"

Andre turned to Candy. "It's going to be a long night!" He didn't mention it, but it was possible that they could succumb to the cold.

"It will." Candy agreed. "But we have each other, so we will manage." He gave her a hug and a kiss before moving on. They saw a line of people, who like them were heading for safely. They went to join them.

They didn't know it, but someone had taken photos of them talking and embracing in the torch light, which would be splashed over the national papers in the morning.

They trudged through the snow for a several hours. There was silence among the travellers, all trying to conserve as much energy as they could. Candy offered to take a turn at pulling the sled, but Andre wouldn't have any of it. She knew he wouldn't be able to keep it up all night.

"Where are we heading? Do you know?" Candy was concerned. She hadn't seen any road signs. She was also worried that with no point of reference, they could end up walking in circles, as sometimes happens when people get lost in the Australian outback.

"We are heading towards Lyon, though it is a very long walk in these conditions."

"We will need to rest somewhere then, if we see shelter on the way."

"Do you need a rest?" Andre asked.

"Not yet, but if I see any barns, we will definitely make a detour!"

Andre didn't argue. He didn't want to admit it to himself, but he was starting to feel tired. All the effort of moving the ice from the door to the roof and now this was starting to take its toll.

"We will join you!" the couple behind them had heard their conversation and were ready for a rest too! Another half hour on, Candy saw it. The long roof line in a dip of the landscape.

"Shall we take a look?" Candy pointed to the roof.

"We're game if you are!" the couple behind them

replied. They had quite enough of travelling for tonight!

"What's going on?" People both in front and behind were asking.

"It looks like some shelter over there!" Candy called out.

"Stay with the sled." Andre told Candy, while he and the man behind him skied over for a look. Seeing them head off the track, others in the line came to see what was happening and headed over to see what had been found.

Andre and his companion found an abandoned farm house, which was falling down; but the barn was a better prospect. The door opened enough to get in. It was dry inside and there was plenty of hay bales inside for comfort.

One of the skiers came back to the rise and gave a big whistle, which was heard by everyone in the long column.

"Come over here! The barn's nice and dry. There's plenty of room for everyone!"

There were lots of smiles at this news as people started to make their way to the barn. Candy started to pull the sled and appreciated why Andre didn't let her pull it till now. It was very heavy! She was quite proud of the fact that she managed to pull it to the top of the rise before Andre came with a severe look on his face.

"You will hurt yourself!" He scolded Candy, as he took the rope from her.

She sighed in exasperation. "I'm not that fragile you know!"

"Sorry!" Andre was contrite. "I'm fully aware of how strong you can be, when you set your mind to something!" He gave her a hug. "That was a good find you made! Come and look at our "hotel." It has all the mod cons of hay bales to sleep on!"

Inside, there was much chatter and sighs of relief as everyone found themselves a spot to rest. Both Andre and Candy now relished the energy bars they had brought with them.

"I wonder if there is phone reception here." Candy murmured, as she dived into her suitcase to retrieve her phone. "They will hear about the avalanche in the morning and be worried whether we made it out."

Andre also reached for his phone and messaged his father. "We are safe! In a barn. Heading towards Lyon." Candy sent a similar text to Celeste, who didn't receive her's till the morning.

Corbin and Fleur were settling for the night when he heard his phone ping in the other room. He padded off to see who was wanting him at this time of night. When he returned, Corbin immediately turned on the TV news. He passed the text message across to Fleur, who was now as anxious as he was. He took the phone back. "Can we reach you by car?"

"No. We are on skis. Will contact you when we reach a town."

At Chambery, more lights had been brought in and emergency services had been called. As a camera panned the landscape, very little of the town could be seen.

"I think we will get a better idea of how things are in the morning." Corbin tried to reassure Fleur. "At least Andre and Candy managed to get out and aren't still trapped under there."

They were horrified the next morning to recognise their apartment building from the air. The roof had collapsed taking all the floors with it to the ground floor, in a tangled mess.

At the barn, Candy went outside for a comfort stop. She had to stay close to the building or she sank into the snow. As she went round the corner, she heard footsteps. To her surprise an emaciated Donkey came trotting towards her. It too, kept close to the building. Candy guessed that it belonged to the farm and had either been abandoned or its owner had died. She also guessed that it was starving and wouldn't last much longer without a feed.

"Bonjour" Candy smiled at the Donkey. "Come with me! We have plenty of feed in the barn." She turned to go back inside, but the donkey stayed around the corner. Candy grabbed a handful of hay and took it outside. As soon as the donkey saw the hay it came charging over and quickly demolished it. Candy brought some more to the doorway and enticed it inside. She had placed a pile near the doorway, much to everyone's amusement.

When they saw the Donkey, there were gasps and silence. The donkey was very skittish at being in a confined space with lots of humans, but her hunger overcame her fear. While she was feeding, Candy shut the door to keep the freezing air out. She also stroked and spoke quietly to it, to keep it calm. Candy noticed how cold the Donkey was and fetched the rug she had brought to cover the sled and draped it over the Donkey.

Dulcie the Donkey immediately felt the warmth from the rug and looked around at Candy with grateful eyes. No human had ever given her something to keep warm before. This human was a keeper! Some years ago her owner had been taken away in a van, and hadn't returned. Dulcie had managed to feed herself through the seasons till now, but this year had been particularly hard, the snow much deeper than usual.

When Dulcie finished feeding, Candy gave her a pat before returning to her position with Andre. Some chuckles from other travellers made Candy look round. Dulcie was following her! When Candy lay down with Andre, Dulcie came and sat down beside her, forcing some people to quickly move out of the way!

"It seems I have some competition!" Andre commented with amusement, as he put his arm around her. "But seriously, what are you going to do?"

"She is going to die very soon if she stays here." Candy was thoughtful. Her mind was already grappling with how to bring Dulcie with them. An idea was forming in her mind.

"I will bring one of the hay bales with me. When we get to the next town in a day or two, I will hire a truck to take us, the sled and Dulcie to Celeste's place."

They heard a contented sigh and looked round to see the Donkey put her head on the straw and close her eyes. She knew this human was going to look after her.

The next morning Celeste carried out her usual routine of picking up the newspaper that had been delivered to their foyer, while her cup of coffee was brewing. On the front page under a banner "Survivors" were photos of Candy and Andre looking at each other with a mixture of relief and anxiety in their eyes. Their love for each other was evident. They were both wrapped up, ready for a long walk in the snow. Scanning through the article of the avalanche at Chambery, Celeste immediately reached for her phone, to receive Candy's message. She tried to call Candy, but was directed to her message bank. Celeste guessed Candy's phone was turned off for now.

"Please call me!" was the message she left.

In the barn, people were rousing from their rest. No-one had slept well. Everyone had their future on their mind. Some were starting their lives again with very little, but the immediate problem was how to get through the next couple of days till they reached the next town. Very few people had the thought or time to bring food with them.

Candy took the bags of food she had brought, off the sled.

"How much of this do we really need?" she quietly asked Andre. "There are lots of people here who have nothing. They will struggle on empty stomachs."

He nodded his agreement. They put aside a small amount for themselves.

"Help yourselves." Candy invited them as she put the bags in the middle.

"That's a good idea!" A lady spoke up. Candy recognised her from the shop where she bought her dress. "How many of us have brought food? Can you please share it with those who didn't have time to grab anything?"

There was silence for a few seconds, then some people started rummaging through their possessions. In the end, there was enough food for everyone to eat something before they set out on their journey, and to eat that evening, wherever they stopped to rest. This restored the spirits of everyone as they prepared to leave.

Candy had spotted a pile of cardboard in the corner of the barn. She ripped a piece off and brought it back to the sled. Rummaging in a bag for scissors, she cut a piece off and started shaping it into four round pieces.

"What are you making with those?" Andre asked with amusement.

"I'm making some snow shoes for Dulcie."

A bale of hay was tied onto a larger piece of cardboard for Candy to pull behind her.

When it came time to leave, Dulcie trotted out behind Candy, only to sink in the snow. Candy came over to comfort her, then lifted one of Dulcie's front feet and strapped the "shoe" to Dulcie's foot. Dulcie didn't like it, but when she put her foot down, she didn't sink, but stayed on top of the snow. Her foot was warmer too! Dulcie then allowed Candy to strap the shoes onto her other feet. Candy was pleased it had stopped snowing, thought it was still bitterly cold.

Their progress was slower now, but they kept up with the remainder of the group. It was with some relief that they spotted some signs for the next towns heading west. After a couple of hours they came to a lake. It was frozen, so Candy used a rock to break ice at the edge, so Dulcie could get a drink. Dulcie was also ready for a feed from the hay bale.

In the distance they could hear helicopters and planes. By lunch time they had come to the small settlement of Lepin le Lac, where one of the locals came out to invite them in for some soup, which was readily accepted. They were happy to hear it was only a few hours walk to the next town where they could get accommodation. The lady put in a call to let them know that they could expect a hundred or so visitors coming from Chambery.

About an hour into the journey to the next town, some four wheel drive vehicles came and started to ferry people in. When they saw a donkey was part of the group, a horse float was sent to transport her. Dulcie hadn't been one of these before, so Andre and the sled went in the vehicle with the driver, while Candy rode in the horse float with Dulcie.

Marcel the owner of the horse float had several horses in stables. He was suitably shocked at the state of the donkey as Candy persuaded it to climb into the box with her. Candy had kept a couple of carrots, which did the trick. Dulcie hadn't seen a carrot since her owner left!

"Is that your donkey?" Marcel wanted to know as they followed the convoy.

"No." Andre replied. Explaining how they had found the donkey on an abandoned farm where they had rested for the night, and that Candy had brought it into the barn and fed it. "The Donkey has adopted Candy. It is just as well we are buying a property where there will be room for her."

"Where are you going to put her in the meantime?"

"We are taking her to Candy's aunt's place. She has a country property about half an hour from ours in the Loire valley."

"Does she have horses?" Marcel wanted to know.

"I don't know. Candy was going to hire a truck to take us and the donkey to her aunt's."

"I will take you."

"Thank you!"

The conversation then turned to general things such as what Andre did for a living and how they were in Chambery at this time of year, being the off season.

"My parents have an apartment there, though I'm not sure whether it will still be there when we next visit. There was an enormous amount of snow on the roof when we managed to escape and it was making suspicious creaking noises."

"There has been quite a few casualties. You and your lady friend are lucky you weren't among them!"

"My fiancé." Andre corrected him. "We are getting married on the weekend."

"Really! That's something extra to celebrate!"

At the stables, it took another carrot to persuade Dulcie to exit the horse float and to follow Candy to the stall that had been allocated to her.

"Do you mind if I give her a check over?" Marcel asked. "Andre told me how you found her."

"Please do!" Candy was happy that a horse lover also cared about her condition. "I believe that Dulcie would have died if we hadn't come when we did."

Candy undid the strap that was holding the rug in place and gently removed it. She saw the tears in Marcel's eyes and nodded. Dulcie felt and saw the rug come off and wasn't pleased! She gave a bellow and with her teeth grabbed the rug off Candy and tossed it about, trying to put it back on again.

"I will get her another blanket." Marcel spoke

with amusement. "I was going to give her a wash, but in this condition, she isn't up to that yet. This lady certainly has some spirit though!"

It was only when another blanket was in place, that Dulcie calmed down and started to feed. Dulcie was also happy to have the "shoes" off. Marcel noted that the hooves could do with a trim, but they were otherwise in not bad shape, given the years of neglect.

"Do you mind if Dulcie spends a few weeks with me?" Marcel asked. I would like my vet and farrier to have a look at her and put a program in place to get her back into condition."

"That would be wonderful! By then we will be in our own home and I can organise some suitable shelter for her."

After Dulcie was settled, Andre phoned his parents, explaining they now had a donkey to look after, much to their astonishment; and that they were staying the night near Le Gue Des Planches. He confirmed that a wedding was taking place on Saturday, and could they bring his grey morning suit, and cream tie.

"You don't want your tuxedo?"

"No, that would be too formal! It will be inside, so we don't have to worry about freezing to death during the ceremony. By the way, we've managed to save a few things for you from the apartment."

"We are very grateful!" Fleur replied for them.

"Where are you keeping the donkey?" Corbin asked.

"Oh! That's another bit of news we have for you! We have bought a house. There will be room for you to have an apartment there when we get it renovated. It is in an acre of land, which is plenty of land for the donkey.”

"This happened yesterday as well? You two have some explaining to do! Can you send us a photo of the place? And, what are the roads like down there?”

"We will send the real estate blurb and they are using four wheel drives to get about. Marcel is taking us to Celeste's tomorrow morning, so we will see you there.”

SUBTERFUGE

When Marcel picked up Andre and Candy, along with the donkey, he thought he had seen them before. It was only when Andre mentioned that his family had a pharmaceutical company, that he realised who they were. Photos of them were in yesterday's paper.

He started thinking of how to get them home without the press following them. He broached the subject while having pre-dinner drinks with Andre. Candy was talking with Marcel's wife Patrice, while helping to set the dinner table.

"I will have to hide you when we leave here in the morning!"

Marcel made the comment as he handed Andre the paper. Andre was silent for a minute as he considered what the weekend would be like, with the press and paparazzi stalking them at the chateau.

"A ride for us both in the horse float?"

"Are you sure? It won't be very comfortable!"

"It will be even less comfortable at the chateau if the press discover where we are going."

When Candy called Celeste, she was able to tell her that they were being billeted for the night and she could expect them to arrive by horse float!

Corbin and Fleur were feeling anxious. Andre had been identified in the press as being at Chambery with an unknown female. Everyone was wanting to know who had obviously won the heart of one of Frances most eligible bachelors!

They had disappeared from view after escaping from his parent's apartment at Chambery. The press were now making their presence felt at their apartment block in Paris. Corbin realised that if they were to achieve the quiet family wedding that Andre and Candy wanted, they needed to use some subterfuge to put them off their trail.

Jean set off in the car alone, with instructions to stop at a café on the road south from Paris. One of their neighbours with a furniture business agreed to bring one of their delivery vans into the basement carpark, where the press were unable to gain entry, to pick them up with their luggage. There were no windows in the back for anyone to see them. The van took a detour to his business, to pick up the wedding present that Corbin and Fleur had picked for them.

"Is anyone with you?" Corbin messaged Jean.

"Yes."

"Come back to Paris. We will get you to pick us up Sunday afternoon."

A message was sent to Celeste to expect a furniture van with a "special delivery."

Candy and Andre took some carrots out to Dulcie and gave her a big hug, telling her to behave for Marcel! By now Dulcie knew that this lady was called "Candy" and that she was calling her "Dulcie." She also realised that Candy was leaving her here! She started braying in distress, after Candy and Andre left, until one of the horses asked what she was fussing about. Her owner would be back for her.

"How do you know?"

"They always do come back."

In the back of the horse float, Andre and Candy had been settled on some large cushions on the floor. The rug that had kept both them and Dulcie warm, had been laundered and was ready for use again. Their luggage also was in with them. The curtains in the side windows had been drawn. A hamper of food, drink and snacks also tided them over on the five hour journey.

"We are on our way." Candy messaged Celeste.

Celeste looked at the family at the breakfast table.

"Will everyone be fine with lunch at one o'clock? We've got some special guests joining us!" She also messaged back "Are Leon and Juliette Blanchet members of Andre's family?"

"They are his Uncle and Aunty" Candy replied after consulting with Andre.

"Do you want them at the ceremony?"

"We haven't had contact with them for years. I prefer to keep to immediate family."

"I wonder why she's asking about family?" Andre asked Candy, who smiled knowingly.

"Aunt Celeste is big on heritage, as you will see when we get there. Most of the Chateau and gardens is given over to tourism, which she runs with an army of workers. She is probably organising the public announcement of our wedding, with your parents approval, of course."

Celeste was indeed organising the public announcement. Family crests had been investigated and family members found. When she was satisfied, a message was sent to Corbin for his approval. He gave it a quick scan and with a little smile handed it over to Fleur.

"Do you approve?"

For once there was complete silence as Fleur digested the implications of their family uniting with Candy's family. She managed to keep her smile as restrained as his.

"Of course I approve!"

In the back of the horse float, Andre and Candy were taking advantage of being alone at last! They didn't demure when they found they were given separate rooms at the horse agistment property. It also occurred to them that they may be separated again at the chateau, until after the ceremony!

When they arrived at the chateau, security directed Marcel to the private quarters where the family lived. Security were pleased to see there was no sign of unwanted vehicles trying to follow the vehicle, or any aircraft or drones in the air to indicate that their presence had been detected.

When Candy and Andre were finally released from the horse float, there was a joyful reunion, with all the family. Marcel joined them for lunch before insisting on returning home. There was too much work waiting for him, especially with Dulcie, who wasn't out of danger yet.

While Marcel was away, Patrice kept a close eye on Dulcie while doing all the chores that Marcel usually did. She also tried a halter on her, something that Dulcie hadn't had on for years. At first Dulcie resisted, but with gentle persuasion, allowed Patrice to try it on. She led Dulcie out of her box and tied her to a post near one of the other horses while she mucked out Dulcie's stall and placed some fresh hay and feed in there for her. Patrice then tried walking Dulcie down to the end of the barn and back. When some of the horses put their heads over their stall to "talk" to Dulcie, she let them have contact. The happy swishing of Dulcie's tail, told Patrice she was enjoying it. Dulcie came to expect her little walk and talk each day while she was confined to the barn.

When Marcel finally arrived home after a very long day, he was happy to hear the progress that Patrice had made with Dulcie. Keeping her happy mentally was as important as her physical recovery.

It was late afternoon when the furniture van pulled up at the chateau. Corbin had googled the chateau to get an idea of what the place was like. It certainly was a big attraction, with a big carpark for visitors, which was empty during the winter months. He noticed it had its own chapel and that rooms were available for visitors to stay.

The family all came out to greet them, including Pierre, who had arrived during the afternoon. Candy spotted the pair of tall blue vases that they had brought with them, which matched the colour of the front door of their home.

"Oh! Thank you very much!" Candy beamed at them both. "I know where they are going to live!"

Corbin shook his neighbour's hand.

"Mission accomplished! I owe you for this!"

His neighbour just grinned. A nice bottle of red will do!"

What did land on his doorstep, was a whole carton of high quality wine, that he savoured for some time.

THE DINNER

Celeste led Corbin and Fleur to their suite, making sure it suited them.

"We will let you rest, if you wish. Pre-dinner drinks will be at six o'clock in the drawing room. Pierre and Andre's rooms are either side of your room. If you need anything at all, just ring 1 on your phone."

Corbin and Fleur were unpacking, when a knock came on their door. It was Andre, who had a sparkle in his eyes they hadn't seen before. He had with him some bags they recognised from the Chambery apartment. He gave them both a long hug. They all knew how close Andre and Candy came to losing their lives.

"Have you got my suit?" he asked.

Corbin picked up the suit bag from his case and put it near Andre, but he patted the bed for him to sit down.

"We both are dying to know how things turned around so quickly between you two!"

Andre began to explain. "After our first meeting Candy had contacted a real estate agent about a home she liked online, in the Loire valley. When I took her to the apartment, she made a joke about escaping. I made it clear, that if she ran away again, I would be going with her! She realised then, that I was in her life to stay. So when the agent sent some information about the house and others, she showed them to me. The one we've bought was her favourite. She gave me her vision of the life we would have there, with our family. It convinced me she was as committed as I was. The clincher was the wedding dress she bought at lunch time; so that afternoon I applied for a marriage licence and put a deposit on the house, which was quickly accepted.

We are compatible in more ways than one. We had a lovely evening together doing homely things that we both enjoyed. She's not only courageous," Andre looked at his father, "She's also resourceful and extremely generous! You should have seen the shoes she made for the donkey so it wouldn't sink in the snow! She also gave most of our food away to people who had escaped with nothing."

Both Corbin and Fleur came to put their arms around him.

"So you've no doubts then?"

"None at all!"

"If your half as happy as we are, you will have a wonderful life together." Fleur commented. "I'm looking forward to knowing her better."

"You will!" Andre grinned, "when you share our house. Do you want the first or top floor? We are putting a lift in."

"That's a relief!" Corbin spoke for them both. "We didn't fancy climbing all those stairs all the time."

The conversation then turned to the house and grounds, and their plans for it. Before they knew it, it was time to prepare for dinner. As Andre walked to his room, Candy was coming out of hers, way down the corridor. She blew him a kiss, but he wasn't having that! He motioned silently for her to join him. Swiftly she was spirited into his room where his lips claimed hers as they embraced.

"I can't wait!" Andre whispered.

"I can't either!" Candy whispered back.

There was a knock on the door. "Are you coming?" His father called out.

"You go ahead. I will be there shortly." As their footsteps receded down the corridor, Candy clung to Andre as they collapsed onto the bed to satisfy their passion.

They gave each other a check over to make sure nothing was out of place when they emerged from his room, and managed to reduced their grins to more demure smiles. When they entered the drawing room they were the last to arrive.

"We were wondering whether you were going to skip dinner!" Henri commented with a raised eyebrow. It was obvious to anyone with half an eye that this pair had been at the very least, cuddling already! "Jack! you might have to put a lock on her door tonight!" to a roar of laughter from the room.

Candy managed to control the panic she felt at the suggestion of locking her in; instead she fixed Henri with a gleam and replied.

"And I will be making sure you won't be able to lock it! No more locked bedrooms for me!"

"Just you wait!" Henri added with a gleam of his own, pointing to her stomach. "When your children are toddling around, you will be looking for that lock!"

Candy had to admit defeat, to join in the laughter in the room. She noticed that Henri and Celeste's son, Gaston was talking to Jillian and her husband Mark. They didn't seem very happy about what was being said.

Before she could find out what it was about, a familiar voice spoke to her.

"Are you all ready for tomorrow Love?"

Candy looked around, it was her mother and father, looking very happy. She gave them a hug.

"I'm ready. Are you all ready to walk me down the aisle?"

"I certainly am!"

"Is everything alright for Mark and Jillian?" She saw them give each other a glance.

"Mark is finding it difficult to find a job. He may have to go back to Australia to his FIFO job, which he was glad to see the back of."

Just then, the dinner gong went, so they filed in to the dining room, where Andre's seat was down the other end of the table with his family.

"I will see you later." Andre gave her a hug before heading to his seat. Candy quickly took the chance to speak to Mark before they too were seated.

"Have you been made an offer you want to refuse?" He nodded miserably. Candy gave him enigmatic smile. "Whatever it is, forget it! I have a much better proposition for you!" Mark gave her a quizzical look that was full of hope. She nodded, but had to leave it there, as she was called to her place between her parents. The exchange between them was noticed by everyone at the other end of the table. Andre recognised the look on Candy's face. She was up to something! Andre and Corbin exchanged smiles.

"What do you think she is up to now?" Corbin asked Andre with amusement.

"I'm sure she will tell us when she is ready."

Both Mark and Jillian were now wondering what Candy's proposition was. Mark found he was entertaining Andre's brother Pierre, with his life as a FIFO, which helped to distract him. Jillian was paying close attention to the conversation between Candy and her parents for any clues.

"How did you find your stay down at Chambery?" Candy's Father asked, "You obviously sorted things out after that initial misunderstanding."

"We did!" Candy smiled as she happened to catch Andre's eye as she looked down the table. He was giving her a quizzical "What are you up to now?" look which made her chuckle. Before they could ask what she was chuckling about, she made an announcement to them.

"By the way, we are buying a house. It is half an hour from here. It has four floors, and is set in an acre of land. I will be needing a full time gardener to sort the wilderness of a meadow, where I want an orchard, a vegetable garden and a place for children to play."

Candy saw Jillian was paying close attention to their conversation, and gave her a little smile.

"The Ground floor will be for parking, offices and a flat for Corbin and Fleur's chauffeur when they are visiting. The next three floors will be split into apartments. One for Andre and I and our family. One for Jillian, and for you, Mum and Dad when you are with us and one for Corbin and Fleur when they visit."

Jillian found she was crying! Tears of relief and joy! She was dabbing the tears away when Mark saw her crying.

"What's the matter?" Mark asked in alarm, as he put his arm around her.

"Nothing's wrong!" Jillian's face was full of joy between the tears. "You are not only getting a job you will love; we are getting a home as well!"

"Dad, can you give the house a check over, for any extra work we will need to do before we start renovating? Also are you going to be busy in the next little while? We will be needing someone to co-ordinate the renovations. I will pay you the commercial rates, of course."

The grin on her father's face told her he was happy to do this project for her. In fact it fitted with them very well. A project like this was just what he wanted as he wound down to retirement.

"We are starting a menagerie already!" Candy was telling her parents. "On our trek out of Chambery we sheltered in an abandoned barn. A donkey there adopted me. I'm calling her Dulcie. She is recovering at a horse agistment centre for now. She was skin and bone when we found her."

"I would really love to know what is being said at that end of the table!" Corbin was muttering.

"I agree!" Andre commented. "Did you see Jillian's reaction to what Candy was saying! She started crying her eyes out, but she and Mark are really happy at what they heard. They watched as Mark and Jillian were now toasting their new life in France.

"You aren't the only ones wanting to know what's going on at that end of the table!" Henri murmured to Corbin. "Please give me a heads up when you find out!"

"She's quite a woman!" Corbin murmured.

"Organising both a wedding and buying a house in the same day!"

"What? Where is this?" Henri was all ears. They had kept that quiet! Corbin filled Henri in on the details he knew. Henri now had a fair idea why Jillian was crying with happiness. She was getting a home and Mark would be kept busy in that acre of land. Gaston would be finding someone else for the casual gardening job at low rates.

After dinner, the men retreated to Henri's study to plan their activities in the morning, while having a few drinks. The ladies retired to the drawing room, where Antionette's portrait had pride of place above the fireplace. Celeste and Camille sat either side of Candy on the sofa.

"Candy," Celeste began. "There is something we would like to do in the morning. That lovely portrait of Antionette was done on the eve of her wedding. We still have the dress she wore. We would like you to wear it for a photo. Would you agree?"

Candy grinned. "If you can fit me into it, I'm game!" The two sisters beamed at each other. They then turned their attention to Jillian.

"Are you interested in dressing up? We have a lovely dress for you and Eliza to wear too!"

"What about all of us?" Jillian asked.

"Do you mean me as well?" Fleur was astonished.

"Of course!" Candy interjected. "Your family is joining with ours, so having you in the photos is a must!

When the men joined them for a nightcap, Candy stood up to join Andre, who put his arm around her.

"What's happening?" Andre wanted to know with a grin. Candy looked at him with a questioning look.

"Everyone wants to know why you reduced Jillian to tears of joy! And Mark is looking like he has won the lottery too!"

"Oh! I know Mark loves gardening, so I'm offering him the job of looking after our garden, which will be a full time job. I happened to mention to Mum and Dad that we had bought a house and that one of the floors will be an apartment for Jillian and them when they are there."

'Is that it?"

"Yes. I think they have been feeling very insecure since they have been here." Candy replied thoughtfully. "And now that worry has been taken away."

Andre saw Candy check her watch.

"Are you getting tired? It's been quite a long day!" He commented sympathetically.

"It isn't that," Candy grinned at him. "I've got work to do!"

LATE NIGHT FOR CANDY & ANDRE

"I believe you are missing this?" Jillian said as she handed Candy her computer. It was after lunch as she were discussing their escape from Chambery. Candy managed to restrain herself from running off to see what emails were waiting for her.

When Celeste gave her a phone, Candy had messaged Marianne to say that she was in Switzerland and that as soon as she could, she would obtain another computer to do any work they had available. Marianne had messaged back "Let us know when you are back online!"

When Candy finally had a moment to check her emails, there was a long list, which Marianne had helpfully listed in order of urgency. Candy knew that ordinary Wi-Fi wouldn't be sufficient for her needs, so she went looking for Celeste, who agreed for her to use their business centre, though a security guard would need to be present.

Andre watched Candy, her laptop under her arm, follow the security guard through the doors from the private quarters to the chateau's business centre.

She had dropped a small bombshell after dinner, telling him that she had a month's work to catch up on! One account in particular, needed to be attended to in the next forty eight hours, or it would be given to another contractor. Also, given that it would put five hundred thousand Euro's in her bank account, it was not to be ignored! She was quite happy to forgo a few hours' sleep to get it done.

"Talking of bank accounts, we need to set up a joint account."

"Monday!" Andre agreed. "His mind still reeling from the income that she was able to command. "I will go to sleep when you do!" When Candy opened her mouth to protest, he stopped her with a gentle finger to her mouth. "It's only fair that we both will be bleary-eyed in the morning! I will be waiting for you to come back!" He gave her a kiss on her forehead.

When the family had retired to their rooms, Andre opened his heavy curtains at the window seat. To his delight, he could see a light on across the quadrangle. Candy was already beavering away, with headphones on, at her laptop. The security guard was sitting across from her, looking suitably bored. Eventually the guard dozed off, which suited Candy, as she found his presence a distraction.

Andre grabbed a cushion and rug, to make himself comfortable on the window seat. Seeing Candy "at work" made him check his own work emails. He was concerned to see one from Eugene the supervisor at the factory, asking him to call as soon as possible! Eugene needed advice on the procedure to manage a suspected contamination! He had so far had held back all products made since it was detected. But, there was evidence of sulphur in the system where it shouldn't be and there was also a nasty looking and smelling sludge in the drain!

Andre quickly stood up and called Eugene.

"Where are you?" Eugene asked with relief when he heard Andre's voice.

"I'm nearby, at Blois. You need to stop production

immediately! I don't have a car, but I will find a way of coming in!"

"I will come to collect you! Where from?"

"Do you know the carpark by the chateau? I will meet you there!"

Andre quickly dressed in his outdoor clothing and rang housekeeping, asking for security to escort him to the carpark opposite the chateau. He was being collected there for an emergency visit to his business at Beaugency. Within minutes, Andre heard the door from the commercial area open, and went out to meet the guard.

Corbin and Fleur heard Andre on the phone and then leave his room. Corbin put his head out the door to see what was happening, only to see Andre heading out the door of the private quarters in outdoor gear with security. Something urgent was going on for him not to come and tell him about the situation. Corbin decided to call the factory. It took a while for someone to answer.

"It's Corbin. Is everything alright?"

"No. Eugene suspects contamination in the system, we don't know what yet. Andre has stopped all production and is on his way in."

"Thanks for that."

Corbin texted Andre. "Let me know if there is anything I can do. What's your plan to sort it?"

In the business centre, Candy saw the guard look around at the door and looked up too, just in time to see Andre stride past, a pre-occupied look on his face. Obviously something had happened at his work! She forced herself to concentrate on the job in hand. She had a feeling that they would be needing her income more than ever!

It took some time to walk through the long corridor to the staff entrance. Andre was given a card with a number to call, to be let in again. The Guard walked Andre over to the carpark, which was empty. The area was quiet at this time of night.

"Will you be right if I leave you to wait here?" the guard asked. It was already bitterly cold and there were signs of mist forming already.

"Sure. He won't be long."

Andre answered his father's message while he was waiting.

"There is sludge to be contained and removed. The whole system will have to be cleaned out thoroughly and also will have to test all ingredients and systems for the source of contamination. Our customers will also have to be advised that there will be a delay in the availability of some products."

"Sounds like a plan." Corbin was happy to leave the clean-up in his son's hands.

While he was waiting, Andre also realised he needed to have a plan available for the supervisors to use at times like these. It was only ten minutes to wait, but Andre was glad to get out of the cold when Eugene pulled up.

"Have you had a nice week off?" Eugene asked as they pulled away. He like everyone else had seen the photos in the newspaper.

"Meeting my wife to be was very nice! We get married tomorrow!" He grinned at Eugene's shocked look. "Being in the avalanche wasn't so great! We nearly didn't make it out of the building before it collapsed.

Trekking for hours in the snow and not knowing whether we would survive it, wasn't pleasant either. We bought a house too! It's going to be a big project to do up for us and the family to live in. Oh! We picked up a donkey that will live with us, to start our menagerie."

"It sounds like you are coming back to work for a rest! How did you meet your fiancé?"

"Dad has contacts that arranged the meeting. It has turned out surprisingly well, given she is a fiery redhead and is fiercely independent."

"So, where will you be living? In Paris?"

"No." Andre grinned at Eugene. It's nice and close to the factory! On the outskirts of Beaugency. My fiancé picked it as she wants a country upbringing for our children."

On the shop floor, Andre found the nightshift had gathered with worried faces.

"Are we being stood down?" one asked.

"Definitely not! We need all the help we can get, to sort out where the contamination is, and clean up so we can get back into production. Has anyone any ideas where we can start looking for the source of the contamination?"

"I've a fair idea." One of the men spoke up.

"Good! I will get you to show me shortly." Andre turned to the other workers.

"Our clean-up of the whole facility needs to start with the drain, where we have sludge that needs to be contained, and removed when we can find suitable receptacles to put it in. I need some volunteers for this job. You will be wearing full PPE and will be on double pay till it's done." Some hands immediately went up.

"Stand over here." Andre advised the volunteers.

"Is anyone from the lab on the floor tonight?"

One hand went up. "Grab some swabs and containers and come with us to check the contamination source. We will also want a swab of the sludge. Also from now on, all ingredients coming into the factory are to be checked for contaminates before they are released for use.

The rest of you, please find some boxes. And start packing all the items that are being processed on the production line. Make sure you wear protection too as we don't know at this stage what we are dealing with."

The sludge clean-up team were sent off to put on some PPE and find some barriers to stop the sludge moving any further into the environment.

The lab technician and the other worker went with Andre to a pile of white powder that was used to make some of the tablets. Andre could see straight away that it had a lemon tinge to it. He nodded to the technician to take a sample.

"Are all supplies put in the same pile?" Andre asked the worker. He confirmed that they were.

"From now, they are to be kept in separate bays, with the date of arrival and the batch number of each to be recorded."

At the business centre, Candy was getting a reply from the real estate agent. She had contacted her earlier, asking whether the owner of the property would be agreeable to them paying rent for four weeks, for the time it would take to reach settlement; so they could have access to the property.

The agent was happy to advise that they would be agreeable to those terms and gave an amount of rent they wanted for the period. Candy immediately sent off the payment to the agent. She then enquired about the availability of three pre-fabricated buildings for the use of living, and one for office space. Advice was given that they would be available on Tuesday, and to arrange a plumber and an electrician to be available to connect up the services.

Happy that she had that organised, Candy continued on with her project. It was one o'clock in the morning before she sent the project off. Candy had also included some ideas for other campaigns in her presentation. She wasn't tired enough yet to retire, so she looked at the next project on the list. Candy was surprised to get a message from Marianne.

"That's perfect! Thank you! Some of your other ideas will be wanted by one of our other clients. I will get back to you on them.

In her email, a message came from PayPal that the five hundred thousand Euros had been deposited in her account, which made her smile. She was setting up the next account when her phone rang. It was Andre.

"I've finished at the factory, but I don't know when I can get back. The fog out there is like "pea soup" we can't see to drive back. Hopefully it will clear before the ceremony."

The guard in the room with her was shaking his head. "It can stay around for days!"

"Did you hear what the guard said?" Candy asked. "He said it can stay around for days! Do you have the "Sat Nav" app on your phone?"

"Not yet!"

"Put it on. Put in the location of where you want to go, so you can navigate your way home. If you have any problems, call me!"

Candy packed up, much to the guard's relief. She returned to her room to put on her lounge suit. Her door was left open while she meditated. A very long hour later she heard the door to the commercial area open. Swiftly Candy slipped out to the corridor where Andre was coming in, to be wrapped in his arms.

When they looked up. Corbin was in the corridor in his dressing gown, waving for them to join him and Fleur, who also had her dressing gown on. Fleur patted the bed beside her for Candy to sit. She looked with admiration at the warm suit Candy was wearing, running her hand down the sleeve.

"Is that as warm as it looks? I wouldn't mind one of those!"

"It is! Andre wants one too!"

"You've been working this evening. Did you get it done?" Fleur wanted to know.

"I finished the most pressing campaign, though I have plenty more to attend to. They can wait till Monday though."

While they were talking, Andre was updating his father on the situation at the factory.

Fleur looked at Candy's bare left hand. She reached into the drawer at the bedside for a ring box. She took Candy's hand and placed the box in it.

"This is a little gift for you from our family. My mother wore it. I have no daughters to pass it on to, so I hope you will enjoy it too."

"Thank you so much!" She gave her mother-in-law to be a hug. "I will treasure it. I know there is a rhyme about mothers losing their sons when they take a wife. You aren't losing your son! You are gaining a daughter!"

Candy opened the box. Tears came into her eyes as she viewed the antique ring. A single ruby was surrounded by diamonds. Candy slipped it onto her engagement ring finger. It was slightly loose, but a wedding ring would hold it in place.

"By the way," Candy spoke to Andre. "I have been in touch with the real estate agent. The owner has agreed for us to rent the property while we are waiting for settlement, so we can have access. I have also arranged for three prefab homes and an office to be delivered there on Tuesday. I just have to arrange an electrician and plumber to be there to connect the services."

"Why so soon?" Andre was frowning.

"I don't want my family to be in the position of "outstaying their welcome" once the wedding is over. Also, it would be a good idea to have someone living on site while the renovations are going on. You too will want to be handy to the factory untill the crisis is over."

'That all makes perfect sense." Fleur smiled her approval.

"How much rent do they want?"

"It's already been paid, for four weeks, which will cover the time to settlement. Next week I will get a copy of the plans for the house. Dad is an engineer, so I've asked him to look over the house, to see if there is anything that needs doing before we start. He has agreed to supervise and co-ordinate the renovations for us." Candy looked at Fleur. "Have you decided which floor you would like yet?"

"Not yet. We would like a look at the place first."

"Has it got any views?" Corbin asked with a smile.

"The top floor has!" Candy answered his smile.

"That's settled then."

"You've made a very good start." Corbin told Andre after he detailed what had been done. "The authorities will have to be informed on Monday, if they don't know already. You have done everything that could and should be done, so there shouldn't be any problem from them."

A local council inspector visited the factory that morning to a hive of activity, with workers in protective gear. The supervisor gave him an update on the action that had been taken, and the results of the lab tests.

"I will arrange a tanker for the sludge to be taken to our regional toxic waste facility. The remainder of the waste is to be destroyed in a furnace."

The inspector left satisfied that measures to prevent further contamination were already in place and a plan to prevent future occurrence were already being implemented.

Candy looked at her watch. It was three in the morning.

"I suppose I should get some sleep before our "dress-up" in the morning." Candy told Fleur. "It won't do to have a bleary-eyed Bride!"

"I have some concealer if all else fails!" Fleur reassured her.

Candy went over to Andre. "I will see you at the altar!"

He took her in his arms and give her a cuddle and a kiss before sitting next to his father, who asked.

"You aren't seeing her back to her room?"

"If I did, I would be staying there the rest of the night!"

Candy woke to a knock at her door. Her mother was bringing in a breakfast tray. Candy smiled at her mother and looked at her watch. It was nine o'clock!

"We knew you had a very late night! So we left it as long as we could before we disturbed you! How does the bride feel this morning?" Camille asked as she came over to give Candy a kiss and a hug. Before she could answer, the sound of little footsteps being chased by larger ones were heard in the corridor! Eliza let out of squeal of joy as she came charging into the room.

Candy held out her arms for Eliza to come onto the bed with her. While the scolding tone of her mother could be heard at the door.

"Eliza!"

"Are you going to help me eat my breakfast?" Candy asked Eliza as she settled herself under the covers with Candy. It had been a long time since she had been able to have a cuddle in bed with her.

"Sorry!" Jillian apologised as she came in to give her sister a kiss and cuddle. "Are you getting excited yet?" remembering how she felt on her wedding day.

"I haven't had time to think about it yet! But I'm sure it will hit me when I start dressing for it. We have the fun of our other dress-up to look forward to first!"

She ate her breakfast, while Jillian and her mother talked about their wedding days, and the little trials they had. Once finished, Candy gave Eliza another hug and a kiss.

"Are you ready to play dress-ups?" she asked Eliza, who nodded. She would do anything for her Aunty Candy!

"I will have a quick shower!" Candy announced, so Camille and Jillian collected Eliza and left the room.

"We will see you in the drawing room in twenty minutes."

Candy scrambled into the shower, revelling in the luxury of hot water cascading over her. She still appreciated the privacy that a normal bathroom gave her. She began to consider the idea of a his and her's bathroom, but the space in their new home would dictate that. Candy's thoughts of her new home made her realise that she was looking forward to seeing her new home more than the wedding! Not that she would be admitting that to anyone! She must organise the electrician and plumber today if she could! With that thought, Candy threw on a tailored pair of trousers and a warm sweater. A comfy pair of shoes completed her outfit. For once, she didn't tie back her ringlets, but let them fall onto her shoulders.

As Candy entered the drawing room, the conversation stopped.

"There you are!" Celeste was the first to speak. "You are looking amazing! Considering how late you went to bed! Did your work take that long?" She came to kiss her in greeting.

"Thank you Aunt Celeste, but no." Candy was able to smile serenely. "I finished about one. In the meantime Andre had an emergency at work. When he finished the fog was too thick for them to drive home. They had to use Sat Nav to find their way, which took another hour. I certainly wasn't sleeping till Andre was back safely! We had a chat with his parents when he returned."

Just then, Celeste's assistant came in.

"The photographer is here!"

Candy looked around. Fleur was hovering on the edge of the gathering. She went over to give her a kiss in greeting, and tucked Fleur's arm in her's.

"Are you ready?"

"I am! You aren't greeting your family?"

"Mum, Jillian and Eliza brought my breakfast in." Candy reassured her, as she and Fleur led the family to be fitted into their outfits.

The next two hours were a whirl of changing into complicated outfits, make up and photographs taken in different poses.

"I'm so glad we don't have to wear these anymore!" Camille was the first to comment about the discomfort of wearing them.

"I agree!" Fleur spoke up. "They aren't very practical!"

Lunch was taken in a room that Candy hadn't been in before.

"It was the "Ladies' Room" back in Antionette's Day." Celeste told them. Candy looked around. It did have a more feminine feel than other rooms in the Chateau.

"Ladies, will you be ready at two o'clock for your pre-wedding photos?" Candy looked at her watch and nodded. She had an hour to make her arrangements and get ready.

"I will see you all then." Candy excused herself. It was obvious to everyone she was on a mission to do something!

Back in her room, Candy quickly put out her outfit, then searched for the local electrician and plumber near their new home. Two calls later, Both were booked. Both the Electrician and plumber were going round to the property to check out the facilities over the weekend to prepare it for the connections that would be needed. Next was a call to the French Telecom to arrange connection of phone and internet. They would come for the temporary connection on the Wednesday. She had just finished, when a knock came at the door. It was Celeste. She had a veil in her hand.

"You aren't dressed yet! What have you been doing?"

Candy checked the time. She had fifteen minutes!

"Organising things!" Candy grinned at her Aunt. She swiftly changed into her dress and shoes. The wrap that came with the dress also converted into a train. She asked Celeste to hook it into her dress at the back. A quick freshen up of her makeup and a comb through her ringlets, and she was done.

"What is that you have there?" Candy asked Celeste, looking at the veil, which matched her dress in colour.

"Something borrowed for you." Celeste smiled as she brought out the tiara and cream net veil, which had lace flowers sprinkled through the veil. "Antionette wore this veil at her wedding."

Celeste secured the tiara high on Candy's

forehead, before attaching the veil to it.

"Two minutes to spare!" Candy smiled as she picked up her train to follow Celeste.

In the Drawing room, Fleur and Jillian were already present in their finery. Eliza was doing twirls in her apricot and cream satin dress, which she loved the feel of. A halo of cream flowers had been secured to her head. There were gasps at the beauty that now joined them. The cream of both the dress and veil complimented her auburn ringlets perfectly. Jillian was in an apricot gown, with cream shoes and fascinator.

Hugs were given before the photos were taken. Candy knew that Eliza wasn't going to stay still for the whole hour of the ceremony, so when she gave Jillian a hug, she reassured her.

"Unless Eliza starts throwing a tantrum, let her move around. If she joins us in the ceremony, that will be fine!"

Jillian gasped! "Are you sure?" It was the one thing she was worrying about! That Eliza would disrupt the ceremony!

"I'm sure!" Candy grinned at her sister. "If anyone complains, you can tell them she has my permission to be with us."

Celeste's assistant brought in a bouquet of cream and apricot roses, with sprigs of lily of the valley and maiden hair ferns interspersed in the bouquet. Candy's eyes shone with joy when she received it.

Footsteps heralded the arrival of her parents and Corbin. Her mother in a lilac gown, with a satin jacket. A cream corsage on her jacket. Her father and Corbin in grey suits with cream tie and corsage. Jack grinned at Candy as they hugged.

"This is the first time I've been in one of these for years!" He wriggled to get more comfortable in the attire.

"This is the first time I've been in one of these as well!" Candy grinned back at him.

When Candy and her mother hugged, she looked at Candy closely. "I hope you will be happy!"

"Believe me Mum! I will be! This has been a whirlwind, but the foundations are there for us to have a wonderful life together."

Corbin kissed Candy's hand. "We've made sure he will be at the altar!" which made her laugh out loud.

The photo session went all too quickly.

"It's time! Celeste called out. "Follow me!" They dutifully fell into line behind her, with Candy and her father in the lead.

At the chapel Candy, her father, Jillian and Eliza were directed to the aisle, while the remainder of the guests were directed to their pews. When Candy and her father reached their position, Andre and Mark had been brought out of the ante room and were waiting at the altar.

When the organ music began to play for their walk down the aisle, Candy suddenly felt nervous! She had to take a couple of deep breaths to calm herself. She saw her father give her a questioning look. She gave him a brilliant smile.

"Come on! We had better not let him think he's being jilted!" Her father laughed as he led her down the aisle.

"I see I'm not the only one who has last minute nerves!" Andre grinned to Mark. No-one had seen him get the shakes in the ante-room. Mark had pulled out a small flask of whisky and poured a generous measure.

"Take a swig!"

As Candy approached Andre, he had to catch his breath as his eye's feasted on the vision of beauty that he was about to commit to.

Pierre was resplendent in a cream and gold embroidered robe, but he might as well not have existed. The bride and groom only had eyes for each other.

The ceremony went to plan, with Jillian and Eliza dutifully standing to one side, untill Candy and Andre were required to kneel for prayers. Candy's cream shoes came on display.

"Shoes!" Eliza said with excitement and went running over to Candy to feel her shoes. Remembering Candy's instructions, Jillian stayed where she was. Candy struggled to prevent a giggle as a big grin spread over her face. Andre heard her struggle and gave her a glance to see what was up. He saw her grin and the movement behind her, and started to grin himself.

Candy put her other hand behind her, and found a little hand was put in her's. When Eliza came to cuddle her, Candy put her arm around her. Suddenly Eliza came in front and lifted Candy's veil to give her a kiss, which she returned.

"Hey! I'm supposed to get the first kiss!" Andre spoke with mock indignation.

"Andre's feeling left out! Are you going to give him one?"

Eliza dutifully went over to give Andre a kiss too, before returning to her position next to Candy. Her father, Mark was laughing silently, unable to say or do anything.

"Do you want her removed?" Pierre asked. This wasn't the solemn ceremony he had envisaged he would be presiding over!

"No!" Candy's reply was emphatic. Eliza loves her aunt. If she wishes to be part of the ceremony, I welcome her here."

"Andre?"

"Eliza's participation is making this ceremony much more joyous than we expected it to be. She stays!"

"Stand for your vows please."

Candy didn't need helping up, but Andre came to help her up anyway. Any excuse to put his arm around her! As they faced each other and clasped each other's hands, the love they had for each other was evident.

Eliza wrapped her arms around Candy's leg and cuddled her. She knew that something very important was happening for her Aunt Candy, and she was making sure she was part of it!

At the exchange of rings, Candy was relieved to find her's fitted. She would have to ask Andre how he knew the right size. When it came time to kiss the bride; after Andre had his kiss, Eliza put her hands up. "My turn!" Andre scooped her up so she could kiss Candy, then they both gave her one too. As Candy and Andre walked arm in arm together to sign the registry, her bouquet back in her other hand, Eliza held both her parents hands as they followed them in.

As they came out of the registry room, Celeste nodded to her assistant who scurried off to put the official announcement out at the front gate of the Chateau.

After the final blessing. The organ sounded to escort the wedding party out of the chapel. What no-one was expecting, was the sound of bells pealing, announcing to the world that a member of the De La Court family had married!

By now the fog had cleared enough for people to move around. A crowd quickly gathered at the gate to see the news!

Under the family crests, was the formal announcement.

"Camille and Jack of the De La Court-Payne family, join with Fleur and Corbin of the Blanchet family to announce the union of their daughter Candice Antionette to Andre Laurent.

Leading the news that evening and headlining the paper the next morning, was a photo of the newly-weds.

At the reception, Candy made time to give Jillian her news.

"The temporary new homes for you and Mum and Dad are being delivered and the services connected on Tuesday."

"Oh thank you!" She gave Candy a hug before looking around to see who might be listening. "We hope to stay till then, but if things go south, it will be only a few nights to find another place to sleep."

"Have you had trouble?" Candy looked at her sister with anxious eyes. She realised she had organised alternative living for her family, not a moment too soon!

Jillian tried to make light of the matter.

"Celeste was slightly put out that I didn't stop Eliza from gate crashing the ceremony." She grinned at her sister.

"Did you explain that I gave you instructions to give Eliza free-reign? Actually, Eliza's participation was the highlight of the ceremony for us!"

"She wasn't in the mood for explanations! Sometimes you just have to wear these things!"

Candy gave her a comforting hug.

"Do you want me to book you somewhere to stay?"

Jillian nodded silently.

Candy pulled her phone out of her bra where she had hidden it and turned it on. Swiftly she found accommodation at Beaugency. She showed Jillian a place that had a park with play equipment opposite. Jillian smiled. Within minutes it was booked and paid for.

"You only have tonight to manage here."

"What are you two up to?" Their mother Camille had come to look over their shoulders.

"I've decided it's time for us to move on." Jillian told her mother. "Our new homes will be ready by Wednesday. We are just organising somewhere to stay till then."

"Is there room there for us?" Camille asked. She too had felt the frosty atmosphere since the ceremony.

Candy went into the site and booked a room for her parents.

"Done!" she smiled at her mother. "Perhaps you can share a taxi if you need one."

"Good idea!" Camille agreed as she gave her daughters a big hug.

Everyone could see something was being organised among Candy and her family, but they kept their council. They would hear soon enough.

After the reception, Candy and Andre found that their belongings had been moved, to a suite separate to everyone else.

"At last!" Andre said as they removed their wedding outfits and curled up together in bed.

"Yes, At last!" Candy echoed his sentiments, as she melted into his arms.

THEIR NEW HOME HOLDS A SECRET

When Celeste and Henri came for a late breakfast the next morning, five suitcases were waiting at the lobby.

"What is going on?" Celeste asked when they reached the breakfast table. "This weekend doesn't end till this afternoon."

"Morning Aunt Celeste!" Jillian gave her a smile. "We are staying till then, but will leave with the others. We are just making sure we are ready, that's all."

"What do you mean, you are leaving with the others?"

Camille got out of her seat and came to give her sister a hug.

"Celeste, dearest! We have had a wonderful time staying with you, but now the wedding is over, it is time for us to give you your life and your home back! We will only be half an hour away and be able to visit."

"You aren't going to live with us?"

"Of course not Darling! That was never our intention! Candy is arranging a temporary home for us until our apartment in her house is ready. Jack is itching to get over and have a look at the house and see how the tradesmen are getting on with putting in the services for our temporary homes."

Celeste was still doubtful. She was now feeling guilty about her display of displeasure over Eliza's part in the ceremony.

"Are you sure I haven't upset you?" Celeste gave her sister a searching look. She didn't want to lose her again after their long separation.

"No. You haven't upset me!" Camille reassured her sister. "When Candy and Andre bought their house, they intended for us to live with them. It is far too big for them to live in on their own. It has four floors!"

Until now, Fleur and Corbin had kept quiet during the exchange, but now Corbin chose to put in a word.

"Yes Celeste! Four floors! They are very kindly giving us a floor. Andre and Candy will have a floor. Camille and Jack are sharing a floor with Jillian and her family."

"And the fourth floor?" Celeste asked with interest. Henri had mentioned Candy and Andre were buying a house, but hadn't given any details.

"Will be office space, parking and a flat for our chauffeur when we are visiting."

"If I had known, I would have told her to look for a place with five floors, so we could have one."

Suddenly Celeste was very envious of her sister's family who were together, but with their own spaces. It would give her the excuse to pass the chateau on to Gaston.

"That's getting into Chateau territory!" Corbin spoke with a twinkle.

"Well! If a floor ever becomes available, let me know! I would like to have a look at this house! When are you all going over?"

There was silence for a few seconds.

"We are waiting for Andre and Candy to get the key, but we are staying over in Beaugency."

"Is that where the house is?" Henri spoke.

"It's here." Corbin showed Henri a photo of the

house and where it was on the map. "Just on the outskirts."

"Can you send that to my phone?" Henri asked Corbin, "And let us know when a tour of the building is on?"

Andre and Candy were also enjoying a late breakfast in their suite, when a call came from the real estate agent, asking when they were collecting their key.

"I was thinking tomorrow, when your office is open."

"Are you still at Blois Chateau? I am coming over there shortly. I can drop it in to you."

Candy asked for the details of her car so that security could direct her to their quarters.

"Time to get ourselves moving!" Candy finished her coffee. "The agent is bringing over the house key."

"We will be quicker in the bathroom if we share the shower!" Andre suggested. Candy laughed. She wasn't sure how much time would be saved.

"Come on then!" She grabbed his hand and led him in, where they delighted in caressing each other as they lathered and washed the soap off. They knew they didn't want to stop, but had to! They had to satisfy themselves with an embrace before they stepped out to dry and dress. They only just made it to the drawing room when the agent was shown in by security.

"It's lovely to meet you both in person!" The agent greeted them. From the happiness on their faces, it was obvious that married life was suiting them! "I hope you will be happy in your new home! There is much work to do!" as she handed over the house keys. "It's been waiting for someone to come along to love it!"

"Thank you! We certainly will love it and bring it back to life again. We will head over later to have a look."

"I will be in touch to organise the final arrangements for settlement." The agent shook their hands before being escorted out.

"Did you say you are going over to the house?" Corbin asked.

"We are thinking of going over, on our way to Paris, after lunch."

Corbin got his phone out. "I will get Jean to come now."

Henri then spoke to Jack and Mark.

"We will give you a lift over to the house and drop you off at your accommodation."

Jack expressed their gratitude. "Thank you. We really appreciate it. Getting some wheels will be a priority this week."

Henri's eyes lit up. "I can take you to the car sales yards. Have you anything particular in mind."

"Just a family wagon that has room to carry things."

Henri nodded. "You have to be practical when there is a family to consider."

There was a call to Camille from security, that the photographer was here with the photos.

"Send them in."

They spent the rest of the morning going through the photos, choosing the ones they wanted to order. The ones Candy loved the most, were the ones the photographer had captured in the church, of Eliza interacting with them in the ceremony. He had the camera on silent, so they hadn't realised they were being taken.

"We will have to frame this one!" Candy pointed to the photo of them both kissing Eliza. Andre went through the photos of them with Eliza.

"We will have to make a montage!"

When Jean made his appearance close to lunch time, he grinned at Andre and Candy.

"You've had an interesting time since I dropped you off! And, Congratulations!" He kissed Candy's hand. "Welcome to the Blanchet family."

"Thank you Jean!" She gave him a hug and a kiss on both cheeks. "It was more interesting than we expected! I trust you enjoyed your days off."

"Actually, I was starting to get bored in the end, so I was ready for my little trip here. Are they your cases in the foyer?"

"No they aren't! excuse me Jean while I sort them."

Andre and Corbin saw Candy head off to their suite with purpose and followed her.

"What's up?

"Just packing! Jean wanted to know whether they were our cases in the Foyer. It won't take long."

By the time the lunch gong was sounded, they were wheeling their cases to the foyer. Corbin and Fleur had also taken their lead and packed as well.

On their way over to their new home, Andre checked his messages and showed one to his father with a smile. It was from the supervisor.

"The inspector came and was happy with our

response. The tanker is now here to pump out the sludge. The other waste is being picked up tomorrow. We just have to scrub the place out and get the clearance from the inspector before we restart production.”

“Well done! Staff can have a couple of days paid leave before restarting production.”

“Are you sure?” Corbin asked with a raised eyebrow.

“Of course! The staff have gone above and beyond their duties the past few days. They deserve a small break, not to mention reward. Besides, I don’t want tired staff restarting production.”

“We are here.” Jean interrupted the conversation, as he passed through the gap in the conifers to stop in the drive. In front were two other vehicles. The plumber and electrician were busy laying pipes and power cables to the positions where the temporary homes were going to be sited.

Andre looked at Candy with amazement.

“You’ve organised it already!”

Candy nodded with a smile. “The phone and internet will be connected on Wednesday.”

There was silence from Fleur as she took in the impressive façade of the home. She looked at the top floor that was to be their home from home. She allowed herself a big smile. This was going to be grander than their apartment in Paris!

“Well!” Corbin spoke when Jean had let them out of the car. “This is a nice little pad you’ve picked!”

“Candy picked it! And it’s not so little! I’m glad you will be sharing it with us!”

The reactions weren't so subdued in Henri's car.

"OMG!" was Jillian's response. Mark just grinned as though he was a cat with cream!

"I think we will be needing a map to find our way round this house!" was Camille's reply.

"If there is too much room for you, just remember us!" Celeste put in a reminder that she was interested. Henri gave Celeste a nod. He definitely was interested too!

The tradesmen saw the cars pull up and downed tools. They gathered the new owners were here.

Candy Andre and Jack went over to meet them and introduce themselves.

"Dad is an engineer; He will be supervising the site while the renovating is going on. We are having our first look at the property to see what needs doing before we start fitting out the interiors. We will get you to join us to get an idea of the work and the finance that will be needed."

They started with the ground floor. Two old doors to the garage space would need replacing. Candy had brought pen and paper to list the obvious things. She drew a rough outline of the floor, marking in three flats on one side, with parking in the middle.

"Jean, do you want a view to the front with formal gardens or the back with the orchard, vegetable garden, play area and donkey?"

"I'll have the back view please!" Jean grinned.

In the middle of the parking area it looked like two large cupboards side by side. Jack opened one. It was empty, but the space went right up through the building to the roof. The other cupboard was the same. It had obviously been used as chutes for laundry and rubbish in the past. He looked at Candy with a grin.

"I think we have our lift well here! If we can use it, it will save a small fortune in adjusting all the floors to fit one."

Candy marked the lift well in.

"What are you using the other side for?" the electrician wanted to know.

"I will be working from home, so I was thinking office space, but I would want a bathroom and a small kitchen there too. I don't want to be up and down stairs all the time."

They all trooped out to climb the double stairway to the first floor, much to Jillian and Eliza's excitement. Eliza had much fun running around in the big open space downstairs, but this was different again.

The large front door opened into a wide marble hall way. Double doors lay on either side, but light from the interior invited you in. Eliza went running ahead to the interior and looked up. Her eyes were transfixed on the leadlight in the centre. She hardly noticed the magnificent double staircase that wound its way up to the gallery on each floor, or the doors to explore opening off the space.

"Plenty of room for family portraits here!" Henri murmured to Celeste.

"Plenty of room for a banquet in here too!" She murmured back.

"This would be nice for Christmas dinners in here!" Celeste said out loud to Candy, who nodded her agreement at the idea. She already had plans for a big Christmas tree in here!"

Candy lead them back to the double doors for this floor. Jillian gasped at the size of the room with another of similar size beyond it. The wallpaper was old and tatty, but there was nothing shabby about the intricate moulding on the ceilings. As they moved through the rooms, Jillian and Mark made decisions on the changes they needed.

They came to a long gallery along the back of the house, which had several doors opening out onto the balcony.

"I want this area." Camille spoke for the first time. She could see it as a nice big living area, with a bedroom and ensuite off it. That was all she really wanted. Jack agreed. She indicated their wishes to Candy, who pencilled them in.

For the first time, Celeste dared to hope she had a place here. Candy was looking at her with a smile, reading her thoughts. They found the other side of the house was similar to the side that Jillian and Mark had claimed, which suited Celeste and Henri very well.

By the time they had viewed the first floor, Eliza was getting tired. Henri and Celeste offered to take Jillian and Mark to their accommodation, which they accepted happily. "I will talk to you both tomorrow." Candy hugged her sister and brother-in-law.

A walk up the stairs to the second floor led them to a large living area overlooking the front grounds, with bedrooms on either side of the building to a large gallery overlooking the back garden. Corbin guessed that their floor would be similar.

Decisions were made to reduce the lounge at the front of the house, to allow for a snug in the winter months. Both Candy and Andre wanted an office space upstairs as well as the business centre they planned downstairs. Bedrooms were kept on the eastern side of the house, with a kitchenette included, to reduce trapsing to the other side of the building where the main living areas were to be.

Corbin and Fleur looked at the plan Candy and Andre had made up.

"If our floor is the same, then your plan will be perfect for us too!"

A tour of the top floor, showed that it was. Both Corbin and Andre were pleased to see there was no sign of water damage in any of the rooms, but they wanted to see the roof anyway. They were puzzled when they couldn't find a manhole.

"There must be a concealed entrance." Candy was thoughtful. She remembered some decorative panelling in the lounge area and went to take a closer look at it. Candy ran her hand over the panel, noticing the Fleur de Lea stood out slightly more than the rest of the panel. She gave it a firm push. With a click, the panel swivelled open. Beyond it was a narrow staircase to the attic.

"Who's game for a look?" Candy grinned at the astonished looks from Corbin and Fleur.

"Lead on!" Andre, Jack and the tradesmen also had grins on their faces. Corbin Fleur and Camille cautiously followed them. Batting away years of cobwebs, they found a large roomy area for storage. Jack noticed tiny pinpricks of light.

"It isn't urgent, but it would be a good idea to get a few quotes for a new roof." Jack advised Andre and Candy.

At the back of the attic, Candy noticed what appeared to be a large chest, with the remnants of a rug over it. As she lifted the rug, it fell apart. Beneath it in the chest, a pair of skeletons, with the remnants of clothing were entwined, protecting each other.

Andre saw Candy's hand go to her mouth, an expression of grief on her face, and came to look.

"It is obvious what happened!" Candy turned to Andre as his arm went round her. "We will have to give them a proper burial, though we will have to find out who they were. I presume they were the owners during the revolution." Andre nodded as he led her away.

The family left the tradesmen to carry on their preparations, dropping Camille and Jack off at their accommodation. Jillian and Mark were already across the road at the park with Eliza, who was revelling in having somewhere to play again!

As they made the journey towards Paris, Candy's phone began to ring. It was Marianne. She had changed the priorities on her "to do" list.

"I tried to ring you yesterday! Where were you?"

Candy smiled as she replied. "I was busy getting married!"

"I think that is a reasonable excuse!" Andre smiled at the exchange, giving Candy a kiss on her neck. She gave his knee a squeeze, as she reached for her laptop.

"If I do my work on the way, I will have more free time in Paris."

"Sounds fair enough. By the way, when do you get paid for your work?"

"As soon as I submit it and Marianne approves it, it is Pay Palled straight to my account. That work I did Friday night is already in my account."

Andre lifted a cover by their feet. "You want to plug in?" Candy smiled her gratitude. He also gave her the wifi code for in the car.

"Get your work out of the way!" Corbin approved. "We are having dinner and a show out tonight!"

"Have you a cocktail dress?" Fleur asked with a twinkle in her eyes.

"I did have, but I think I left them at Chambery."

"I will look out something for you."

"Thank you!" Candy replied, before turning her attention to her work, her headphones in place.

While she was working, Andre and his parents had plenty to talk about. They were wondering about shared costs such as power and water; and what about the rates and maintenance on the property.

"Each apartment will be on a separate power circuit, so you only pay for what you use. The same for water too. We will work out how much in area each apartment will take and your rates will be in proportion to that. We are intending to create a sink fund for the family to pay into. Whenever something needs doing, we will have a meeting to sort any issues like that."

"That sounds very reasonable." Corbin was impressed. The arrangement was much better than in some apartments they had been in.

"We've had word from the other residents at Chambery, wanting to know whether we are interested in the rebuild of our building. We aren't sure yet. We will have to go down sometime soon though, as they have retrieved some items from our apartment."

They were on the outskirts of Paris, when Candy sent off her work and packed away her laptop. Some minutes later a message from PayPal came to her phone. She showed it to Andre with a smile.

"I wish our clients were that quick to pay!"

It was dusk as Candy looked around her, at the low rise city around her. In the distance she could make out the unmistakeable silhouette of the Eiffel Tower in lights.

"Is this your first visit Candy?" Fleur asked, seeing Candy's interest in the passing streets.

"It is!" Candy admitted with a happy smile.

"Welcome to Paris!" Corbin beamed. "We will have to give you a tour in the daylight."

'I will look forward to it!"

As they travelled into the centre, the car deviated from the wide avenues to narrow suburban streets, with residential apartment buildings overlooking them. A roller door opened for them to enter a basement car park. Candy collected her items into a tote bag she had brought with her from Chambery. She felt a little envious that Fleur didn't appear to need one. Candy used her's like a security blanket, with her essentials at hand wherever she went.

"Your thoughts?" Andre asked Candy as they alighted from the car, noticing she was in a reflective mood.

"I'm just envious that Fleur doesn't seem to need a handbag! I would be lost without mine!"

Andre grinned. "You won't be needing that big bag tonight!"

"I agree! But I will be wanting a small one for my essentials!"

"You can choose from one of mine that I no longer use." Fleur spoke with a big smile. She remembered being in need of a bag wherever she went, but in her present lifestyle, it was rarely needed.

On leaving the lift, Candy noticed that their apartment was the only one on their floor. The foyer to their apartment held double doors with intricate panelling. A Butler and a maid stood ready to greet them. Andre led Candy over to be introduced.

"Amélie, Duval, please meet my wife Candy."

"Welcome Candy." They both smiled.

"Bonjour and Thank you!" Candy replied with a big smile, putting her hand out to shake their hands. She didn't know it, but she had just scored points for making physical contact. Most employers never made contact in this friendly way.

Andre led Candy through for a tour of the apartment. down a wide corridor lay the living areas in an L shape. A separate corridor held bedrooms.

"This is our bedroom and bathroom." Andre showed her the large bedroom and ensuite with a free standing bath in the middle of the room. He began to kiss her, but the sound of footsteps and the sound of suitcases being wheeled made them break off.

"I suppose we should be sociable!" Andre muttered as he led her to the living area. A large drawing room held antique furniture. Candy could see a dining setting and kitchen beyond.

Corbin and Fleur were already seated with drinks in hand and some nibbles in front of them.

"It will be a while before we eat dinner, so tuck in!" Corbin told Candy. "What do you think of it?"

"It's a very spacious base for life in this city! I'm impressed." Candy replied. In comparison, the unit I used to live in was..." she looked around to compare the area she used to live in, "about half the size of this room!" she finished with a grin.

This brought laughter, as none of them could imagine living in a space that small. Candy told them about her life in Perth, untill Amélie came to her.

"Madam Candy, I have some gowns for you to look at." She gave Candy a smile.

"Thank you, Amélie." Candy returned the smile as she stood up to follow her. In her bedroom was a rack with four gowns, with matching shoes. Two of them were black, one was a sea green, but the one she lingered over was a blue satin.

"I will try this one." Candy said as she lifted the dress off the rack. Amélie immediately took it off her to place it on the bed for her. Amélie assisted to do up the zip of the gown and placed the shoes near her feet to try on.

"There are a couple of extra things to finish." Amélie said as she left the room briefly. She returned with a white fur cape and a couple of boxes of jewellery. A blue enamel necklace in art-deco style with matching earrings were given to Candy to try on. "Will you be needing an evening bag or purse as well?"

"I will, thank you Amélie."

Candy freshened her makeup and tied her ringlets up at the back of her head.

"I have just the right ornament for your hair!" Amélie offered. "Yes please! Candy accepted.

When Candy entered the living area, she asked; "Will I pass muster?"

There was stunned silence for a few seconds before Andre stood up and came over to Candy. The admiration in his eyes told her that she did.

"Can you get our Tuxedos out please Duval!" Corbin spoke to the butler. "An ordinary suit won't do!"

Fleur stood up to examine her daughter-in-law, a definite twinkle in her eyes as she took in the beauty before her.

"You will definitely pass muster! I have a feeling there will be more eyes on our table than the stage tonight! I had better find something suitable to wear too." As she took herself off to find Amélie.

As they were dropped off at The Red Windmill theatre restaurant, Candy noticed some camera flashes, but didn't take too much notice as there were other patrons arriving as well.

As they enjoyed their dinner, Andre could feel lots of messages coming through to his phone. He took a quick look in case something was amiss at work, but to his dismay they were messages from his old flames, who hadn't been put off at all by his marriage. Some were wanting a meeting; others were offering to be his mistress. He quickly put the phone back into his pocket, vowing to remove them from his phone contacts! He hadn't taken too much notice of who else was in the audience till now. Andre was even more dismayed to see a couple of his old girl friends in the audience. They gave him special smiles when they made eye contact. He just hoped they didn't come over to introduce themselves!

Candy noticed that Andre was looking distracted.

"Is everything alright?" she asked, squeezing his hand in reassurance. Andre took her hand and kissed it.

"Not quite!" he said, looking at her with anxious eyes. He decided to be truthful, so she knew if any of them made a move.

"Before we met, I had a number of...ladies chasing me. They were after the lifestyle that the money I earn could give them. Word must have got around that we are in Paris. Being married doesn't seem to have deterred them at all. I've just had a flood of messages! Some wanted to arrange to meet, and others... offering to be my mistress!"

"Oh I see! So the race is now on to see who can be first to get you out of our bed and into theirs?"

"That's about it!" It was Andre who now squeezed Candy's hand to reassure her. "I will be deleting them all of course, but I am also glad we are moving to the country! They will have to find someone else to chase! When will our temporary house be ready?"

"It's being delivered Tuesday. The internet and phones are being connected on Wednesday."

"We will want a few days to find some furniture and get it delivered."

"What is the busiest time of day for you? Morning or afternoon?"

"Mornings, why?"

"What if we both work in the morning and take the afternoon off to search for furniture? We will get an idea tomorrow how much time we need to get everything we need."

"Sounds good to me!"

Tables were now being cleared, ready for the show to begin. Andre noticed that the couple behind them were straining to see around him, so he moved his chair round next to Candy; to be given grateful smiles from the people behind him. He also was grateful for the excuse to put his arm round Candy. Andre gave Candy's neck a nuzzle. When she looked round at him with a smile, he claimed her lips for a long kiss. Not missed by most people in the room! Some of whom were members of Corbin's club. There would be a fair amount of chat next time Corbin made an appearance, wanting to know how his "gem" was settling in.

Candy enjoyed the cabaret. Shows like this one were few and far between in her old life. She realised how fit and athletic the dancers were and wondered whether she should get a dog to keep her company when she was home alone and take them for walks with Dulcie to keep herself active.

After the show, Candy and Andre were waiting in the crowd for Jean to bring the car, when a voice next to her spoke.

"Madam Candy?"

Candy looked around to recognise the face.

"You were one of the viewers!" she spoke quietly.

"I see you've landed on your feet! Were you...?"

By now Andre Corbin and Fleur looked over to see who Candy was talking to.

"Was I, and am I pregnant?" She paused. "Yes I am." Candy felt Andre's arm tighten protectively around her. The man showed her his police badge.

"I gave a full statement to Interpol when I arrived in Switzerland, But if you want an interview, I will be home in the morning."

He nodded as Andre pulled Candy away.

"Our car is here!"

"What was that all about?" Corbin asked once they were in the car.

"He is one of the police officers that successfully penetrate the Dark Web. I recognised him as one of the viewers that were paged every time I moved around. I believe he wants an interview in the morning."

"You don't have to!" Andre was feeling upset that she had to relive her abuse all over again.

"I know, But if the French authorities want reassurance that I am here legally and of my own free will, it is best to get it over and done with." She gave him a hug.

"You're right of course!" Andre sighed, before giving her a kiss and cuddling her.

"Do you have an office in your apartment?" Candy asked as they reached the foyer.

"We certainly do!" Corbin smiled. "Come and inspect it!"

"You aren't going to work now, are you?" Andre was ready to protest.

"No." Candy reassured him, reading his mind. "But I will set up ready for the morning."

"I will let you off!" Andre was relieved. He didn't like the idea of her turning into a workaholic! Corbin showed her into a large room off the drawing room, with views to the buildings and rooftops opposite. A large desk dominated the room. She was shown where to plug in her laptop and the wifi code. She spotted the printer in the corner, going over to exam how this model worked.

"I may need to copy a document." Candy explained. Looking around, she then asked; "Do you have any spare chairs for the interview in the morning?"

"How many do you want?"

"At least two. I expect immigration will be visiting with the police."

Corbin looked at Andre. "I will get Jacques to sit in on the interview."

"Jacques?" Candy asked.

"Our Lawyer."

THE INTERVIEW

When Andre woke the next morning, Candy was kissing his forehead. He promptly pulled her down to kiss her on the mouth.

"Morning my sleeping beauty!" she murmured, which made him roar with laughter.

"The only beauty in here is you! I see you've already had your shower!" Noting Candy was already dressed for work.

"I'm just about to have a quick breakfast before I get started. I'm not sure how much time I will have before the visit."

"I will join you." Andre said as he sprung out of bed to put on his dressing gown.

Duval had heard Candy in the shower, so he knew someone would be wanting breakfast soon. Coffee was already brewing when they entered the kitchen.

"Morning Andre, Morning Candy. Please take a seat."

"Thank you, Duval. We hope you slept well."

"I always sleep well, thank you Andre. Are you having your usual? What would you like Candy?"

"A small bowl of cereal and some fruit please. Did Corbin mention last night that I would be getting some visitors this morning?"

"Not yet. Who can we expect?"

"Jacques the family lawyer will be sitting in on an interview with me. I am expecting a visit from the French police and immigration, I presume to check that my paperwork is in order, and that they want an account

191

of the circumstances that brought me to Europe.”

“May I ask about the circumstances? Also, why would they be questioning your paperwork? That would have been dealt with on arrival.”

Candy told Duval about her time in captivity and how she came to Europe without a passport, finally her encounter with the officer last evening.”

“You were given documentation on arrival?”

“I have it here.” Candy showed him her passport with the document she had received in Switzerland.

“Where will you be holding the interview?”

“In the office.”

“Make sure the door is kept open! In fact I will make sure it can’t be closed.”

Candy looked at Duval. “You think I am being set up for something?”

“I believe you are. I shall make arrangements for your protection. They won’t be visible, but they will be here, and be able to defend you in an instant. Also, don’t allow them to move behind you for any reason!”

“Thank you, Duval. It will give me peace of mind.”

Candy looked at the time. She needed to start work. She quickly finished her coffee and her breakfast, before coming round the table to Andre. He stood up to cuddle her. He didn’t know how she could be so calm in the face of danger.

“I will see you at lunch time.” Candy kissed him before heading to the study. Duval had already adjusted the study door to stay open. He had also disappeared, she presumed to organise her protection.

Candy placed four chairs, facing each other, in front of the desk, before making a copy of her passport and document. Candy had been working a couple of hours when she heard Duval bring someone in. She quickly shut down her laptop to place it in her tote bag along with her passport and entry document.

"Madam Candy, Monsieur Jacques is here for you."

"Thank you Duval." She gave him a smile of gratitude.

"Good morning Monsieur Jacques. Thank you for coming." She came forward to shake his hand. He took her hand and bowed over it. "I have made a copy of my travel documents, in case of any issues."

Jacques took a quick look. "There isn't any reason to question these. If they want to take you anywhere, for any reason, you will not be going!"

Candy gave him a smile. "I won't argue!" She heard Duval speaking to someone at the door. She took a deep breath. "Here we go!"

"We will stand behind our chairs and won't sit until they do! If necessary use them as a barrier."

Duval appeared at the door.

"Your visitors are here, Madam."

"Thank you. Please bring them in."

The police officer was in uniform. The other man with him was in a suit.

"Before we commence the interview, we will introduce ourselves." Candy began. "I am Candice Blanchet and this is Jacques, our family lawyer.

"You are Candy Payne." The police officer interrupted her.

"I was. I married on the weekend." Candy spoke smoothly. "Who am I speaking to, please?"

"It's obvious, isn't it? You don't need...."

Jacques interrupted him in a testy tone. "If you won't identify yourselves, this interview is over now!"

Candy saw them reach for their pockets.

"STOP!   Keep your hands away from your pockets!"

"We are only getting our notepad and pens out." The man in the suit spoke.

"That will not be necessary." Candy produced some paper and pens. "Please take a seat."

The men remained standing.

"You are under arrest, Candy.   You are to accompany us to the police station."

"On what charges?" Jacques asked as bluntly.

"Illegal entry to Europe, and prostitution!"

Candy couldn't help showing her astonishment at the prostitution charge. While she was struggling to stop herself from laughing out loud, Jacques answered for her.

"I have already checked her entry documents. They are in order. She has made a copy for you."

Candy managed to recover her composure to answer the accusation of prostitution.

My father-in-law acted as my benefactor, by paying for the plane to bring me to Europe; also my care at the clinic in Switzerland to recover from injuries I sustained while I was a captive in Australia. He also provided some clothing for me to wear. I have not received a financial allowance of any kind since my arrival, as I already had my own income from my job in Australia, which I have continued with."

"You have received nearly €750,000 since you arrived in France. How do you justify that?"

Candy was able to give them a big smile.

"I work freelance in marketing. It involves making advertisements for an advertising firm in Australia. One account in particular had a budget of A$5 million. My payment for making the advertising was €500,000. The rest of my income was from other accounts that I have done for the firm. I will give you the details of the firm if you wish to confirm that the details I have given you are correct."

"We are still taking you to the station for a statement!" as the officer spoke both he and the other man reached into their pockets. Candy froze as she saw a pistol in the officers' hands, which they started to lift towards them.

Two shots rang out as they were shot from behind, to slump on the floor.

"Take her out. We will deal with these two."

Candy quickly grabbed her bag before Jacques put his arm round her, to lead her past the bodies on the floor, then out to the lift. Jacques turned on his phone to send the message.

"It's over. She's unharmed."

"Bring her to the office."

Jean was waiting in the carpark as Jacques brought Candy down in the lift. He gave her a hug and a kiss on both cheeks, before handing her into the car. Jacques joined them for the ride to Head office, which was also in a heritage building. They were escorted up to Corbin's office, where Fleur and Corbin were waiting with Andre.

Andre came rushing over to take her in his arms.

"Are you alright?" He asked.

"I will be. I don't know whether to laugh or cry!

Do you know he tried to ping me for prostitution!" With that she collapsed into giggles, which turned to tears. Her reaction continued for several minutes. While Andre was comforting her, Jacques told Corbin about the interview.

"It was just as well the protection unit was there. She could have been taken anywhere otherwise. When you arranged to bring her to France, did you have any competition?"

"I did. I have a fair idea who's behind it. It will be interesting to know whether there is a money trail to these men from him."

Once Candy had recovered, she went to sit with Fleur, who also gave her a hug.

"I'm sorry I've caused so much trouble!" Candy began.

"This isn't your fault!" Fleur stopped her. "We will find out who was behind this "visit" at some point. We are just glad we were able to protect you."

Candy sighed. "I expect we will be needing some security at our new home as well."

"It would be wise." Fleur agreed.

"I've already put it in place." Andre spoke as he came over to them, to give Candy another hug. "I couldn't bear it if anything happened to you!"

Candy looked at him with tears in her eyes.

"I couldn't bear it if anything happened to you either."

"We might as well go for some lunch." Corbin spoke. "There hasn't been much done around here this morning anyway."

Lunch was almost a festive occasion, as they relaxed after a fraught morning.

"Have you anything interesting planned for this afternoon?" Fleur asked Candy as they were finishing, "or are you working?"

Candy looked at Andre. "The plan was to create a joint account for us, then go shopping for furniture."

"I would love to join you for the furniture shopping, if I may?" Fleur looked at them both hopefully.

Andre nodded with a grin. He knew better than to refuse when shopping was involved.

"We would love you to come." Candy agreed.

"We will have a cup of coffee while you are at the bank." Corbin replied for Fleur. "Remember to come back for us!"

A pleasant afternoon was had while they browsed and selected items for their new home and arranged delivery.

"Have we got everything?" Andre asked as they prepared to return to the apartment.

"Not quite. We have bed and bath linen, and kitchen ware to get, but that can wait till the morning. I take it we will be making a trip to see the house installed in the afternoon?"

"I would love to come, but I need to catch up with work. I will get Jean to take you."

That evening, they chose items for the house together, arranging for Candy to collect them in the morning. A furniture van was going to follow them down to the house. Candy and Jean were about to leave the apartment when Andre called.

"Have you left yet?"

"No. We are in the carpark."

"Can you pick me up? There's an issue at the factory."

"Is it another leak?" Candy asked with concern.

"No, but it has the potential to be as serious. I'm just glad I brought in a system that checks everything that comes into the factory." Andre looked at Candy with anxiety. "We detected arsenic in one of the ingredients!"

"You think it was deliberately put in there?"

Andre nodded.

"Is there any way of separating the arsenic from the ingredient?" Andre had to have a long think about it.

"I'm not sure, but we may have to try, if we can't get another source of the ingredient. One thing is for sure, I wish head office was at Beaugency. When dad retires, I will be moving it down."

"We will have a business centre in our home. Would that be suitable?"

"It just might!" Andre brightened at the idea.

A NEW BEGINNING FOR THE FAMILY

After dropping Andre off at the factory, they made their way to the house, to find a large truck with a long tray backing out of the drive.

"I wonder if it is the first or last one." Candy murmured to Jean, as they waited for it to leave. To her joy, it was the last one. When they turned into the drive a man stopped them. It was their security officer. After introducing themselves, and advising him of the furniture truck that was coming, he waved them in.

"We will park up near the main house." Candy told Jean. 'In fact, I will open the doors so you can turn around."

She could see her father helping the plumber connect the homes and office to the system. The electrician was there too. She waved to her Mother and Jillian who had Eliza in her arms. Both Camille and Jillian had sets of keys in their hands as they watched everything being installed. The large front garden now looked very small with four buildings in it.

Candy got out to open the doors to the ground floor, when both Camille and Jillian came running up to wrap her in their arms. Eliza also joined in the cuddle; so happy to see her Aunt Candy was here!

A little toot from Jean made them look round. The furniture truck was behind him. Candy quickly opened the doors to the ground floor for Jean, who parked to one side. The driver of the truck got out for a look. There was room for the truck in there too.   This worked out well, as some of the furniture was being stored there for Corbin and Fleur.

"Where did you say my new home was going to be?" Jean asked Candy when she had a spare moment from organising the truck driver and his mate.

She took him over to the corner.

"Imagine there is a wall from the back to the front here. You will have a third of it."

"It's huge!"

"Enjoy it!" Candy beamed. "I will made a little patio area out the side for you as well."

"Who will have the other two thirds?"

"Duval and Amélie can fight over it."

The grin on Jean's face, told her he was going to enjoy that.

The next hour was busy as the furniture was moved into their new home. Candy then unloaded the car to make up their bed and install the linen in the house. Their truck had just left, when another two trucks came in with furniture for the rest of the family. While Jillian gave instructions to the driver, Mark came over to see Candy.

"What's the first thing you want done." He asked.

"A priority will be a stable for Dulcie and a shed for her feed. If you can find or make a swing for Eliza in the Oak tree, that would be nice for her too. If we can't get planning permission from the council, we will incorporate a place for Dulcie and her feed in here." Candy pointed towards the four large arched windows at the back of the house. "You will be wanting a shed or workshop as well, won't you?" Mark nodded.

Candy showed Mark the boundary of the staff quarters, the business centre, and the parking area.

"The rest of the area we can play with for Dulcie, your workshop and storage area. Will you be wanting a vehicle for work?" Candy asked as she looked at the floor, which was laid with small bricks. Not suitable for keeping a donkey.

"If we keep Dulcie in here, we will need to lift some of these bricks and lay some concrete, with drainage towards the outside and a sump. Some time before spring, we will need to go to a nearby plant nursery and get some fruit trees and some seeds to start a garden. If I start a garden account with a budget of €20,000, will that be sufficient for you to gather everything to get the garden started? We will of course need a book and receipts to record the expenses."

"I'm going to share your Dad's car till we get ourselves established. That €20,000 will be a good start."

"Speaking of expenses. Your salary of €50,000 per year. Is it okay to pay you fortnightly with the tax taken out?"

"That will be good." He didn't ask when their first pay day would be. They were getting low on funds, but they would manage somehow. Candy had read his thoughts though.

"I know things are tight financially for you, so I will give you €1,000 to tide you over till pay day."

She dived into her bag and gave Mark an envelope. There were tears in Mark's eyes as he gave her a hug.

"It's okay." Candy gave his shoulder a gentle tap to comfort him. "It's what family is for, when things get tough."

"We have a couple of weeks to sort a home for Dulcie and her feed. I will get onto that account for the gardening too, tomorrow."

Jean saw the little exchange between Candy and Mark, realising she was helping him out of a tight spot, financially.

Candy's phone rang. It was Andre.

"How are you going at the house?"

"Our furniture is in and the bed is made. The furniture trucks for the rest of the family are here. Are you ready to be picked up?"

"Not yet. We are testing to see whether we can separate the arsenic from the ingredient. It will be another hour before we will know the result."

"Let us know, Love, when you are ready!"

"I'm ready, already!" which made candy laugh as she disconnected.

"He will be at least another hour." Candy told Jean. He will let us know when he's ready to be collected."

When the tradesmen had finished, they came to Candy with their invoices. She had checked that everything was working and offered to pay them on the spot. The look of shock on their faces was plain to see.

"I am paid when I complete a job. I am extending the same courtesy to you." Candy explained. In a few weeks I will be in touch with you about the work we want done in the main house."

They quickly produced their card readers and left with beams on their faces.

A message soon came through from Andre.

"What were those payments for?"

"The Plumber and Electrician. Everything is working as it should, so I paid them."

Candy then had a chat with the security guard.

"How many hours are you working each shift?"

"We work twelve hours, Madam."

"Come with me." Candy told him. "I will show you your facilities, while the renovations are being done. You will have your own space in the house when they are completed."

She led him to the office building, showing him the canteen area and bathroom. A much happier guard left the office building. He had considered this job a temporary position, but from what she said, it could be worth hanging on to.

Candy visited Camille and Jack's home, where they were cracking open a bottle of champagne, that they were sharing with Jillian and Mark. They had informed her that dinner had been ordered and was being delivered for everyone.

"Are you sure you won't join us?" Jillian asked Candy. "Even a tiny one?"

"A tiny one!" Candy agreed.

Jean put his head in the door. "I'm just picking up Andre."

"Good!" Tell him that dinner and champagne will be waiting for you both."

"I have to drive back tonight!"

"They need you to drive somewhere tonight?"

"No. I have to drive Monsieur to work in the morning."

"Then drive back in the morning. We have a bed for you." Jean didn't need much persuading.

A tired but triumphant Andre joined them on his return.

"We did it!" Andre cuddled her when Jean showed him where the family was gathered. A place was made for them both while drinks and food were served up. "We have separated the arsenic, so we can get on with production again. I will have to look into the storage of it in the morning."

"The authorities will have to be told?"

"They will. They will be able to tell us how to dispose of it."

After dinner was over, both Andre and Candy were feeling weary.

"Will you excuse us for having an early night?" Candy asked the family. "It has been an emotionally draining day for us. I was nearly kidnapped this morning and Andre has had to deal with arsenic placed in one of the ingredients at his factory. We have got through it, but we need a rest now."

There was silence for a few seconds, before Camille and Jillian came to hug Candy. Jack and Mark came to hug Andre as well.

"Why didn't you tell us!?" Camille asked half accusingly.

"We were far too busy till now, but it is catching up with us. Dad, can you give Andre a lift to work in the morning? Jean has to return to Paris early."

"Just give us a call when you're ready." Jack beamed at Andre. "We will be up."

As they crossed the drive to their home, an owl could be heard in the trees surrounding the property.

"Does anyone want a hot chocolate?" Candy asked as they entered the living area.

"Sounds good to us." Both Jean and Andre had broad smiles at her suggestion.

"Put your feet up then." Candy told them as she put the kettle on. Andre pulled off the rug that Candy had slung over the couch and placed it over him. Jean did the same with the rug over his chair. They both grabbed pouffes that were near their chairs for their feet.

"This is the life!" Jean grinned as Candy brought in their cups, then snuggled under the rug with Andre.

"You know, those flats you are going to make for us are too large! We will need maids to keep them nice!"

"You think so?" Candy laughed at the idea of the staff needing maids. "I could split it into four, with an area for security at the front."

"What are you talking about? Andre wanted to know. Candy showed him the rough drawing she had made.

"How about giving the front area to security, but put Dulcie and her feed etc. along the side. Have storage at the back corner, then this area along the back of the house, could be made into flats for Jean, Duval and Amélie."

"So we all have the same view? That sounds fair."

"What's this area?" Andre asked.

"That will be Mark's workshop. He is very handy at building things."

"He will be able to put up walls for us?"

"He will."

"Then swap the storage area for his workshop."

Andre was very happy they wouldn't have to hire a builder as well. Between Jack and Mark, the building side of the project would be covered.

After they had finished their chocolate, Candy showed Jean his room and bathroom, which was on the other side of the living area. He was touched that she had made his bed for him. No employer had done that for him before.

Candy put out breakfast cereal and bowls for the morning, so Jean wouldn't have to hunt for things. Another touch that he appreciated when he came out.

Andre was surprised at the comfort of their room, which was much smaller than the one in the apartment in Paris. He appreciated the space to walk round the bed without bumping into anything. There was plenty of room for their clothes in the built in robes provided. The shower took up the whole width of the bathroom. The wide vanity unit gave them plenty of room for their toiletries too. They would be very comfortable in here while they waited for their apartment to be ready. They would visit his parents on the weekends.

When Jean collected Corbin in the morning, he was asked how his night in the new house went.

"It was far too comfortable!" Jean grinned at him. "They put on dinner and some champagne. We had our feet up with a warm rug and hot chocolate before bed, which was already made for us and breakfast was already put out when I came out this morning!"

Corbin felt quite jealous. "No wonder you didn't come back last night! We missed out there! Are you going to take Andre's car down for him?"

"I will. Jack took him to work this morning."

"I will give you his work computer to take down too. You had better check at the apartment whether there are any clothes to be taken down for them."

When Jean returned to Beaugency with Andre's car, computer and clothes for them both, they were very grateful.

"Can I drive you to the station and get you a ticket back to Paris?" Candy offered Jean.

"Yes please." Jean hadn't been on public transport for years! It also made a change to be driven. He noted that Candy was a very careful driver, so Andre's car was in good hands.

Candy collected Mark after dropping Jean off and took him to the bank to establish the Garden account. It would need his signature as well as her's. She noticed the petrol tank was under half full, so took it to fill it up.

"Do you need anything before I take it to Andre?" Candy asked.

"A quick trip to the hardware?" Mark suggested.

"There is no such thing as a quick trip to the hardware!" Candy laughed. "It's a bit like telling a woman to have a quick look at clothes or shoes!"

Their quick trip resulted in a trip to the house with Mark's loot, which included some timber and a swing.

"How has your morning been?" Andre kissed Candy as he greeted her.

"I put Jean on the train back to Paris; took Mark to the bank to establish a Garden account and a not so quick trip to the hardware."

"How much did you establish the account with? It hasn't come through the phone yet." Andre asked with a quizzical smile.

"You will be waiting forever!" Candy smile back.

"Seeing it was my idea to have a full time gardener, I took €20,000 out of my account. He has been instructed to log and keep receipts of all expenses."

"That's good. I have started a spread sheet of the expenses of the property. The garden will be part of it." He gave her another kiss. "Just make sure the next top up of the garden account is out of our joint account."

"I will." Candy agreed. "I will message you what I'm spending when I'm using our joint account, so you don't have to scramble to find out what's going on."

"Is it nearly lunch time?" Andre asked. It had taken most of the morning to organize a suitable method to process the large amount of the contaminated ingredient to the council's satisfaction. They hadn't been happy to hear of another contamination, but were relieved that it had been caught before entering processing.

"It is!" Candy gave Andre the keys to the car.

"Who filled up the car?" Andre asked. He knew it wasn't that full when he last used it.

"I did!" Candy smiled. "I used to always fill up when my car was down to half a tank. I could never run out that way."

"What sort of car did you drive?" Andre was interested to know. Not many ladies of his acquaintance drove.

"I had a Mazda. That's a small to medium car."

"Do you want a similar model again?"

"I think I will need a larger model, for carrying the children, prams, not to mention groceries. After all I expect to have it for ten years or so, depending on how well it runs."

"We will have to have a look online to see what model suits." Andre suggested.

By now they had found a café and served their lunch.

"This is nice!" Candy commented. "I usually have a quick sandwich at home when I'm working."

"When I join you, we will be making it a much longer lunch!" The desire in his eyes telling her how much longer!

"Your office will be ringing to see whether you're coming back for the afternoon!"

"We should be like the Spanish and have a siesta every afternoon!"

"It sounds nice, but I'm not sure I would want to be having such a late dinner every night!"

"We may have to compromise on just having a siesta at lunch!"

Candy was drinking her coffee, when her phone rang. It was French Telecom, advising they would be arriving in thirty minutes.

"I will be there."

"Telecom are coming to connect the phone and internet. Can you take me home?"

"Of course! Will that be another bill we can expect this afternoon?"

"I'm not sure. If you don't hear anything, you will know it is coming later."

When they arrived at the gate, the van was following them in.

"I just might get some work done this afternoon!" Candy kissed Andre as he dropped her off.

Andre returned to work for the afternoon, but precious little work was done. His mind was at home with Candy.

DULCIE COMES HOME

Marcel went out to the stables. It would be another week before Dulcie could go home. He had carrots in his hand. It would take some months to return her to normal condition. Two weeks of care had changed the gaunt donkey a little. Her bones no longer stuck out so much.

It was her attitude that had changed the most. Her downcast attitude had changed to a vibrant personality that he loved. It was time for Candy to see the new Dulcie.

Candy was in the ground floor of the house with Mark. He had a laser device to measure distances and some chalk to mark the area he was marking out. It was time to make the stable for Dulcie. They had already put down a concrete pad, with heating imbedded within it. Candy had arranged with a local farmer to deliver a large trailer of hay. They just had to build the walls and doors for the stable and storage area.

Candy's phone rang. It was a video call from Marcel.

"Hello Marcel! How is Dulcie?" Candy asked. She could see that he was in the stable. Dulcie was already at the door to her stall, waiting for the carrots that Marcel brought with him. Suddenly she could hear Candy's voice! So the horses were right after all! She let out a big "He Haw", looking around for Candy as she did so.

Marcel, grinned at Candy as he brought the screen up for Candy to see Dulcie. She was looking around, a bright light in her eyes that wasn't there before.

"Oh Dulcie! You beautiful girl!"

Dulcie was getting frustrated. He could hear Candy, but where was she? She snorted and stamped her feet at Marcel. She didn't like this game much!

"Dulcie!" Marcel put the phone up near Dulcie's face. "Candy is here!" He tapped the screen and grinned.

"Hello Dulcie!" Candy waved.

Finally Dulcie saw her! Candy was on the screen! She lunged forward and gave the screen a big lick, which made Candy laugh.

"We are getting your home ready for you Dulcie. You will be coming home soon!"

"How are things going there?" Marcel wanted to know.

"We are restoring the stable area of our new home." Candy advised Marcel. "It is on the ground floor. She panned the camera around the area. "We have put down a concrete pad, with heating in it. Meet Mark, my brother-in-law." Mark waved at the phone. "He is putting up the walls and doors to the stable and store room today. I have ordered a large trailer of hay as well."

"Is there any other feed or medication you want us to buy for her?" Marcel had his back to Dulcie. She tried to put her head over his shoulder so she could see Candy again, and gave a big snort, showing her displeasure that she wasn't in the conversation now.

"Dulcie's quite vocal, isn't she!" Candy laughed.

"Dulcie's very vocal!" Marcel grinned. As he told Candy the items she needed to get.

Dulcie had to content herself with the fact that they were talking about her. Could this mean she was going to see Candy soon?

Candy saw the horse in the next stall come over to "talk" to Dulcie, who answered them. She realised that Dulcie would miss the interaction with the horses when she left.

"If you hear of another donkey that needs a home, let me know. I can see that Dulcie will appreciate the company."

"Are you sure?" Marcel asked. "I have heard of one that will need to be rehomed soon. I would like Dulcie to have some more condition on first, before she shares her stable with another one.

"I'm sure!" Candy reassured Marcel. We will build a second stall so that Dulcie doesn't have to share her food."

"That sounds like a sensible plan." Marcel approved. Will next Saturday be suitable to bring her up?"

"We will look forward to it!" Candy waved to Dulcie, who had her head over Marcel's shoulder again.

"Bye Dulcie!"

Dulcie snorted when Candy's face disappeared from the screen. Marcel put his phone away and stroked her. "You will see Candy again soon!"

Candy gave him a nudge, looking for the carrots she knew he had brought with him. Marcel fished in his pocket to bring them out for her. Dulcie knew the routine now. The halter would go on next and she would be going for her walk.

Today there was a change in routine. Marcel took Dulcie outside and put her in a paddock. The snow was gone, though the ground was still hard and the air was cool.

"I will be back later, Dulcie." Marcel told her as he went to collect the next horse and brought them out to the next paddock. Soon all the horses were out in the paddocks. Some had a gallop after being in their stalls, or lay on their backs for a scratch. Others immediately started feeding on the short grass that was available, just glad for a change of scenery.

"You must be going home soon." One of the horses came for a chat at the fence.

"You think so?" Dulcie brightened as this news.

"He usually starts putting horses outside about a week before they leave, to get them used to being outside again."

Candy called Corbin and Fleur.

"I won't be able to visit this weekend. Marcel is delivering Dulcie our Donkey to us on Saturday. He will probably need to stay overnight as it a five hour trip each way."

"Will Andre be coming?"

"I will give him the news when he comes home at lunchtime. I will get him to ring you."

Mark was attaching timber for the frame of the stall to the floor.

"We are making two stalls now?" he asked with a grin.

"We are!" Candy grinned back. "I could see Dulcie was interacting with the horse in the stall next to her and realised that Dulcie will feel lonely on her own. She will adjust better with another donkey for company.”

By the time Andre came home, the framework for the stable and storeroom was in place. Candy was helping to hold the hardboard for the walls while Mark secured them into position. A brick wall would also be built as a barrier to the car park, for both noise and fumes.

“We are going to need an air vent and extractor fan in here for when everything is built.”Candy mentioned to them both, as they stopped for their lunch break.

Andre looked around and nodded. “We will put it on our list to do.”

I’ve got some good news!” Candy’s eyes were sparkling as she prepared their lunch. “Marcel is bringing Dulcie up on Saturday!”

“What about our weekend with Mum and Dad?”

“I’ve told them about Dulcie and that I won’t be able to come. You can still go and visit them though. I told them that you would ring them.”

Andre wasn’t very happy that they would be apart, but she was right. He hadn’t had any time with his parents alone since the incident. Candy had her family here too.

“Where are you putting Marcel?” Andre wanted to know.

“I will give him this house for the night. I’m not sure whether he will bring Patrice. I will stay with Mark and Jillian.”

Andre phoned his parents. “I will still see you on

the weekend!”

“Good!” Fleur answered for them. “We will look forward to it!”

“Pour that later!” Andre ordered Candy as she went to make their coffee. “We have some time on the weekend to make up!” and led her to the bedroom.

Dulcie knew something was up. Instead of leading her outside to the paddock, Marcel gave her a wash and an extra brush before leading her to the horse float. She started to resist.

“You want to see Candy don’t you Dulcie?” Her ears pricked up at Candy’s name. “Yes, Dulcie, I’m taking you to Candy!” He brought out a carrot. “Come on! It’s time for you to go home to Candy!”

Dulcie reluctantly let herself be led into the horse float. The last time she was in here, Candy was with her. If Candy wasn’t at the other end, she would make him sorry! Dulcie started munching on the hay they had put in the holder in front of her. If she lifted her head she could see out as well!

It took a while to get used to the motion of the float, but eventually she even had a little nap as the motion lulled her into a snooze. There was the occasional stop during the journey, but it was the slamming of the car door and the unlocking of the float behind her that made Dulcie alert again.

She started looking around. She heard Marcel talking and was that Candy answering him? She gave a neigh as she called to Candy.

“Yes Dulcie! I’m here!” Candy called out louder to her.

As the backflap was lowered, Dulcie looked around. Candy was here! and some other people as well. One of them was a little girl. She had a carrot!

"Donkey!" Eliza beamed to Jillian.

"Yes, Eliza. This is Dulcie!"

"Dulcie have a carrot?" Eliza asked. She held out the carrot when Marcel led Dulcie towards them. Dulcie gave a little whiney and snatched the carrot out of Eliza's hand and chomped on it as she was stroked and hugged by Eliza. Candy took over the halter.

"Come on Dulcie. It's time to see your new home."

She obediently followed Candy through the gate and fence which had been erected that morning. Long grass was all around. Candy showed Dulcie her stable, which had the door open. Fresh hay lay inside and a holder for water was secured to the wall. Candy then led Dulcie to the paddock at the back where she removed the halter.

"Dulcie, this is your paddock now."

Dulcie looked around. The large paddock was surrounded by tall trees, which was much nicer than Marcel's paddocks that were open and had strong winds ripping through them. Jillian, Mark and Eliza had come with them. Eliza ran over to a swing in the tree by the house where Mark gave her a push. Eliza's laugh rang out in the paddock.

Near the house was a trough of water. Dulcie trotted over for a drink. Also near the tree was a garden setting. Marcel joined the family for lunch. He was heading back to his stables as he had a horse that needed close attention. Candy brought out a nose bag with some oats for Dulcie so she didn't feel left out. Dulcie had learnt by now, how to drop her head low to get it off when she was finished. Dulcie then wandered off to have a good look at her new domain.

When Marcel called goodbye to Dulcie, she briefly looked up before continuing to graze in the paddock. Eventually Dulcie wanted a rest. She remembered the stable she passed on the way in. She sauntered over and walked in. Candy was behind her. She came in and gave Dulcie a cuddle, before shutting the bottom door. After Candy shut the top door, which had a pane of Perspex in it, Dulcie lay down with a happy sigh. She was home with Candy at last. Dulcie noticed there was another stall next to hers. Was she going to have company?

In Paris Andre was relaxing with his parents, catching them up with events in Beaugency. He was looking forward to getting back to Candy though, and the excitement of settlement on the house on Monday. They could get a copy of the house plans at last and make a proper start on planning for their new home.

"We have tickets to the Opera tonight. It's a shame Candy isn't here. Will you still come with us?"

"It's a shame to waste a ticket. I will come."

A little while later he received a text from Candy.

"Dulcie has settled in well. – Took herself off to her stable by herself. Eliza is smitten after giving her a carrot. Marcel returned home after lunch. Missing you! XX"

That evening Andre dressed up in the Tuxedo that he had left at his parents' apartment. There wasn't much need for it at Beaugency. His parents had splashed out on a private box overlooking the stage and the downstairs stalls. Andre was enjoying the spectacle of the show when the movement and swish of a skirt told them that they had company.

They all looked round to see one of Andre's old flames come and sit next to him. Andre raised his eyebrows at his parents and shook his head. He wasn't happy that he had been cornered like this! He ignored her and continued watching the opera with a stony face. The enjoyment of the evening had gone for him.

Andre felt a tap on his shoulder. He turned his head only slightly to find she was attempting to kiss him on the mouth. Andre swiftly turned his head away so it landed on his cheek and pushed her away, to the accompaniment of flashes from cameras. He stood up and walked out.

"What is the matter with you Andre? You are acting like a monk!" she had chased after him.

"There is nothing wrong with me! I just happen to be in love with my wife, who can't be here with me! Find someone else to chase after!" Andre turned and walked out of the Opera House. He called Jean.

"Jean, where are you hiding?"

"Are you ready to be picked up? Did it finish early?"

"No. I'm coming to join you! Where are you?"

"I'm in the carpark across the road. Level two."

Andre dodged the traffic coming down the street and found Jean within minutes. He sat in the seat next to Jean with a sigh and removed his bow.

"That's the last one of those I go to!" He looked at Jean with frustration. "You would think that once I was married they would let up! I've just been cornered in the box with my parents by one of my old flames!"

"She made a pass?" Andre nodded.

"With all the paparazzi in attendance too! It will be on the front page tomorrow!" Andre looked at the time. "Can you drop me back at the apartment, and tell Mum and Dad I've left a note."

"Where are you going?" Jean asked as he started the motor.

"Back to Beaugency. At the very least, I need to tell Candy what happened before the papers get out in the morning."

In the apartment, Duval was surprised to see Andre return alone with his Tuxedo in disarray.

"Some pen and paper please Duval." As he headed to his room to pack his overnight bag and collect his car keys. Andre wrote the note and put it on the silver platter Duval had handy. "Make sure they get it please."

Andre sighed as he took a last look around the apartment. He was not intending to return here again. He took the key to the apartment out of his pocket and left it with the letter.

Corbin and Fleur weren't impressed with the invasion of their box and the interruption to their enjoyment of the evening. They heard the short exchange in the corridor, and became worried when Andre didn't return.

As soon as the curtain fell, they exited the box and the theatre.

"Is Andre with you?" Corbin asked Jean when he called him.

"No. He's gone back to Beaugency. He's left you a note."

Both Corbin and Fleur were shocked to see Andre's key with the letter.

"They've forced him out of Paris for good." Corbin commented as he passed the letter to Fleur. There were tears in his eyes. Their enjoyment of Paris was tainted now too. "We need to make other plans for our future."

It was late and Candy was taking advantage of her time alone to catch up on some of the accounts waiting for her attention. The first thing she knew of Andre's change of plan, was him coming in the door with his Tuxedo askew and his overnight bag, which was thrown on the floor. He came over to give her a kiss.

"Finish what you're doing. I will change and put the hot chocolate on!"

A message was waiting on Andre's phone.

"Call us! We will visit next weekend."

When Andre and Candy applied for a copy of the house plans, they also enquired about the history of the home's owners. The document they were given listed the owners who built it, as Mathieu and Estelle Chevaler. The Revolution came ten years later. The property lay empty for some years before another family took over the property.

Candy googled their names, to find paintings of them both, which were now in the art gallery in Paris. In the painting, Estelle was wearing a gown very similar to the one she saw in the loft.

Candy's next step was to enquire at the local council whether any members of the Chevaler family were buried at Beaugency. She explained that they had bought the property that the Chevaler family had built. The council clerk looked up their records.

"No, madam. It is known that their children were taken abroad. There is no record of the resting place of Mathieu and Estelle."

"I believe we have found them." Candy spoke quietly. We want them to have a proper burial and a memorial.

"What?!"

"During our first inspection of the property, we found a chest in the roof space. Inside are a pair of skeletons entwined. The remnants of their clothing look very similar to the garments they wore in their paintings in the Art Gallery."

"We will of course arrange a burial for them.

What sort of memorial were you thinking of?”

“I was thinking of creating a garden and a bronze statue of them together at the front of our home. We are going to renovate the property first before we make the garden and memorial.”

“People will want to come to visit. If you value your privacy, I suggest that the statue and garden be made in one of our public parks.”

“That’s a good idea.” Candy agreed. She didn’t mention that she still intended to have a garden and memorial in the grounds.

“How soon do you want the burial? Is there any urgency?”

“We intend to replace the roof in the next couple of months. We would like them to be at rest before we start on the replacement.”

“I will let the Mayor know. You can expect a visit from the council.”

The next morning, Candy was talking to her father and Mark in the office, when several cars and a hearse pulled up in the drive.

“It looks like the council are here. We had better go and meet them.”

Candy was pleased she had dressed in a classical and elegant outfit that was fitting for such a meeting, as the delegation were all dressed formally, including the Mayor who had his regalia on.

“Good Morning and welcome to my home.” Candy began. “My husband is needed at work this morning, otherwise he would be here to welcome you too.” She introduced her father and Mark.

“What is all this?” the Mayor wanted to know,

pointing to the buildings out the front.

"They are temporary dwellings and an office for the family to live and work in. They will be removed once the renovation is complete. Do you wish to have a tour of the house, or inspect Mathieu and Estelle's remains first?"

"We will do a tour first." The Mayor decided.

"Are there any services to these buildings?" the building inspector asked.

"Yes. I hired an electrician and plumber to connect them to water, sewerage and electricity. We also have phone and internet services. My father is currently working on the plans for the renovations to submit to council."

"I will go through the house with you later." The inspector spoke to Jack. "Have you done any work on the home yet?"

"Yes. We needed a stable for Dulcie the donkey that Candy rescued down by Chambery. Given that the area was a stable previously, we have built one, with updated facilities, such as a concrete floor with inbuilt heating, which can be hosed out. The contents of the stall is being removed to a compost area which will fertilise the orchard, vegetable garden and front formal gardens when we establish them."

Candy led the delegation into the ground floor, where the inspector had a good look at the stable. They all were interested in the markings that Mark had made on the floor, for the office space, living quarters, his work shop, security area and the parking.

"We have ordered an extractor fan and will be building some air vents for the parking space. We will also be installing an elevator for the building." She showed the delegation the cupboards in the centre of the parking area. Candy then led them up the stairs to the first floor.

"The next three floors will be accommodation for our family." Candy advised them. Indicating the three apartments on the current floor. When Candy led the delegation into the central area with the stairway, there was silence for several seconds as they took in the grandeur of the area.

"What plans do you have for this?" the inspector asked.

"Apart from the elevator access, it will be left as is. If any paint is required, we will match it with the current colour scheme."

Candy led the delegation up the staircase to the second and third floors, showing them the proposed changes for the living spaces.

"Are you ready to view Mathieu and Estelle now?"

The mayor nodded. Candy led them to the drawing room and pressed the wood panelling. There was silence as the stairway to the roof space was revealed.

The silence continued as Candy led them up to and through the roof space. The Inspector was having a good look around at both the roof and the area. When Candy led them to the chest, the funeral director came forward to lift the cover. He nodded to the Mayor who came forward to offer a silent prayer, along with the other councillors.

"They will be taken to the funeral home to rest untill the funeral is arranged for them. You wish to attend?"

"Of course! Does anyone know whether there are any living descendants who may wish to attend?"

"We will look into it." The Mayor advised her.

Six week later, a procession to their resting place was arranged for Mathieu and Estelle. Their coffin was carried on a carriage drawn with four white horses. Walking behind it were their great grandchildren, followed by the Council, Andre and Candy.

THE SCAN

Candy was at the three month mark of her pregnancy. There was no telling bulge of her abdomen yet, but she could feel that her breasts were increasing in size. She would have to get some new bras soon! It was time to do some shopping and make an appointment with the doctor.

"What have you got on today?" Andre asked as they had breakfast together.

"Well, I need to do some shopping and make an appointment. I'm three months into my pregnancy now, which means its officially viable. I'm due for another scan to check that all is well."

"What do you mean by viable?"

"In the first three months, if there are any problems with the baby, it is more likely to miscarry or be lost." Something drastic will have to happen for me to lose it now."

Andre looked at her stomach.

"You wouldn't know it!

Candy smiled. "But I do know it! My bras are getting too small!" and, I will start showing my "bump" in the next month or so. That means clothes that will expand with me! I've only got that pinafore I bought at Chambery.

"Does this mean you are going to transform into a Rubens for me?"

Candy grinned at him. "I had no idea you fancied Rubens' ladies!"

"This means I won't have to go to the gym as

much either!" Andre looked happy.

"You don't want one in our house? I will be needing something to help me get back into shape after the pregnancy."

Andre became thoughtful. It won't hurt for us to have a few items, for bad weather when we can't get outside. At home it won't be competitive, and we won't be intimidated by all the posers that usually inhabit the gym. Where do you want to put it?"

"Do you want it on our floor or downstairs where anyone in the house can use it?"

"We will see how much interest there is from the others. If not, we will keep the equipment on our floor. Let me know when you're having that scan. I want to come."

"Are you sure?"

"Of course! It's time I met our daughter or son."

A visit to the doctor brought good news. Her weight gain was within normal limits. Candy was given appointments to visit the practice nurse each month. A referral to the hospital ante-natal clinic was given too, along with a request for an ultra-sound.

"Keep tomorrow afternoon at one 'clock free for the scan." Candy messaged Andre.

When the time came for them enter the scan room, Andre squeezed her hand. She squeezed it back.

"I believe you are more nervous than I am!" Candy chuckled at Andre.

"You will have to show me what's where." Andre said when the technician showed the foetus on the screen. A fast heart beat could be heard.

"Is that normal?" Andre asked.

"It is!" the technician reassured him, as she pointed out the head and body, arms and legs. She was doing measurements of the baby's head when another foot appeared briefly by its ear. The technician ran the scanner round to the side of Candy's body. Another heart beat could be heard at the same time.

"So you do have another one hiding in behind there! congratulations you are having twins."

The shock on Andre's face was obvious. Candy had a big smile on her face. Andre looked at Candy. She wasn't shocked at all, but her happiness was plain.

"You knew?"

Candy nodded. "I had a scan in Switzerland. It was only a tiny blob then, but we heard the two heart beats. I didn't get my hopes up too high untill now, unless something happened to one of them.

"No wonder you were so protective!" Andre grinned at Candy as he remembered their first conversation! She laughed as she remembered it too.

"I expect we will start collecting things for the babies now?"

'It's early yet, but if I see something we will need, I will get it."

"What about their names?" Andre asked.

"If they are boys, Jack and Corbin will be there somewhere. If they are girls, Fleur and Camille will be part of their names too. That leaves us their first names to choose."

As Andre prepared to return to work, he gave Candy a big hug.

"I should have brought my laptop home! I can't see myself doing much work this afternoon though!"

"Do they need you to be there physically, at all times? I would have a check that all is going well, and come home. You have a lot to think about. If they need you, it won't take long to be there. After all, they ran it most of the time, when you were based in Paris."

An hour later Andre came home. He found Candy out the back giving a carrot to Dulcie and Dudley who had joined the family. Dulcie was almost back to normal condition now, and was ruling the stable!

Candy had some good news for him. The Council had given their approval to start the renovations.

THE HONEYMOON

"You know, we never had a honeymoon!" Andre commented that evening as they were snuggled up on the couch after dinner. "Where would you like to go?"

"Well, I still haven't seen Paris yet, or Versailles. Of course we wouldn't be going to any of the nightlife! I would love to see the garden at Giverny and a day or two on a barge would be nice. But what about you! Where would you like to go? "

Andre was amused. "You obviously don't mind tempting fate! I thought you might want to go somewhere in the sun. I will ring Mum and Dad and see if they have room for a couple of strays for a few nights."

Andre put through a video call to Corbin. He and Fleur were in a café eating their dinner. Candy recognised a certain café owner behind them.

"You are in Chambery!" Candy called to them. Fleur waved to them with a big smile.

"We are! That was good spotting Candy. We have decided to sell our apartment in Paris and will rebuild with the other owners of our building. We will come down here for the summer months, when there is no danger of avalanches! We have some of your clothes to give you too, Candy. We will see you tomorrow."

"We have some news for you too! The council has approved the renovations for the house, so we can get started." Andre's excitement was plain. "We have decided to have our belated honeymoon. Do you have room for a few days while we do the tourist trail in Paris,

Versailles and Giverny?"

There was astonished silence for a few seconds, before they recovered.

"Of course! Do you mind if we gate-crash and join you? We don't suppose you want any evening outings organised?"

Andre and Candy looked at each other and burst out laughing. "We will pass on the evening outings thanks." Candy replied for them. "Andre says I'm tempting fate by wanted to come back to Paris!"

"You aren't wanting to stay to supervise the building?" Corbin asked.

"No. We have Jack supervising the work. We have already gone over the priorities of what needs to be done. Besides, we are only a phone call away if they need our input."

"Will we see you for lunch or Dinner?" Candy asked.

"Expect us for dinner." Fleur informed her. "We won't be rushing to get up and leave Chambery. It is still cool here, but all the spring flowers are out."

Candy and Andre bid them goodnight and organised to clear their workloads by tomorrow. They didn't want work interfering with their holiday.

When Candy checked on Dulcie and Dudley the next morning, they were already out in the paddock. Jillian and Eliza had let them out. Dudley was receiving extra pats and cuddles from Eliza, which he loved. Dulcie was giving him the cold shoulder this morning, so he was quite happy to have some fuss from their human family.

When Candy asked Jillian if she could care for the

donkeys for the rest of the week as they were having a belated honeymoon, she came to give Candy a big hug.

"Of course! You have given so much to our family, it's time you did something for yourselves! Where are you going?"

When Candy told her the activities they had planned, Jillian sighed.

"I wouldn't mind doing that myself. It will be a while before we can go though. The renovation work is a priority and of course getting the grounds organised."

"We can't wait till the renovations are done to have a break." Candy spoke quietly. "We have twins coming. I expect we will still be in our temporary home when they arrive."

"Are they..." Jillian wasn't able to say the name of the man who had captured and abused Candy.

"They are Barry's. I told Andre I was pregnant when I met him. He accepts the pregnancy as I have."

"What if he hadn't?" Jillian showed her concern.

"I would have had a separate life from Andre, and still bought this house for the family. I had enough to buy it anyway, without Andre's input."

"Really?" Jillian was astonished.

Candy nodded. "I had a good deposit for a home saved when I was taken. Homes here are much cheaper than in Perth." Jillian was helping Candy to muck out the stables and put in fresh straw as they talked.

"Mummy! Dudley is doing something to Dulcie!" Eliza came running round the corner of the house to them. Candy and Jillian looked at each other with astonishment and tried not to laugh out loud. They had a fair idea what Dudley was doing!

"Is he? We will leave them alone for a bit. Would you like some fruit and a story?" Jillian asked as she picked Eliza up and took her through the gate to their home. Candy followed them, wondering whether Dulcie was still fertile. Time would tell.

Candy sat herself down to begin working, when her mother knocked and came in. Her face beaming.

"Jillian has just given me your news! How exciting!" She came to give Candy a hug. "You are happy about it, aren't you?" remembering how Candy came to be pregnant.

"I am! I'm just happy that they have made it to this stage. We are going for a belated honeymoon tomorrow, so I'm getting work out of the way!"

That evening Corbin and Fleur came with a large bag of clothes that Candy had left behind at Chambery. Andre noticed the negligees with a gleam in his eyes.

"You will be able to bring them with you!"

Candy smiled until she came across one that was almost see-through. She had a flashback to her week in captivity. Andre saw the change in Candy's expression and how she screwed it up into a small ball before taking it to the bin.

"What's up?"

"That particular gown just gave me a flashback! The others are fine." When she came back, he gave her a cuddle.

"You are safe now, you know."

"I know." Candy still needed the comfort of his arms to feel safe. She clung to Andre for several minutes before she was able to relax again.

Both Candy and Andre came to see the donkeys before they left, which made Dulcie suspicious! She knew something was up! When they offered her their carrots she knocked them out of their hands and stomped off in a huff. Dudley had no such qualms and came to eat them for her and accepted all the fuss too.

While Candy and Andre were absent, Dulcie sulked. On the first day she stayed in her stall, treating Dudley with silent distain. Jillian had to clean up as best she could before changing the straw and feed in her stall. Dudley lapped up all the attention while Dulcie was in her mood.

Meanwhile, Candy and Andre were having a lovely time. They arrived in Paris in time for lunch. Corbin had already booked them in to a restaurant where they had a leisurely meal. A drive along the river to visit Notre Dame, then a visit to Sacre Coeur to see the view of Paris, before visiting the nearby art quarter. A painting of poppies came home with them.

It was late afternoon when they joined the queue for the Eiffel Tower. Evening twilight came while they were on the viewing platform. A sea of lights coming on below them. The light breeze freshened, giving Andre the excuse to put his arms around Candy to keep her warm.

Corbin and Fleur elected to have a meal at a local café while Candy and Andre rustled up some omletes at the apartment. They checked their phones. All was well.

When they rose the next morning, rain was beating on the windows.

"A day for indoors!" Andre commented. Candy agreed.

"What about a visit to the Art Gallery and the Louvre? I would like to see the paintings of Mathieu and Estelle."

Andre called Jean to drop them off at the Art Gallery. A walk through the galleries followed. When they came across Mathieu and Estelle's paintings, they lingered. Candy couldn't help herself, and pulled out her phone to take a photo of the paintings. A security guard came to see why Candy was taking photos. While she was explaining that they had bought the home that Mathieu and Estelle had built and that she wanted a photo of them to grace the main staircase, a curator came to listen.

"It was you who found them recently?"

"Yes. They have been laid to rest now."

"We may be able to do better than your phone photos for your home. Come with me!"

Candy and Andre were led to the storage area for the many paintings they didn't have room to display. A large guilt framed painting was pulled out, of Mathieu and Estelle with their family around them.

"We can arrange for the permanent loan of this painting to you while you and your family live in your home."

"Thank you!" Candy had tears of joy. "We have started to renovating our home, which will take about six months."

The curator gave Candy a card to call them.

"When you are ready, we will install it for you."

While they were having lunch at the gallery café, Andre asked "Are you going to get rid of the phone photos?"

"No. I will find a spot for them!"

"I thought you might!"

By the time they called Jean to take them to the Louvre, the rain had eased to showers.

"You know it would take a week to see everything in here!" Andre advised Candy as they entered the glass pyramid, for the complex. They had to be satisfied with seeing the main attractions.

Corbin had taken advantage of the wet day to check in at Head office and visit his gentlemen's club, while Fleur had a meeting with her friends. That evening Candy insisted on cooking a meal for them all at the apartment.

"Please give the recipe to Duval!" Corbin asked Candy. "I would like to have that one again." He added "It's going to be fine tomorrow. Where are we going?"

"We were thinking of a trip to Giverny to see Monet's garden in the morning, with a look at Versailles on the way home."

"It sounds good to me!" Fleur commented. She always enjoyed visiting places with nice gardens. She was waiting to see what sort of gardens that Candy and Andre were planning for their home.

That night when they retired, Candy remembered to put on one of the negligees she had brought with her.

"I wondered when I would get to see them on." Andre grinned as he reached out to her to kiss all the places it didn't cover, then removed it to kiss all the places he had missed.

A pleasant morning was had at Giverny, walking in Monet's gardens and home. Candy was surprised how bright the interiors of Monet's home were, in contrast to the more muted tones of his paintings. The garden had grown a great deal from the time Monet lived there too! It certainly gave Candy ideas for her garden at home.

The afternoon visit to Versailles was an eye-opener for Candy. They were greeted by magnificent gates in gold.

"I'm thinking, maybe we could have some gates for the front of our place." Candy mentioned to Andre.

"Do you mean instead of security?"

"Yes. If we installed cameras as well. Over time it would be cheaper and more private for us. There has been the occasional day when the guard couldn't be there for some reason anyway."

"They were herded through the main living areas, including the magnificent ballroom with its numerous mirrors, to reflect the jewels of the nobility in the candlelight. Candy loved the femininity of Marie Antionette's bedroom, knowing full well she wouldn't get away with replicating it in their room at home. She admired the terraced and manicured gardens with their statues too, but was glad their own garden would be much more manageable than these ones.

Candy didn't demure when they were steered into a restaurant for dinner on the way home. Corbin showed Andre a message he had been sitting on since lunch time, from his assistant. Not wanting to interrupt their day, he had left it till now.

"Please come into the office when you can. We have received a takeover bid." It was followed by details of the company and the offer they were making.

"It's not happening!" Andre's tone was final.

"Are you sure?"

"I'm positive! The trouble we've been having all makes sense now. They've been softening us up for this! My challenge now, is to make our company completely independent of them."

"Is that possible?" Corbin was doubtful.

"It will cost money, but yes, and we will be able to guarantee our products remain safe."

"Then do it!" Corbin gave Andre his blessing.

"I will let you do the communicating while I get on with changing the factory."

"Back to work tomorrow?" Candy asked Andre as she squeezed his hand. He nodded as he squeezed her hand back.

"We have a lot on our plates, haven't we?"

"You just concentrate on the factory. I will sort the rest. Did you want to return after dinner? We have a bed for Jean if he prefers instead of making the return trip tonight."

"I would prefer it. I have no doubt that they will have heard something at the factory, and will want reassurance they aren't being sold out."

When Jean turned into the drive, there was no sign of the security guard. They checked in with Jack and Camille, to be told that the guards hadn't been around for the last couple of days. They had found more lucrative work elsewhere.

"We will manage without them." Andre gave Candy a grateful look. "Candy suggested we make alternative arrangements for our security. We will just be doing it sooner than later."

Candy nodded. "I will contact fencing and gate firms, along with security camera firms tomorrow for some quotes."

At the factory the next morning, Andre found the workforce waiting for him, with anxious faces.

"You've heard about the takeover bid? Well, It's not happening! In fact, we have a lot of work to do to add a new process to our production, so we don't need that particular company's product. We will be making it ourselves."

"The big smiles on their faces told Andre he had done the right thing, even if the profits for the firm for the next year would be negligible.

When Andre came home for lunch, Candy had commandeered Mark to find the boundary markers for their block of land and to mark them for the fencing and the gates. It meant some trimming of the fir trees. The logs to be kept for other projects – the tree house among them.

THE NEW ARRIVALS

Candy was feeling uncomfortable as she sat down to attend to her latest batch of accounts. She had warned Marianne that she may have to take a break soon, but the accounts kept coming.   Candy still had a month to go till her twins were due to be born, but she had a feeling that the children weren't going to wait for their due date. Her bag for the hospital was packed and went everywhere with her. Bassinettes and other necessities were also ready for their arrival.

Progress on the renovations were going well, but they too were at least another month or more away from being complete. There were frequent visits from both Corbin and Fleur and Henri and Celeste to check on the progress. They along with everyone else were waiting impatiently for the day when they could move in. Jean, Duval and Amélie had been for a visit and approved their new quarters.

The installation of the gate, fences and cameras had worked better than they had hoped. The control panel was activated in the office during the day, then switched to Andre and Candy's home at night.

Andre too was happy that his new system was operating. It had taken a few months and some anxious days to set it up. Once the takeover bid had been rejected the product had been withdrawn by their supplier. Andre had anticipated this and had made sure that alternative product was on hand.

When Andre walked in the door, Candy was

sitting at the table, the laptop in front of her, but her eyes were closed and her hands were clutching her stomach as she did some deep breathing that she had been practicing in her antenatal classes.

"Is everything alright?" Andre asked with concern. When Candy opened her eyes, her smile as she gave him a kiss didn't quite reach her eyes.

"It may be a false alarm, but I may be in labour. It is too early to go to hospital just yet. Can you put the kettle on while I finish this? I will let Marianne know that there will be no more work till after the twins are here!" Candy started to type furiously. The five minutes it took to finish and send the account was just enough before another contraction came and stopped her in her tracks. This one was stronger than the last one! She swiftly shut down her computer to concentrate on her breathing, before making herself relax after it.

"Are you sure you want this?" Andre held up her cup as he took their drinks over to the couch.

"I'm coming now." Candy spoke as she joined him on the couch. Andre put his arm around her to cuddle her, putting his other hand on her stomach as Candy took some sips of her drink. They were discussing how their morning had been when another contraction made Its presence felt. Andre could feel the hardening of Candy's stomach under his hand. He noticed that the twins were quieter than usual. He was used to having his hand kicked when he laid his hand on Candy's stomach.

"How far apart are your contractions?" Andre asked.

"About five minutes, I think. I suppose I should call the hospital and tell them that my labour has started."

Andre pulled out his phone and gave the hospital a call. He was put through to the labour ward. The crisp no-nonsense voice of the ward sister came through clearly.

"It doesn't matter how many minutes the contractions are apart, Monsieur. Madam Candice is four weeks early, please bring her in now please!"

"I will." He grinned at Candy after the call. "We've got our orders!"

"I will just finish this first!" Candy downed her cup of coffee, before Andre helped her out of the couch. He finished his as well. While Candy fetched her bag, Andre called his assistant to give her the news that he might not be back this afternoon.

As Andre locked up their home, Jack came out of the office next door. He saw the bag in Candy's hand. He had a big grin on his face.

"Are they finally making an appearance?"

"It looks like it!" Candy managed to say as another contraction began. She had to stop talking to breath. As she stepped down onto the ground, clear fluid ran down her legs. Mortified, but also pleased it hadn't happened inside, Candy asked Andre to fetch a towel.

"These babies are definitely coming! That fluid that just ran down my legs was the amniotic fluid they've been living in."

Before Andre could open their door, Jack had

slipped back into the office and grabbed a towel off the rack.

"Use this!" he said as he threw it to Andre.

"Thanks!" he said, as he laid it on the seat.

Camille and Jillian came out when Jack told them of Candy's development, but their car was already being driven out of the drive. At the hospital, Candy insisted on staying with Andre as he parked the car. A couple of stops were required on their walk to the labour suite.

"I'm staying with her!" Andre insisted when the nurse assigned to her tried to direct him to the waiting area, where a couple of men were pacing up and down.

"Very well! Put on this gown, hat and cover for your shoes please."

In the prep room, Candy was changed into a gown, before a set of observations were done. Her stomach was palpated to check the position of the twins and the dilation of her cervix was also checked, before a foetal heart monitor was attached to Candy's stomach with a belt.

"You are half dilated already!" the nurse commented. "We will be moving you into the birth suite shortly. I will just let the doctor know."

While the nurse was out of the room, Candy put her arms out for Andre to cuddle her. She had a look of fear in her eyes.

"What is it?" Andre asked, concerned as he held and kissed her. "You know that you are being well care for."

"I know!" Candy had tears in her eyes. "But just then I couldn't help thinking of being in that room and having to do this all on my own."

"But you're not! "I'm here, and I'm not going anywhere!" He held her close as the next contraction came.

"Can you give my back a rub?" Candy asked Andre. "It's aching worse than my stomach!"

"Harder!" Candy was saying as the nurse returned. She took a quick look at Candy's cervix.

"As soon as this contraction is over, we are moving you. Your hard work is about to begin!"

"Sounds like fun!" Andre commented as he and the midwife helped Candy to walk to the delivery room, down the corridor. Andre could see it was set up as a theatre, tiled from floor to ceiling, an adjustable table in the centre of the room, with covered trolleys along the walls. Two clear plastic bassinettes and humidicribs were also in the room, along with a smaller table with resuscitation equipment next to it.

The nurse adjusted the table so Candy could sit with support. Candy was being helped to a comfortable position when the doctor came in to review her. Another contraction was starting.

"I want to push!" Candy told them.

"Blow! Don't push! The nurse told her after both she and the doctor examined her.

"Madam Candice! We can see one of your twins is showing signs of distress. We need to do an emergency caesarean now. Nurse call the team!"

"Can I have an epidural? I need to be awake, please!" Candy pleaded once her contraction stopped.

'Very well then. Candice can you turn around so

you are side on to the table for the epidural to be inserted? Monsieur do you still wish to stay?”

“I’m staying with her, regardless!” Andre’s tone was firm.

Candy was given a pillow to hold in front of her as she was asked to lean forward. Andre was standing in front of her. Cuddling her to him. A number of staff had now entered the room.

She felt something damp on her spine, and told to keep still as a sharp scratch could be felt. Candy was given assistance to lie on the now flat bed. Andre was given a seat next to Candy’s head, as a screen was wheeled into place, obscuring their view of the procedure.

“Can you feel this?” The anaesthetist asked.

“No.”

“Or this?”

“No.”

“This?”

“Yes.”

“You can begin.” He told the Obstetrician.

Andre held and squeezed Candy’s hand, giving her a kiss.

“You are so brave!” he murmured. “If that was me I would make sure I was asleep!”

Candy was able to smile. “I didn’t want to miss seeing them come into the world! They heard a cry.

“Here is number one! It’s a girl.” the doctor Briefly held up the baby for them to see, before handing it to a nurse who, with a towel in hand, took her to the resuscitation table. She was a dark pink.

"I will bring her to you in a minute."

Behind the screen, they could hear suctioning, before a second cry was heard.

"You have a son! Congratulations." He will join you shortly too."

Andre looked over the screen to see the boy was on the resuscitation table, receiving some oxygen as he was being checked. His colour was darker than the girl who was now a brighter pink. She was being wrapped in a blanket and brought over to them.

"Meet Mum and Dad." The nurse laid the baby in Candy's arms.

"Hello Charlotte Fleur!" Candy kissed her forehead. Andre leant forward and gave her a kiss too. The baby's eyes had been shut, now opened. She heard her parent's voices, which were much clearer than when she was in the womb. She screwed her eyes up at the bright light, but could make out two faces looking at her. Candy noticed her eyes were blue green like her father's eyes.

"She has Dad's eyes!" Candy spoke in wonderment. I think she should be Jacqueline Fleur."

"Here is your son." The nurse was standing next to Andre. He turned around with a grin. The boy was now a healthier pink, like his sister. As Andre took the boy into his arms and looked into his face, something unexpected happened. A rush of protective love came over him. It no longer mattered that he had not conceived him. There was now a bond that would last all their lives. Andre brought him down to Candy. They gave him a kiss too.

"Hello Laurent Corbin!"

"Would you like a family photo?" their nurse asked.

"Yes please!" Andre brought out his phone. Photos were sent to the family, who promised to visit when they were permitted. Corbin and Fleur sent a message.

"We are on our way!" They knew Andre would be wanting some company tonight, to talk about the experience he had shared with Candy. They both were delighted to hear that the children had been named after them.

It was a long week, for both Candy and Andre, before she was allowed home with the twins. Although Candy had established a routine in hospital, with the help of her nurses, she felt nervous when doing it alone at home, which the babies picked up on and grizzled more.   She was very relieved that both Camille and Jillian popped in each morning to see how she was coping. One thing Candy was most grateful for. Being back in Andre's arms!

Candy had sent Marianne a photo of the twins and told her she was now home. After a week, no new work was sent. It was then that Candy realised that she had been replaced. Keeping in mind that Christmas wasn't far away, it was time to find new work. Dusting off her CV, she sent her resume to an online work agency.

Within hours, Candy had several phone calls, wanting her to come to Paris for an interview. She knew that she had to do this, but how? Candy made a couple of appointments, for the following day. She would ask Jillian to come with her, to care for the twins while she was in the interviews.

In the end, both Camille and Jillian came, jumping at the chance to spend some time in Paris. When Candy informed Andre of her plans for the day, concern, then admiration chased across his face, as he realised that if Candy wanted to continue her career, she needed to make this move.

"You may not be paid what you were receiving before." Andre commented.

"Of course not! I'm not expecting to. I'm literally starting over again and will have to prove myself. I am used to budgeting, so managing with a lower income isn't a problem for me." She realised that Andre's spreadsheet of expenses was on his mind. "Perhaps in the next few days, we can get Jillian to mind the children while we go through the spreadsheet together to see what expenses we need to cover and what changes we can make to reduce costs?"

Andre gave Candy a kiss. "You've read my mind! We will make it a date!"

Candy was offered a position with both of the firms she attended for the interview. One required her to be in Paris to work, which didn't suit. The other required her to attend the office for a weekly meeting, which she could live with. The pay was also reasonable too, with the potential for bonuses.

Within days, Candy was submitting her work. She also came to an arrangement with Jillian to mind the children while she was working. Both Camille and Jillian joined Candy on her trips to Paris for her meetings, dropping her off while they did some sightseeing or shopping. Jillian was also happy she was now receiving her own income, something she hadn't had since she had Eliza.

A month later Candy received a call from Max, her employer in Australia.

"I'm sorry Candy. Since Marianne left our office over a month ago, it has been chaos! Are you available to do some work for us?"

"Send me the accounts and date for completion. I will fit them in."

SETTLING INTO THEIR NEW HOME

Candy stepped out to admire the decorations on the tall pine tree that now stood in the central area of the house. It's smell assailed everyone who entered the space. It was three weeks till Christmas and the family were adjusting to their new apartments.

Celeste had placed an adjustable table in the middle of the space. On it stood a large vase of flowers. The painting of Mathieu and Estelle and their family now supervised the area. When the Curator came to deliver the painting, she stood in silence for several minutes, taking in the beauty of the space. She had a smile on her face once the painting was in position. The family had come home.

The temporary homes and office had now been removed. Heavy frost now covered the front garden area where the buildings had been. Mark was now enjoying the quiet period after the build. He had been stretched, attending to all the tasks required to make the building habitable for everyone and attending to the back garden. It would be several months before spring planting began. All the trees in the orchard had been pruned for the winter months and the vegetable garden prepared for spring. Candy and Mark had worked out a plan for planting the front garden, which included a fountain.

Mark was pottering in his workshop, where he had timber that he was using, to make some furniture. Their furniture looked lost in their apartment, but they didn't mind. Mark and Jillian had all the time in the world to make their home how they wanted. Jillian was loving her new job of caring for the twins. Eliza also loved the little errands she was given, to help her mother care for them too. Jillian also realised that once the children were at school, childcare would be a good career for her.

Both Candy and Andre were enjoying the space their apartment gave them, after the modest space of the temporary home they had been living in. The large kitchen family area and sun room at the back were used the most. They both appreciated being able to work from their apartment when they needed to.

Most mornings Candy took the twins down to Jillian on her way to the business centre. Near lunch time, Candy would collect them from Jillian, so she had a break and have lunch with Mark while Candy and Andre had family time together. It was a rare occasion when both the twins were having a nap when Andre came home. If Candy had free time in the afternoon, she would take the twins down to see Dulcie and Dudley, have a walk round the back yard to check the gardens or take them for a longer walk down the road to Beaugency.

Dulcie and Dudley now spent most of their time in their stable, only leaving when they were forced to, to have them cleaned. Candy would lead Dulcie out, while Jillian swiftly cleaned the area. Sometimes she lead Dulcie out to the back yard for a walk around, but after a few minutes, the cold ground underfoot penetrated Dulcie's feet, she then pulled hard to be returned to her nice warm stall again. Dudley followed Dulcie's lead and didn't tolerate the cold hard ground either.

On one occasion Candy left the top half of the stable doors open to give them some fresh air. Candy and Jillian had hardly stepped around the corner with the wheelbarrow, when there was a furious bellow from the stable to have the door shut again!   Much to the amusement of Jean, Duval and Amélie, who happened to be in their quarters that morning.

They too, were enjoying their new home. They had wondered how they would adjust to being in the country, after the bustle and convenience of the Paris streets. But they were well catered for in their personal spaces down stairs and they now had a dedicated staff room upstairs, with views to the front garden.

Corbin and Fleur now made use of the space to spread out, that they hadn't had before. Corbin had not only an office, but a library for the books that he treasured. In the formal areas they had plenty of room for their other treasures, plus any more they spotted on their travels.

Fleur found she was spending most of her time in the large sunlit casual area overlooking the back garden. In the move she found a small tapestry she had bought years ago, but never made. Fleur also had her own room that she had decorated to her taste, mainly for entertaining any ladies that came to their apartment.

In the months after their move, there was a steady stream of visitors to see their new home. Both Corbin and Fleur now enjoyed the fact that Andre and the family was only a floor away. They did miss the fact that they could no longer just pop out to the local cafés and restaurants, but it was a nice excuse to go for a drive to town at Beaugency. Friday evening was now set aside for the whole family to get together for a few drinks and nibbles while catching up with each other.

Corbin and Fleur were happy to find that Beaugency had a thriving arts centre, which they patronised. They also now enjoyed performances without having to please other patrons with formal dress codes expected in Paris.

Camille and Jack loved their new apartment overlooking the back yard. Although Jack was glad the build was finished, he was feeling restless. Camille recognised the signs. Jack was used to travelling! They had been in one place for ten months.

"Where would you like to go?" Camille asked one morning.

Jack grinned at her. "Somewhere in the sun."

"Costa Rica? It's just across the Atlantic. We will go after the new year."

Celeste and Henri were enjoying their new apartment too. It was smaller than their one at the chateau, but with just the two of them, they didn't need any more space. The biggest change for Celeste was not having to organise the workforce every day. She realised that she needed something new to challenge her, but what? She wasn't quite ready for volunteering just yet. It took a visit into Beaugency to find her new project. As they passed the land next to their property, there was a "For Sale" sign up. Celeste asked Henri to stop the car, so she could take the details.

"What do you have in mind?" Henri asked. He knew that whatever Celeste was planning, it wouldn't be a small project!

"I would like to make a tearooms and some nice gardens for people to walk in, or even a mini golf course. If the area was extensive, establish some woodlands for people to wander in too. It would be mainly in the spring to autumn months. I'm missing the contact with visitors I had at the chateau. With this project, I can shut the door before dinner time and not worry about catering for guests. I would only need a few staff as well too. A gardener, of course, someone in the kitchen and a waitress. What do you think?"

"You mean make a mini chateau café?" Henri was grinning at Celeste. "Having mini golf among nice gardens would be quite a tourist attraction. It would take a while longer for the woodland to be a feature. Perhaps you could also put in some ponds for people to fish as well. That is also a popular pastime. Give that number a call!"

They found that the available property consisted of fifty acres, which conveniently had a stream. It was being separated from the neighbouring farm, which would one day become a residential development. The land was a reasonable price, so they put in an offer, which was accepted.

Henri had a detailed plan of the tearooms drawn up, with a map of the gardens, mini golf, woodland and fishing ponds in a proposal to the council at Beaugency. To their surprise, it was quickly accepted, with a request for the timeline they expected to have it up and running.

Fortunately, Henri had approached a builder for a quote and an estimate of when they could have it built if approved by council. It was expected to take six months for the build of the café, establish a carpark and the gardens. Work would also start on the ponds and woodlands which would be ready the following year.

It was mid -January when the builder began the build. A cover was placed over the site to protect both the workers and the equipment. In the next six weeks the pad, walls and waterproof roof cover was in place. The roof tiles had been delivered and they were waiting for the windows to be installed.

"Have you heard about the pandemic?" Henri asked Celeste, over breakfast.

She nodded. "Do you think it will come here?"

"We should take it for granted that it will. They are going into lockdown in Italy. People can only go out for essentials like food shopping. We may have to do it here too, so it may be some time before the tearoom is finished."

"I will go to the nursery today to see how many plants we can get to make a start on the gardens. I will go to the supermarket on the way home."

Next door Jack and Camille were in a sombre mood. They had returned from Central America a couple of weeks ago and were looking forward to another trip. News of a pandemic sweeping Europe was in the news, with countries shutting borders. If they left here now, they may get stuck somewhere and not be able to get back. Their travel plans would have to be put on hold for now.

Mark and Jillian had also heard about the pandemic and were very glad they not only had a roof over their heads, but a job that was onsite.

Corbin also was worried. If a lockdown came to Paris, they would have to shut head office. He remembered the business centre downstairs. He messaged Candy.

"Can I talk to you about the business centre?"

"Of course! Come down."

Candy had already had a phone call from Paris, asking her to connect to the office by Zoom that afternoon for an extraordinary meeting.

She and Andre also had heard about the pandemic. She at least could work from home. They presumed that pharmaceuticals would be an essential service that needed to be kept operating. He realised that extra precautions would have to be brought in, to protect the workers.

By the next day, all trucks delivering to the factory, were stopped at the gate. A staff member in protective gear and mask was to check the driver's temperature and give them a mask to wear while they were inside the complex. All workers in the factory now had to have a temperature check before signing on. If they or any family member became unwell, they were to stay home and receive a medical certificate before they returned. Staff also had to have photo ID cards made and carry them when attending work.

In the next week, three of the factory workers had to go into quarantine while they and their families recovered from the virus.

Corbin called his assistant in Paris.

"Are you able to relocate to Beaugency?"

There was silence for a few moments. "Not really. My mother is in hospital. They think she has the virus, though they won't let me see her."

"Are you well yourself, with no temperature?"

"I have a cough, but feel okay."

"I want you to take some leave, and close the office. Forward all calls and emails for the office to me at Beaugency. I will run it this end. You will need a medical certificate before you return to work."

Candy took Corbin down to the Business centre to show him all the facilities.

"You can open it up for business meetings, or section it off for separate offices."

"Have you been using it?"

"I have been using the back section in the mornings. I have a Zoom meeting this afternoon, though I can take it in my office upstairs. You can have full use of the area if you wish."

"The front section should be fine for me. Managing without my assistant will take some adjustment though."

"If you need help, just let me know." Candy offered.

That afternoon, Candy attended the meeting via Zoom. She noticed that some of the staff were missing.

"As from today, all staff need to work from home. Depending on the how the economy goes, we may have to shut the business. If that happens, if and when the economy recovers, you will be called for your availability to work."

Candy was now glad that her work from Australia was back on stream.

The café was a hive of frantic activity. The builder had got wind of the fact that there were plans for a lockdown in the next day or two. They had no idea of if or when they would be working again. By the time they went home, the roof had been tiled and the windows and doors were on. Fittings for the kitchen and serving areas also were installed, with power and water connected. Tiles were delivered for the floors and also some tables and chairs for patrons.

Celeste had a large tent erected for all the plants, to protect them from any late snow and frosts. As soon as the weather improved, she would be planting them out.

That evening Celeste and Henri celebrated with some champagne. Their bank account had been reduced somewhat, but their venture was ready for business as soon as the lockdown was lifted. She would have a word with Mark to see whether he could lay the floor tiles for her.

Mark had joined Celeste at the nursery. A fountain was picked out and assistance given to load it to take home. He had a list of seeds for planting and also some bushes and trees he wanted for the front garden.

The nursery manager kept the list of items they needed to order in and took his number. Between them, Celeste and Mark had just saved her from ruin.

"We will find a way to get these to you."

When Andre came home from work, he couldn't believe his eyes to see the café apparently finished. A large tent next to it. Inside the gates, Mark was unloading a large number of plants and a fountain.

"I'm just making sure our garden projects stay on track during lockdown." He grinned to Andre.

"You think it will be that long?" Andre asked, looking at all the plants that needed to be planted.

"It could be. Australia has just closed its borders to everyone without a special visa."

Upstairs, he found Candy was preparing their dinner. His kiss was followed by a longer cuddle than usual. She looked at him questionly.

"I'm just grateful that we have each other and our little family." Andre kissed her and looked at the twins who were babbling and looking at mum and dad with interest, from their bouncers. "I just hope that nothing happens to us."

"The only thing that should happen, is that Jacqueline and Laurent will have a sister or brother."

Andre looked at Candy with shocked eyes, he was drawn to look at her now flat stomach.

"Are you sure? Isn't it a bit too soon?" he asked anxiously.

"I'm late. The worst that can happen is that I need another caesarean. Though I hope to have a normal delivery this time." Candy hugged Andre and gave him a long kiss to reassure him. "We will be fine. Our new son or daughter will be something to look forward to."

"Another early Christmas present?" Andre asked.

"It will be close." Candy smiled.

It was April and signs of spring were everywhere. Mark had marked out the areas for planting for Celeste. He had nearly finished tiling the café and had raked the load of gravel that had been delivered for the carpark. A sign was also being made for the entrance.

Celeste was slowly planting the garden beds. She was doing an hour at a time as part of her "exercise." She heard a car pull into the carpark. Removing her gloves and pulling up her mask, Celeste went to see who was visiting and to inform them that they weren't open yet.

It was the mayor, here to see how the project was progressing. Like Andre, he was amazed at how complete the building was.

"You're a long way from home? Aren't you?" the mayor asked, recognising Celeste from the Chateau in Blois.

"I live next door." Celeste smiled. Our son runs the chateau now. Would you like a look?"

"Please!" the Mayor followed Celeste in.

There was silence as the mayor took in the space of the café. The picture windows giving views in the main space, contrasted with the cosy nooks in the turrets. The almost finished tiling on the floor, to the completed serving area and kitchen. Tables and chairs were stacked, waiting for the floor to be finished. He liked the silhouettes of the knight and Damsel on the toilet doors and also the circular light fittings, suspended from the ceiling. The lights resembling candles. Double glass doors led out to the gardens beyond.

"Very well done!" The mayor beamed. "Do you have a menu organised yet?"

"I do. I just have to print them and place them in plastic folders. There will be a board put up as well."

"Can you send me a copy? Also will you be having a formal opening?"

"Of Course! When the lockdown is over."

"It would give the council pleasure to assist you to open your facility. It isn't every day that a tourist attraction is opened in our area."

"We would be delighted and honoured." Celeste beamed, as she led him out to inspect the garden areas.

She pointed out the groves of trees planted at the back, with paths leading into them, were to be woodland to walk through. Celeste also showed him the contoured landscape with trees around the hollows which would be fishing ponds.

"Have you taken a photo of it yet?" the Mayor asked.

"I was waiting till we had finished."

"Do you mind?" the Mayor pulled out his phone. "The Council would love to see what has been completed so far."

"Please do."

When Celeste returned to their apartment, another champagne was called for. Having the council's participation in the opening, guaranteed their venture's success.

In the coming months, their home became a haven from the disruption the pandemic brought with it. Supermarket shelves emptied, before sanity and rationing was imposed. Some medications also became scarce too as hoarding began. Difficulty with some supply chains meant that Andre had to ration supplies to their customers.

"I think I need to go into quarantine." Andre told Candy when he came home one lunch hour. He had a large box with him. "Some of our staff have been working with it. We should prepare for it now."

Candy couldn't help showing her alarm.

"Have you got symptoms?"

"No. By then it would be too late."

Candy wasn't happy about the idea at all, but nodded her agreement.

"We will have lunch first!"   Candy was determined to have a last normal meal with him before they started their separation. The set look on Candy's face told Andre he would have a fight on his hands if he tried to argue!

Over lunch, Candy had questions she needed answers to.

"What happens if you get really sick and need hospital? I've heard all the services including the ambulances are overloaded. And who is to run the factory while you are away? It would be too dangerous for your father to do it? Are any of the supervisors authorised to step into your shoes for the payment of wages etc.?"

"That box I've brought home has personal protective gear in it. If I need you to take me to hospital, you are to put it on before you take me to the hospital."

Andre had to have a think before he answered her other question.

"I can get Dad to sort the wages remotely, but if there were any issues that needed someone to go in to make decisions, you will have to do it."

Once lunch was over, for once their dishes were left. Candy called Jillian.

"I'm bringing the twins down for a little while. We have some sorting to do up here."

"I will explain later." Candy said as she handed the twins to Jillian, who could see immediately that something was wrong.

Back upstairs, Andre was putting food into the kitchenette.

"I will use the stairs instead of the lift from now

on to make sure I don't give the virus to anyone else."

"You will need to tell your parents to use the lift only. I will ask Jillian to tell everyone downstairs. Also, can you divide our office space?" Candy asked Andre while she moved the children's cots to the family area. She also moved a single bed for herself to sleep in the room next to them. As she took some of her clothes out of their wardrobe, Candy felt distraught. The fact that she wouldn't able to see or touch Andre for an indefinite amount of time was hitting home.

Andre was still in the office when she finished.

"I will give you a video call when it's the children's bedtime." Candy called out to him. She couldn't keep her grief out of her voice. Andre heard it and came out, but by then she had already gone into the lift.

Jillian asked Mark and Eliza to entertain the children while she found out what was happening with Candy and Andre. When Candy returned, Jillian took her into her bedroom.

"I can see by the look on your face that something drastic has happened. What is it?"

"Andre is putting himself in quarantine. They are still getting cases of covid at his factory. I've just had to move myself and the children to the other side of the apartment." She nodded at the look of horror on Jillian's face. "He hasn't any symptoms yet, so I don't know how long this will go on for. Andre is going to use the stairs only. Can you tell Mum and Dad and Celeste and Henri to use the lift only too?"

Jillian agreed as she cuddled her sister, who was obviously close to breaking down. Candy took some deep breaths and forced herself to be calm. She could hear Laurent was starting to grizzle with a tired cry, despite Mark and Eliza's efforts to entertain him. It was time to get them settled.

"Thanks for looking after them for us." Candy's smile didn't reach her eyes that were full of despair. "Can you keep your phone on at night from now on. If I ever need to take Andre to hospital.."

"Of course!"

Candy was on auto-pilot as she took the twins through their evening ritual of their bath, then read to them before settling them in bed. Laurent quickly settled to sleep with his favourite toy, but Jacqueline was looking at Candy with puzzled eyes. She knew something was wrong with mum, but she didn't know what. She put her arms out to Candy. She picked Jacqueline up and gave her a long cuddle.

"It's alright darling." Candy whispered to reassure her, before giving her some kisses and returned her to bed. "I will see you in the morning."

Candy rinsed the dinner dishes and put them in the dishwasher. They could wait till the morning. Candy left the family room door open while she went across to her office space. After putting in a couple of hours work, tiredness got the better of her. With a sigh Candy packed up and returned to the children. Jacqueline was sleeping now too. Quietly she shut their door and retreated to her bed. It was only then that Candy allowed herself to release the emotions she had been holding back. Putting her head in her pillow she was racked by the grief that separation from Andre had brought.

Corbin and Fleur had a pleasant evening together watching their favourite programs. Corbin offered to grab a nightcap before they retired for the night. While he was in the kitchen, he heard a muffled noise. There was silence, then it came again. Yes, someone was crying and it was directly below them. It could only be Candy. What was she doing there? He went straight to Fleur.

"Something's going on downstairs! I can hear Candy crying beneath our spare room."

"Perhaps they have had a tiff?" Fleur asked, remembering some of the rows they had over the years.

"I think it's more than a tiff, by the way she is crying!"

As Corbin and Fleur made their way along the corridor on Andre and Candy's level, towards the room Candy was in, They heard Jacqueline start to cry. They looked at each other with concern. The children were over this side too. They heard Candy take a deep breath as she tried to control her tears and then her movements as she moved from the bedroom to the family room to pick Jacqueline up and take her back to the bedroom, making soothing noises as she went.

"I'm sorry Mummy disturbed you!" Candy was saying through her tears. "She's upset at the moment."

Corbin tapped on the door and walked in with Fleur, to the sight of Candy sitting on a single bed. Tear's streaming down her face, and rocking Jacqueline to comfort her.

"What's going on?" Corbin asked as Fleur swiftly came forward to put her arm around Candy. Surely it isn't that bad."

"I'm so sorry I disturbed you!" Candy spoke through her tears. "Hasn't Andre told you? He's put himself into quarantine. I'm just not handling the situation very well." Her tears flowed again.

"When did this happen?" Corbin was stunned.

"At lunchtime when he came home from work."

Andre was trying to read a book to make himself sleepy, when he heard footsteps out in the corridor, then his parents' voices talking to Candy. He could hear her crying. He knew that she had been upset at the new arrangements and had now broken down over it. He reached for a mask and slipped out into the corridor.

"Has he got symptoms?" Corbin asked with concern.

"Not yet, but it would be too late if he leaves it till he has symptoms." Just then there was movement at the door. Andre was in his pyjamas, a mask on his face.

"You have some explaining to do!" Corbin said not unkindly as he motioned him away from the room. If Andre wasn't already infectious, he obviously expected that he soon would be. Andre took him across the central area to his office. Corbin stood at the doorway while Andre sat in his chair a couple of metres away, to tell him of the events at the factory.

"This morning I arrived at work to find one of the workers on the production line, full of covid symptoms, which they've apparently had for some days. Also the security had been doing only random checks of staff temperatures, instead of checking everyone that came on site. After making it clear that their actions had put the lives of all the staff and their families at risk, the security was sacked and the worker was sent home. A check was done of everyone on site. Another six were sent home. Production has been halted and the last week's produce has been destroyed. Cleaning has been started. I have told the staff that if there isn't enough staff to keep going, I will close the factory."

"How close was the worker to you?" Corbin was concerned.

"Close enough to infect me and everyone else. They were coughing all over the staff and me. At the worst I will be infectious by tomorrow or the next couple of days." Andre was looking miserable. "I had no choice but to separate from Candy and the twins, not to mention the next little one."

Corbin nodded his agreement. "When's it due?"

"Another early Christmas present." Andre managed a grin.

"We will take them up to stay with us for now. Candy's going to need some support while she adjusts to being apart."

"It's a good idea." Andre agreed. It had comforted him that Candy was only across the corridor if he needed her. He now felt more afraid of what the coming days would bring. "I have food for about a fortnight. I have also brought home some protective gear. If I need to be taken to hospital, she can put it on and take me." Andre saw Corbin was going to protest, but stopped him.

"You can't take me, Dad. If you get it, you have more chance of dying. I won't let you do it!"

"Your right of course!" Corbin sighed. "What about managing the factory?"

"The supervisors are in charge when I'm not there. I will get the office to send the wages to you to approve remotely." They could hear Laurent had woken up.

"I will get them upstairs. Try to get some rest."

CARING FOR ANDRE

Andre knew immediately that he had the virus. It was the second morning since he had self-quarantined. He put on the kettle to make a coffee. When Andre poured it, he couldn't smell a thing, and his breakfast had no taste.

He rang the factory to tell the supervisor that he officially had Covid. He would work from home while he could, but if they needed someone to come in physically to sort an issue, they were to ring his wife Candy.

Andre was missing Candy and the twins. There were video calls to him several times yesterday, which was better than no contact. Andre could see Candy was still finding it difficult to be apart, by the sadness in her eyes when she talked to him. Neither of them spoke of it as it was their new reality for now. After the first couple of calls, Candy broke down again, but at least now, she had Fleur to support her.

When Candy and the twins made their first call of the day, Andre was still in his dressing gown, which was unusual, as he was usually in his suit by now.

"Did someone sleep in this morning?" Candy joked.

"It will be sleep ins for me from now on." Andre's reply was matter of fact. "I hope your breakfast tasted better than mine! I will be working from home for now while I can. I have told the factory to call you if they need someone to physically come in to sort things."

As they were talking, a little hand with a plastic spoon came up to feed some fruit to Candy's mouth. It ran down her chin, which made them both laugh.

"Thank you Darling." Candy hugged Jacqueline, who was beaming, now that Mummy was laughing again. Another spoon came up to feed Candy. It was from Laurent. She managed to eat that mouthful.

He too received a hug. Laurent had heard and seen his Dad on the phone and put a sticky hand out to touch the screen. Andre put out a finger to the screen that Laurent tried to grab, but had to content himself with their hands meeting on the screen. Andre blew a kiss to the screen. Laurent responded by putting his lips to the screen, which made it almost impossible to see anyone on it.

"Bye for now." Andre said in parting. He was now understanding why Candy had been so emotional on their parting. He was starting to feel emotional about it too.   Andre forced himself to have a shower and get dressed, before taking himself off to his office.

Once Candy finished their call, her eyes became bleak as she looked at Corbin and Fleur. "He's got it."

"Are you sure?" Fleur was now worried.

"I'm sure. Andre has lost his taste and smell. A classic sign. Also he is choosing to work from home for now." Candy changed the subject. "Fleur do you have a sewing machine? If so can I borrow it?"

"I do! What are you thinking of making?" Fleur was intrigued. Candy hadn't shown any sign of dressmaking skills before.

"I'm going to make some gowns, hats, shoe covers and masks; in case I need to attend to Andre. The supply in the box he gave me won't last long. I want something that can be washed if necessary."

"What fabric are you going to use?" Fleur now wanted to get involved.

"I have lots of sheets that I don't need at present. They can be put to good use in my little project for now."

"Our little project." Fleur corrected Candy with a smile. "Is it nearly time to take the children to Jillian?"

Candy checked her watch. "It is. I will search my linen cupboard on the way back up and print off some patterns while I'm at it."

"I will have a search of our cupboard too, and set up the sewing machine."

"How is Andre? And what have you got on this morning?" Jillian asked, when Candy left the twins with her.

When Candy told her of Andre's condition and the intention to have a sewing session to make protective gear, she nodded. "I will tell Mum and Celeste. They will want to help too."

When Candy returned to Fleur's apartment, it was a hive activity. Both Celeste and Camille had brought sewing machines with them. A pile of linen was waiting to be transformed. When Candy produced the patterns, both Celeste and Camille pounced on them and started to arrange them on the fabric they had laid out.

"We need to make a couple of bags for used linen too." Candy told them. "We shouldn't be touching our protective gear once we take it off."

"How are we going to set it up?" Fleur wanted to know.

"I will set up a table outside Andre's door with clean gear and hand sanitizer. On the other side I will have a box with a linen bag inside and also a bin for used gloves. We will use my washing machine to wash the linen on a hot wash. The bag and linen will be washed together and dried in the dryer on the hottest setting.”

“What table will you use? Celeste wanted to know.

“Our dining table won’t be in service while Andre is ill, so I will use that. Our kitchen bin has a foot pedal to open it, so I will use it too.”

“I will get Corbin to help move the table. Is it very heavy?”

“It is solid.” Candy admitted.

Within half an hour, Corbin, Mark, Henri and Jack had moved the table into position. The box for the linen bags and the bin were also ready. Andre heard the noise out in the corridor, but had to restrain himself from popping out to see what they were up to. He knew that whatever was being organised, Candy was behind it.

Andre was glad he hadn’t gone into work. His mind wasn’t on the job, and also he had started to cough. A dry annoying cough that had him reaching for water. There wasn’t any medications he could use to sooth his throat in the ensuite. He made a video call to Candy.

Andre could see there was activity going on behind her. “Have we got any soothers in the house? I have a cough. What are we up to?” he asked with interest.

“Oh, we are just making some protective gear that can be washed.” Candy replied airily. I will pop down and look for those soothers for you.”

Candy found the soothers she wanted in the main bathroom cupboard. She also found a thermometer, some wipes and a bucket she may need later. Some bags to line the bucket were also placed on the table. Candy dressed up in her protective gear. Hearing Andre in his office, she knocked the door and entered. He was on the phone, so she placed the soothers near him and turned to leave. Candy found her sleeve being grabbed. The call was quickly finished.

"Are you running away?' Andre asked as he stood up.

"I didn't want to interrupt, that's all!" Candy replied as she went into his arms for a long hug.

"I'm needing more than a hug, but I don't want to infect you." Andre's misery was plain.

"Have you any protection left?" The sparkle in Candy's eyes told him she wanted him as much as he wanted her. Candy found herself being led through to their bedroom.

All too soon, they had to part, with a final hug to sustain them.

"I had better go or they will be sending a search party!" Candy sighed.

Back up at Fleur and Corbin's apartment, the production line was going well. They all stopped to look at Candy as she entered the room.

"I found and delivered the soothers." Candy reported, "among a few other things we may need later."

"What other things?" her mother Camille was interested to know.

"A thermometer. Some wipes for if and when he becomes too unwell for a shower and a bucket with bags for a liner for when his cough becomes productive. I'm thinking we will have to make a fire pit out the back for all the things that can't be washed. It wouldn't be right to put it in the general rubbish and infect someone elsewhere. I will have a talk to Mark where the most suitable place will be."

No-one mentioned it, but they all saw how Candy was much calmer after her little visit down with Andre. They just hoped she didn't get the virus too!

Over the coming days Andre struggled with the virus, till late one evening, Candy received a text.

"Can you take me to the hospital. I'm having trouble breathing."

"I'm coming." She replied.

Knocking on Fleur's door, she told Fleur of her errand, and asked her to keep an eye on the twins.

There are bottles of milk in the fridge and nappies in the top drawer between their cots if they need them before I get back."

Candy quickly put on her protective gear and knocked on their bedroom door before entering.

She knew Andre was unwell, but his appearance shocked her. Hunched over, with his hand on his chest, he was gasping and having to use his chest muscles to breathe. There was a look of panic in Andre's eyes as he looked at her. She could hear he had fluid in his lungs. She quickly rang Mark.

"I need help in a hurry! To get Andre into our car for the hospital. Put some protective gear on before you come in."

"I'm coming!"

She heard him running up the stairs as she went to open the door.

"We are in here!" Candy called.

Sitting next to Andre, she put one of his arms round her neck, her arm round his waist. Within a minute Mark came in and took his other arm. They took him to the lift. Andre tried to protest, but they carried on.

"You are too weak to manage the stairs!" Mark spoke firmly. "It is easy enough to clean the lift before anyone else uses it."

In the car, Andre was placed in the front while Candy drove. Mark sat in the back in case he was needed. As they approached the hospital, there was a line of cars. Candy noticed that quite a few were turned away. Candy noticed that Andre was trying to cough up the fluid in his lungs, but couldn't, causing him to be in distress.

When it came to their turn, Candy advised the official of Andre's complaint.

"Sorry!" He said. "They can't take anymore covid patients. You can try Orleans, but they aren't much better.

Candy turned the car around, but parked the car on the side of the road.

"Before we go anywhere, we need to get some of that fluid off your lungs! Have you any bags to cough into in here?" She searched the glove box. There was a plastic shopping bag.

"This will do! Can you lean forward Andre?" giving him the shopping bag to hold, she then cupped her hands. With a chopping motion, thumped his back over Andre's lungs, something she had learnt from a physio, she had gone out with some years before.

"Now cough!

To Andre's relief, some of the fluid came up.

"Some more?" Andre nodded.

Candy didn't know it, but she now had an

audience. Some of the drivers had seen her pull over to give Andre the physio. They watched as she did the chest thumps to Andre's back, and saw the relief on Andre's face afterwards.

They tapped her window for instructions to help their loved ones that had been left to fend for themselves too.

"Where will you take him?" Mark wanted to know.

"I'm taking Andre home. There is no guarantee we will get the help we need anywhere else." She looked at Andre. "It's going to be hard work to get and keep that fluid off your lungs!"

"I'm already feeling better!" Andre managed to say. "I can do it with your help." He squeezed her hand.

"I will sort the lift." Mark offered after he helped Candy get Andre back up to their apartment.

"Thank you Mark." Candy expressed their gratitude. "It would have been difficult without you."

Candy then started what would be a long hard night, dislodging the now sticky fluid from Andre's lungs. Andre now had an elevated temperature too. In between sessions she was sponging him down, or when chills set in, keeping him warm.

To Fleur's surprise, the twins slept through till the morning. When she heard them cry out, with no response from Candy, she went to attend to them. Candy obviously wasn't back yet. Fleur changed their nappies and gave them some breakfast. She had given them some toys to play with, when there was a knock at her door. It was Celeste.

"Candy will need to be relieved soon. Are you able

to help or have the twins kept you busy during the night?”

Fleur was shocked. “The twins slept through for us. We thought Candy was still at the hospital. When did she get back?”

“We saw them go and come back. They were only away for about half an hour or so. She has been giving Andre physio through the night. We could hear the occasional slapping and Andre’s coughing afterwards. I expect they both will be very tired by now.”

“Of course I will help! I will see if Jillian is ready to take the children.”

When Celeste and Fleur quietly let themselves into Candy and Andre’s apartment, both Candy and Andre were asleep, with a look on exhaustion on their faces. Candy was sitting in a chair next to the bed, holding Andre’s hand. Both Fleur and Celeste noticed that Andre’s breathing was almost normal.

Before Fleur or Celeste could speak, Andre was woken with a spasm of coughing, which also woke Candy.

“You should be getting a rest!” Andre said to Candy.

“Yes she should!” Celeste spoke, announcing their presence.

“I will give you one last lot of physio before I go.” Candy declared. “So that your mother and Celeste know what to do if you need any during the day.” She turned to Fleur and Celeste.

“Have you fresh bed linen, PJ’s and some wipes? Andre is too weak for a shower today.”

“We don’t have the wipes yet.” Fleur advised her.

"How come you aren't at the hospital?"

"We were turned away. They don't have the room for any more covid patients. Apparently Orleans isn't much better, so I brought him home." Candy fetched a pack of wipes she had placed in the ensuite.

"Put these in the microwave for twenty seconds. They will be nice and warm to use."

Candy then turned her attention to Andre, showing Fleur and Celeste the correct position for Andre to be in and the technique for the chest thumps, making sure the lined bucket was in position. They were surprised at the amount of fluid and phlegm that Andre was able to cough up.

"You've been doing this all night?" Fleur asked in shock.

"She has!" Andre spoke as he squeezed Candy's hand. "I would be dead now without it. I was literally drowning when she started last night."

"I had no intention of letting that happen!" Candy said as she cuddled him. "I will see you later."

Both Fleur and Celeste gave Candy a pat on her shoulders as she passed them.

"Be careful how you take those off!" Celeste reminded her. "It's easy to make mistakes when you're tired."

Candy nodded. They all had heard of people getting the virus after taking their protective gear off incorrectly.

It was some days before Andre's secretions finally stopped and a swab showed he was no longer infectious. He just had to recover his strength.

There were celebrations when the precautions

they had put in place could be dismantled. It was decided to pack everything up and place them in the attic. If they were needed for anyone else, it was a simple matter of bringing them out again.

Andre was overjoyed to have his family back home, and to be able to have Candy back in his bed again. When Candy brought Laurent and Jacqueline back upstairs from Jillian, she asked.

"You want to see Daddy?"

Laurent immediately started looking for Candy's phone, but she took them into their apartment where Andre was waiting on the couch with outstretched arms.

Laurent and Jacqueline had big grins as they snuggled into Andre's body. For several days Laurent didn't want Andre out of his sight, clinging to him every time he moved. Eventually life in the household returned to normal.

In a few months the twins had something else to interest them. Mummy's tummy was growing. She told them that a baby brother or sister was coming soon.

A BROTHER FOR LAURENT & JACQUELINE

Andre was in his office at the factory. After months of disruption, production was back to normal. Andre's recovery from the virus had been slow. He had been effected by tiredness, but insisted on returning to work. He was also still coming to terms with the fact that the virus had nearly killed him. It was only for Candy's care that he was still here.

During his recovery, physical activity including love making was reduced, which caused him much frustration and anxiety. Andre was also grateful that Candy had been so accommodating in suggesting positions that were more comfortable and less tiring. Their loving relationship and the twins, were the only things that gave Andre the will to carry on.

Andre was also anxious about how the coming addition to their family would affect Candy. He just hoped for her sake that she didn't need another caesarean. She had brought home the latest scan with a gleam in her eyes.

"What do you think we are having this time?"

"You can see what it is?"

Candy nodded and wrapped her arms around him.

"A girl?" Andre asked hopefully. "A sister for Jacqueline?"

"It's a boy." Candy replied, giving Andre a kiss. "A brother for Laurent. We will have to aim for a girl next time."

"Oh good! Are you sure you're up to having

another baby when you haven't had this one yet?" Andre asked with amusement.

Candy noticed that Andre didn't seem at all excited that his own son was coming, and said so.

Andre gave Candy a reassuring kiss.

"It's strange that you say that. It's just that I'm more relaxed about it this time. One thing that won't change, is my relationship with Laurent. When he came I expected that I would form a relationship with him as I got to know him, but the moment he was put in my arms, that was it! I would move heaven and earth to protect him!"

"And he knows it!" Candy had tears in her eyes as she hugged him. She hadn't expected Andre and Laurent to form such a strong bond, but they had, and she would be forever grateful that they did.

Candy attended prenatal classes by zoom, which wasn't quite the same as being the same room as other mothers to be, and comparing how they were travelling on their journey to being a mother. It was good to refresh herself on the breathing and relaxation techniques, which had helped her so much during Candy's last labour.

One thing that did shock Candy, was being told that fathers were discouraged from attending labour and would be allowed a short visit post labour. No other visitors would be allowed in to visit. The information was also sent by letter.

This news didn't suit Candy at all! She couldn't imagine going through labour without Andre, so she started to look at alternative ways of delivering her baby.

Having her baby at home, with support appealed to her. Candy started looking at the availability of private midwifes. To her delight, Candy found one in Beaugency. Katriane was happy to take Candy on as her patient. She also liked husbands to be present. After a visit to check on the facilities, Katriane enquired whether Candy would like a water birth, as their spa bath was able to have the water temperature regulated, and also the bathroom had a heater which would be made a comfortable temperature for when the baby emerged from the water.

Candy also visited the obstetrician that had attended her last labour. When Candy advised him of her intention of having her baby at home, he looked sceptical. However, when she advised him that Katriane was caring for her, he nodded his approval.

"Tell her to call me if there are any issues. I will come to give you both a check afterwards."

When Jillian heard about Candy's plan to have her confinement at home, and the reasons for it, she asked what the costs were, for she suspected that she too was expecting, but was waiting till her pregnancy had progressed before making it public. She was pleasantly surprised that she could afford the care too.

Monthly visits were made to make sure all was progressing according to plan. A delivery pack was left with Candy with instructions and her phone number.

Andre wasn't sure he liked the idea of having a baby outside the convenience and safety of a hospital, but after seeing Candy's determination, he kept his misgivings to himself.

After a few months, Katriane was delighted to find she had two mothers to care for at the mansion.

Andre was at work when Eugène gave notice that he was coming, ready or not! The gentle contractions that Candy had felt in early labour when the twins came were absent this time. From the first they were firm and strong. Candy knew she had no time to waste.

Candy had to breathe through a contraction before she pulled out her phone to call Katriane and texted Andre. She also asked Jillian to take the twins.

"Eugène is in a hurry! Please come home. You will find us in the bathroom."

At the factory, Andre received the text and was glad of the excuse to leave. Despite all the measures he had in place, there were lots of challenges to keep the factory running smoothly and keep covid at bay. He rang the supervisor to tell him he was leaving early.

"My wife's in labour. I will see you tomorrow."

"Good luck." Was his response.

When Andre reached their apartment, he noticed the table with protective gear outside. In their bathroom, he was surprised to be greeted by a completely peaceful scene. Candy was sitting relaxed in the bath, Katriane, dressed in a swimsuit was with her. A small trolly with birthing kit was next to the bath, along with a table, scales, suction machine and bassinette.

"Come and join us!" Candy invited him, before another contraction came to claim her attention. "I want to push!" Candy told Katriane, who made another check.

"Concentrate on your breathing. You are nearly

fully dilated. When I tell you, you can push. If you want to change your position, just say and we will help you.”

Andre swiftly undressed to his underwear to enter the bath next to Candy.

“Is there anything I can do?” Andre asked as he put his arm around her.

“Just hold me! It helps me to have you here. When the next contraction comes, I will get you to massage my back. All the pain is down there.” As Candy spoke, another contraction started. She grabbed Andre’s hand and pressed it to the area in her back that was aching.

“Push!” Candy said with a little grin. “Hard!”

“I thought that was your job!” Andre grinned back as he complied.

“Yes!” Katriane agreed. “It’s time for you to bring Eugène into the world! Take a deep breath and bear down as much as you can.”

Candy found she needed to turn around and squatted on the shelf she had been sitting on, hanging onto the side of the bath as she bore down.

“Keep pushing.” Katriane encouraged Candy as she started to ease off. So she took another breath and tried again. Candy could now feel something between her legs.

“Well done!” Katriane told Candy. “His head is delivered. We are just waiting for Eugène’s body to turn, then I will get you to push some more.”

“He doesn’t need to breathe yet?” Andre asked, feeling a little alarmed.

“No.” Katriane reassured him. “Eugène is still

receiving oxygen from the placenta. We have plenty of time to establish his breathing before it stops giving oxygen from Candy." She turned her attention to Candy.

"It's time to push again, a nice steady long one."

Candy took the biggest breath that she could and started to bear down again. About half way through, Katriane told her to start panting instead of pushing.

"He's here!" Katriane announced. "You can sit down now."

As Candy turned around to sit down, Katriane was bringing Eugène to the surface to lift him out of the water. Although the room was very warm, it was a change in temperature to the water. Eugène gasped and gave a little cry. Katriane lowered Eugène back into the water, which calmed him again. Gently she brought Eugène to Candy and Andre, where Candy took him into her arms.

"Hello Eugène. Your Mummy and Daddy are here." Andre said as he gave him a kiss.

Eugène's eyes flew open, to see two faces looking at him. He recognised his father's voice, which was much clearer now.

"Hello my beautiful boy!" Candy added as she kissed him too. Eugène recognised her voice too!

While they were talking, Katriane clamped and cut the cord.

"Candy, can you put Eugène to your breast?" Katriane asked. "We need to stimulate the placenta to separate from the uterus."

Candy put Eugène to her breast and immediately felt another contraction. She was pleased that Eugène sucked strongly. Shortly afterwards, the placenta was delivered and placed in a bowl that the midwife had ready.

Eugène was handed to Katriane for a top to toe check while Andre helped Candy into the shower and to dress in clean leisure wear before resting in bed. When Katriane brought Eugène in to the bedside, she also did a set of observations on Candy and checked the pad she now had in place. The flow was normal.

"I have called your Obstetrician to visit you." Katriane informed Candy and Andre, who was sitting on the bed next to Candy. "It is usual for a doctor to check newborns, but I also want him to check you as well, Candy. I have checked the placenta and believe you still have some left in your uterus. It needs to be removed before it causes you any problems."

"What sort of problems?" Andre wanted to know.

"Haemorrhage or infection." Katriane informed them. She put a bluey pad under Candy. "I will be keeping a close eye on you for the next twenty four hours. Do you have a spare room nearby where I can put up my camp bed?"

Her phone rang. It was the Obstetrician, saying he was on his way. Did they object to him bringing a medical student with him.

"They are welcome!" Candy grinned. "You had better open the gate and carport." She told Andre. "They may want an escort up here."

"I will go down to meet them." The midwife offered. 'I have some extra equipment to bring up with me."

Outside they could hear some voices.

"That is my family."

Katriane smiled. "They may visit untill the doctor comes."

Andre ensured the gate and carport were open before letting the family in. Laurent and Jacqueline were fascinated to see their new brother. They had ten minutes before Andre had to ask them to come back later, as the doctor was here.

CANDY'S LIFE IS AT RISK

Charles and Simon were led out of the lift by the midwife, bringing several bags with them. They both noticed the staircase and were glad they hadn't had to use it. They were also very grateful for the Personal protective equipment (PPE) that was waiting for them outside the apartment. PPE was now very short in supply everywhere. Charles made a mental note to find out where this household sourced their supply, as he wanted some too.

Katriane went ahead to check on Candy and prepare her for their visit. The family filed out, promising to come back later. Only Andre stayed behind, sitting next to Candy to hold her hand. Candy was placed in position, ready for Charles to exam her. When Charles and Simon entered with the PPE on, he now understood why it had been left out.

Charles eyes immediately checked Candy's appearance. Her skin colour and sparkle in her eyes, reassured him that she wasn't in any immediate danger.

"I see congratulations are in order." Charles greeted Candy and Andre, as he went over to the crib. "This is my student, Simon who is on his final placement. It's a shame to disturb little Eugène but we will do his check first."

Simon then proceeded to check Eugène from his head to his toes. Eugène protested loudly at being disturbed by being undressed, and having numerous checks done, including having an object stuck in his ear, another one making a ringing noise; a bright light in his eyes, having his limbs moved, and being given a fright (when checking his startle reflex).

Eugène was given a feed to help settle him again, before he was wrapped firmly in a blanket and returned to his bassinette.

"There aren't any problems with feeding?" Charles asked, as Eugène was returned to his bassinette.

"None." Candy was pleased to report. "He attached straight away."

"Right, it's your turn!" Charles spoke, as he and Simon sat themselves down on chairs provided at the foot of the bed. Candy was propped up on pillows, armchair style, Katriane brought over the placenta, showing the area where the membrane was missing.

"We have to do a curette, Candy. We will give you some gas. You will feel it, but you won't care."

"Shouldn't this be done at the hospital?" Andre asked with some concern, as Katriane gave Candy a mask to breathe into and turned on the cylinder it was attached to.

"Usually." Simon answered for Charles. "but at present there aren't enough staff to care for patients properly. Believe me when I say your wife is getting the best possible care here at home."

Andre gave Candy's hand a squeeze as they began the procedure. A speculum was introduced to keep the cervix of the uterus open. A device with a camera and a light was introduced to examine the interior of the uterus. The missing material from the placenta was found. The curette was performed to remove it.   As Charles withdrew the device, Simon stopped him.

"What was that lesion?" Simon asked.

"Show me." Charles said as he handed the device to Simon. Simon went back in, and searched till he found the spot he had seen.

"It's here." Simon said matter of factly as the camera was now focused on the area in question.

"Well spotted!" Charles also spoke calmly, though his heart sank at the sight of the lesion. They both knew they were looking at a lesion that was well known for being an aggressive cancer.

Candy took the mask off. She could see by the serious expressions on both Charles and Simon's faces, that they had found something that she needed to know about.

"What have you found?" Candy's tone was as matter of fact as theirs.

Charles looked at Candy with sympathy in his eyes. "What are your plans for having more children?"

"I intend to have a sister for Eugène."

"We have found a cancerous lesion that is known to be very aggressive. If we don't remove your uterus now, and I mean right now, you will die. I know of a little girl born yesterday that is now an orphan and is in desperate need of a loving home."

"I would love to give her a home, if you can arrange it." Candy replied, "However, can I please keep my ovaries so I can harvest some of my eggs? I want the option of using a surrogate for our family in the future.

"Candy!" The anguish in Andre's tone was plain. "If we have to choose, your life is much more important than any children that we may have had."

"Andre Darling, if Eugene is also affected, I will still want the option of being able to have children that are healthy. The Invitro system will make sure of that."

"Candy has a point." Charles now spoke. "Eugène will have to have checks till he is your age, Andre. I agree to take the uterus only, for now. I will put Candy under twilight sedation for it. Eugène will now have to be bottle fed untill we know whether there has been any spread. If there is, then we will take some scans and start you on chemotherapy Candy, as soon as your eggs have been collected."

Candy nodded. She was feeling numb from the shock of the news and the need to act so quickly. She turned her head to Andre, who gathered her to him to comfort her.

"I will put in a canula." Simon offered. "You want some bloods before we start?"

"Thank you, Simon. Ca 125, and the hormones. It needs to be marked "Urgent".

Katriane was now on her phone to Jillian asking her to please collect Eugène and to make up some formula as they had to do a procedure that needed all of her attention.

"What's the procedure?"

"A hysterectomy."

While Charles and Simon were preparing, Katriane gathered the tin of newborn formula and some bottles she had seen in the kitchenette, and some nappies to place them in the bassinette. Katriane was wheeling Eugène out into the central space when Jillian and Camille came rushing out of the lift with shocked looks on their faces.

"What has happened?" Camille asked.

"We have found cancer in the uterus. We are

acting to save Candy's life."

Camille nodded, tears in her eyes as she and Jillian turned to take Eugène downstairs. It was going to be a long night.

Back in the bedroom, The canula had been inserted and the blood samples taken. The curette pack had been put aside and another surgical pack was being unpacked.

"Do you want a catheter inserted and intravenous fluids set up?" Katriane asked Charles.

"That would be helpful." Charles thanked her.

"Are you sure you want to stay?" Charles asked Andre when they were ready to begin.

"I'm staying!" Andre's reply was firm. "She both wants and needs me to be here to support her."

He gave her a kiss and squeezed her hand before they administered the sedation. Katriane placed Candy on oxygen and monitored her with an oximeter, before also checking Candy's blood pressure at regular intervals.

Andre didn't take much notice of the procedure, as he kept watch on Candy's face for any signs of discomfort. He noticed that Katriane administered pain relief on Charles' instruction, which kept Candy comfortable.

"We are finished." Charles announced, as he moved his chair back from the bed. "Katriane please keep the oxygen on till Candy wakes up. If her blood pressure is normal when the IV fluids are finished you may disconnect them. Ring me if there are any issues."

"That's promising." Charles commented as he and Simon checked the uterus after its removal. He looked at Andre as he spoke. "There doesn't seem to be any sign of the lesion on the outside. We can only hope it didn't enter the blood stream. We should have the results when I check on her tomorrow."

"Thank you. We are very grateful." Andre managed to say. He was now feeling drained, but knew he had to muster the energy to see the family.

After helping Katriane to make Candy comfortable, Andre went to the kitchen to make Katriane a drink and a meal, which she appreciated, as she continued to monitor Candy at the bedside.

"I'm going downstairs to see the children. Call me if you need me." Andre said as he departed.

Jillian's door opened as Andre came out of the lift. They had obviously been listening out for him to come down. His mother and father were first out the door to come to comfort him.

"How is she?" Camille asked anxiously from behind them.

"She is resting comfortably. The sedation hasn't worn off yet. We just have to wait for the results now. How are the children?"

"They have been very good, playing with Eliza, thought they are starting to get a little tired now. Eugène has had a feed. He made a face to begin with, but has accepted it."

"Have you eaten yet?" Jillian asked. She had Eugène in her arms. "Mark has made a beef casserole if you're interested."

"Lead me to it!" Andre realised he was starving! "I will take them off your hands afterwards."

"Are you sure?" Jillian was anxious. "What about

Candy?"

"Katriane is staying the night to care for her, so I will keep to our normal routine as much as possible."

When Andre, Corbin and Fleur took the children upstairs, Candy was awake, and sitting up. Laurent and Jacqueline didn't quite understand they couldn't climb over mummy just yet, but were satisfied that they were able to have a cuddle with her before they went to bed.

Andre had a busy night, tending to the twins for drinks and nappy changes, along with feeds for Eugène. Candy insisted that Andre bring Eugène in with them when he was fed, so she could have a cuddle too. In the morning Andre rang the factory. He would be working remotely until Candy was able to help care for the children.

In the morning, Candy was happy to have both the canula and the catheter removed, carefully making her way to the shower under Katriane's supervision. Changing into day clothes helped Candy to feel more normal. She was also grateful for the pain relief offered; for the discomfort she was feeling at the operation sites. Two small puncture wounds now adorned her abdomen where the fallopian tubes and ovaries were detached from the uterus. A deeper discomfort could be felt from the cervix which was now closed off.

Before Katriane departed to attend other appointments, Candy promised that she would relax and not do any heavy lifting. (including the children)

"I'm here to make sure she behaves!" Andre came out to thank Katriane, who smiled.

"I will see you tomorrow." Katriane promised.

Later that afternoon, Candy couldn't help feeling nervous, when Charles called to be let in the gate. She had kept herself occupied during the day, keeping her mind off his visit. Candy started by doing some work on the accounts that were waiting for her. Helping with Eugène's feeds, and resting on the bed to do some meditation to keep herself calm.

When Charles and Simon came out of the lift, Candy came out to meet them with a purposeful stride and a smile.

"Have you been resting at all?" Charles asked with a raised eyebrow.

"Of course!" Candy smiled. "Andre is home to keep me on track. Do you want to do the examination first before our chat? Andre is waiting."

"I'm glad to hear it! And yes, we will do the exam first." After his check, Charles gave his verdict. "All is looking well with your wound sites. Come to see me if anything changes. I will check it again in six weeks."

Candy and Andre took Charles and Simon through to the lounge room. Candy had a note pad on the table in front of her.

"I will give you the good news." Charles smiled at Candy. "There is no sign of cancer cells in your blood, so we won't have to rush for scans and chemotherapy, but as a precaution, I will remove the ovaries once we have collected your eggs.

Starting from tomorrow morning, Candy are to take your temperature before you get up. When your temperature rises, you both will attend the clinic. Candy will be given an injection to mature the egg follicles before being placed under sedation to have your eggs extracted. Your ovaries will be removed at the same time. Andre, we will need a semen sample from you to fertilize the eggs before they are frozen.

Candy, you can expect the menopause to begin straight away. Your GP will be able to help you with treatment of any unpleasant symptoms that go with it."

"Is there any bad news?" Andre asked.

"The little girl we told you about, has received Covid from her mother. She isn't expected to live."

"If she recovers, I'm still interested. I don't suppose I would be allowed to visit her."

"I don't expect so, but I will ask. You do realise you are putting yourself as risk?"

"Of course! But I know she probably will die if she doesn't have any personal contact. Simon said they haven't enough staff to care for patients and I know that any contact she is getting will be minimal. She needs to know that someone cares."

Andre was shaking his head, but gave Candy a hug. Only she would consider doing such a thing for an orphaned, not to mention infectious child.

Candy was surprised to receive a phone call from the co-ordinator of the children's ward a couple of hours later. The only thing stopping their approval was the lack of PPE which was essential for contact. When Candy advised that she had her own washable set, she was advised to present herself in her PPE at reception. A member of staff would escort her to the baby and give her instructions on the handling of the infant.

"Please be extra careful!" Andre took Candy into his arms and cuddled her, when she gave him the news.

"I don't want you going down with it too!"

CHARLOTTE JOINS THE FAMILY

Candy followed the nurse to the children's ward. The long room, segregated into cubicles, seemed subdued. Only the occasional cry of a child indicated that it was occupied. Nurses rushed between the cubicles.

In a separate room with an incubator, lay a little girl. Candy automatically followed the nurse's lead in cleaning her gloves as they entered the room. Candy now was wearing a plastic shield as were all the other staff. Candy could see straight away that the child was in distress and had to stop herself from rushing over to her. The nurse showed Candy where the nappies were and where to dispose of them. All care had to be given through the portholes. She would bring in a bottle for Candy to feed her, and to note how much the child took.

"Has she a name?" Candy asked.

"She is Baby Marchand."

"I shall call her Charlotte."

"Very well." The nurse allowed a small smile to show on her face. "I will be in with Charlotte's bottle shortly."

As soon as the nurse left, Candy took stock of the supplies in the room. The wipes were nearly empty, only one spare nappy was available and there were very few tissues to wipe secretions. She noticed the sheet Charlotte was lying on needed changing. There were some blueys in the cupboard along with a spare sheet.

"Hello Charlotte Darling." Candy said as she opened a portholes to place the sheet and bluey inside.

"Let's make you more comfortable."

After changing their bed at home, with Andre in it while he was ill, changing the baby's sheet was a much easier exercise. Candy had no idea that she had an audience watching from the door, as she confidently lifted Charlotte from the soiled area of the sheet and placed her on her side on the prepared clean area.

Candy could see that Charlotte had mucus in her mouth, and wiped it away with a folded tissue, before changing her nappy. Candy quickly removed the soiled sheet and placed Charlotte back in the position she had found her, cradling her in her hands. Candy then began to gently touch and massage Charlotte, from head to toe. When Charlotte started to cough, she quickly turned her onto her side to help remove the mucus she was coughing up. At that point, the nurse came in with Charlotte's bottle.

"You've done well." She commented. "The only thing is, that sheet was supposed to go on tomorrow. We don't have any spares."

"Do you have a spare towel?" Candy asked. "If I wash the sheet at the sink and wring it in the towel, it will be dry by the morning."

Candy could see by the nurse's expression that her suggestion wasn't usual procedure.

"I will get a towel."

Candy put her arm round Charlotte as she fed her, her bottle. Before she was half way through, Charlotte went to sleep; Candy could see from exhaustion. She sat her up and rubbed her back to burp her. When she burped, Charlotte also started to cough and bring up phlegm. After that was dealt with, She offered Charlotte the bottle again. Charlotte was ready for it this time. She polished it off, and was looking for more. Candy looked round to see the nurse at the door. The nurse beamed when she saw the empty bottle.

"That's the first time she's finished one."

"She wants some more." Candy beamed back.

Charlotte took another half bottle before she turned her head away. Candy left Charlotte lying on her side facing the door, sleeping soundly.

Before Candy left, the co-ordinator asked if Candy could come in, every four hours during the day for Charlotte's feeds. As soon as Charlotte was non-infectious she could take her home.

"Certainly. Just call me after the first bottle, what time you want me."

The nurse who had escorted Candy in, also escorted her out, making sure Candy took her PPE off in the right order and disposed of it into the bag she had brought correctly.

The next week passed in a whirl of caring for Eugène and the twins at home and visits to the hospital to care for Charlotte. Candy and Andre also made a visit to family services to apply for the adoption of Charlotte. A case manager made a visit to their home to check that they were able to care for Charlotte. She noted that Charlotte had her own room ready for her.

"Charlotte's been looking for you!" one of the nurses commented when Candy came in one morning. When Candy opened the port and put her finger in Charlotte's hand, she looked over at her and gripped her finger tight. Candy also noticed that she didn't cough or bring up any phlegm during her visit.

That afternoon, Candy received the call that they had been waiting for. That Charlotte was now clear and could she come to collect her.

Charlotte wasn't sure what Candy was doing when she dressed her, but her eyes were fixed on Candy when the incubator was opened and Candy was able to lift her out to hold her for the first time. Charlotte's eyes looked around at her new world, but she mostly looked at her new mum.

"Hello, my gorgeous girl. I'm here to take you home." Candy gave her a kiss and a cuddle.

Charlotte didn't know what mum was saying, but she now knew she was loved. Candy wrapped Charlotte in the warm rug she had brought with her.

"Do you have a baby seat in your car?" the nurse asked, as she took Charlotte from her for the journey out to the car.

"Yes, we have two." Candy smiled. "Our son Eugène was born the day after Charlotte. We are all prepared for them both." At the nurse's shocked look, Candy added, "We had twins last year. We are accustomed to caring for two babies together."

Charlotte gave a cry of discomfort as she was exposed to the December air for the first time. The nurse quickly brought the rug up to shield her from the cold.

When Candy brought Charlotte into their apartment, both Laurent and Jacqueline came toddling over for a look. Andre was sitting on the couch feeding Eugène.

"I will swop you." Andre said as Candy sat down

next to him.

As Candy took over Eugène's feed, Andre introduced Laurent and Jacqueline to their new sister.

Five days later, Candy advised Charles of the change in her morning temperature. She was booked in at the day procedures clinic for that afternoon.

Leaving the children with the family, Candy and Andre presented at the clinic. Andre gave Candy a kiss and a cuddle before they were separated. After signing the consent forms and changing into a hospital gown, Candy was led to a bed in the ward.

"Are you all ready for this?" Charles asked when he came to see her.

"I am!" Candy smiled at him.

"We will be using the same sites as before. You can expect to feel uncomfortable and sore afterwards, and remember, no heavy lifting for six week! How are you coping with your latest pair of twins?"

Candy beamed. "They are both doing well and gaining weight."

"We will see you inside." Charles said as he walked off to prepare.

Candy didn't actually see Charles in the theatre, as the anaesthetist had already put her to sleep.   It was a couple of hours later, before Candy was awake and ready to go home. She had read how some women had a feeling of loss, after the onset of Menopause and the end of their fertility. All Candy was feeling now, was a great sense of relief that a potential source of cancer had been removed.

When Andre came in to collect her, he took her

into his arms for a cuddle.

"I'm just so relieved they are gone." Was Candy's reply when Andre asked how she was feeling.

Jillian had been revelling in her pregnancy. She was enjoying the reminder of how well she had felt when she had Eliza. It was a pity that she had agreed to having only one more. When Candy came back from having her eggs extracted at the clinic, she casually mentioned.

"I just need a surrogate now to complete the family."

"You've got one!" Jillian mentioned just as casually, but couldn't help smiling. At Candy's incredulous look, she nodded. "I love how well I feel when I'm pregnant. Mark doesn't mind as they are for you. I will be having plenty of contact if I feel the need to mother them."

It was a long five weeks later that Candy had her final check after her hysterectomy. At bedtime Candy disappeared into the bathroom, before emerging in one of her nighties. She tried, but failed to keep a smile off her face at Andre's face lit up with joy and happy expectation.

"No more interruptions!" Candy murmured as she joined him.

"Only our little ones!" Andre murmured as he reclaimed his love.